FIRST
AID

MATTHEW LEDREW

FIRST AID

AID

THE XANDER DREW SERIES

Published in Canada by Engen Books, St. John's, NL.

Library and Archives Canada Cataloguing in Publication

Title: First aid / Matthew LeDrew.
Names: LeDrew, Matthew, 1984- author.
Description: Series statement: The Xander Drew series ; 6
Identifiers: Canadiana (print) 2020040668X | Canadiana (ebook) 20200406701 |
ISBN 9781989473986
  (softcover) | ISBN 9781989473993 (PDF)
Classification: LCC PS8623.E424 F57 2020 | DDC C813/.6—dc23

Distributed by:
Engen Books
www.engenbooks.com
submissions@engenbooks.com

First mass market paperback printing: December 2020

Cover Image: Ellen Curtis

For
Ellen

PROLOGUE

Shots were fired.

"Jesus!" Des Freeman yelled, taking cover behind a large barrel of salt. Three bullets punctured it in rapid succession, ricochets from the metal heat-proofing along the building's far wall, he assumed. It couldn't have been his men firing at the intruder: he'd only just entered. Nobody was that fast.

He heard several sharp pops in a row -- handguns, his men on the ground -- before a sharp burst of automatic weapons fire rang out like a staccato clang. The warehouse was alight with muzzle fire that cast shadows on the wall in front of him: shadows of a man walking with confidence among the hail of bullets, finding his way from point to point without ducking and diving as his men were.

Des turned, his gun at the ready, and peered through the crack between barrels of salt. White grains found their way into a flesh wound he didn't know he'd had, and he fought the urge to hiss in pain, biting at his lip.

He could see the money.

Bobbing in a narrow dock that ran up the warehouse's centre was a small ship, no bigger than a pleasure craft, and yet it reached both sides of the dock as though it had been made for it. In fact, the dock had been made for the boat. On the dock of the boat were barrels that looked identical to the salt barrels, but he knew they weren't. They were open, and the smell that came out of them when they'd been cracked was not the acrid stench of sodium, but that gamey, worn smell of used money.

The money was always used. Nobody ever used new bills. New bills had a greater chance of being tracked.

Des could see the barrels of money from between the barrels of salt he hid behind, the light from the gunshots making contradictory shadows from them. One of the barrels was tipped, small bound bundles of bills spilling onto the dock of the ship. Some had rolled out into the scant space of water between the boat and the dock, becoming nothing but bubbles.

There was a flash of bright light, and then his view of the barrels was obscured by shadow. Des looked up, panting loudly as his face drenched with sweat, and saw the profile of the man who'd entered their warehouse, standing just a few feet in front of him.

His face was shadowed even though there was fire all around. He was hidden behind the awning of the upper section of the warehouse, and it took Des's ringing ears a moment to realize that the automatic fire had stopped. The man wasn't tall -- he wasn't short either, but he had expected someone taller from what he'd been told. The man had dark brown hair -- nearly to the point of black the way it was wetted. It clung to him like tar, slithering along the edges of his soft jaw like snakes.

He wasn't breathing heavily, as Des would have expected. As Des was. He was standing with his shoulders squared, his eyes following back and forth along the expanse of the building. He looked like a hunter, but not one Des had ever seen. He looked almost mechanical at times, as if scanning and waiting. It was unnerving to see something clearly human acting in a way that was undeniably robotic: as though it had been birthed whole from the Uncanny Valley.

Des raised his gun and swallowed hard, preparing to take his moment.

Before he could, the man moved, ducking and darting to their left, around the side of the boat opposite from where he'd come. Des had enough time to wonder, briefly, what had caused him to move, when the answer came. Two more shots rang out at the same instant fresh holes exploded in the barrel of salt next to him, exploding the white sand out onto the boards. It went between them and down into the sea below, where it mingled with the already salt water there and became indistinguishable.

Three more shots came, and then a scream. It wasn't the type of scream that came from being shot though -- Des could tell the difference. He'd shot his share of men in his time, but none, he thought, quite like this one. He'd heard stories of this one. They'd started months ago but were few and far between. Now they were a constant and consistent narrative, the difference between the oral tradition of storytelling and twenty-four-hour media.

He swallowed, raised his weapon, and stood.

There was blood. Everywhere.

There was blood coming from the ceiling, where his gunners had been, dribbling down like raspberry syrup from the rafters and connective plates. There was blood on the floor in striped voids, working its way along the floor from their sources but being lost between the boards and finding its way into the Pacific Ocean below. It was spattered on the wall, edging its way down like condensation off an icicle's tip.

It was in the hair of the man who stood alongside the body of Angel Leonardi, sliding down his face and covering his hands as though it were grouping there.

The only thing not covered in blood was the money. The money, and the boat itself, was ablaze. It stood between them, and now that Des was standing, the flames were the only thing between he and the man covered in the blood of his men. The room stank with the bacteria of it, the ink from the bills wafting up into the atmosphere as Des trained his weapon.

The Man's breathing was hard now, in a way it hadn't been before. His shoulders arched and fell, then arched, then fell. They were sloped in as though pointing to something just in front of his chest. His breath was hard and wet with saliva and blood that had been drawn across his mouth, either his own... or someone else's.

The flame between them arched, and in that moment, Des remembered what he was here to do. The money was burning. He raised his weapon and took aim squarely at the Man's solar plexus.

The man covered in blood did nothing. He was looking out over the fire towards Des, but made no motion to even acknowledge his presence.

Des swallowed, his hand shaking, and fired.

The shot rang out, the first in minutes, a thunder that snapped through the halls of a warehouse. The man jolted back, his blood adding to the spatter on the wall behind him, and let out a hard, guttural bellow.

He did not fall over.

The Man stepped forward on a shaky foot, the blood pluming from his shoulder at first a deep red, then fading to an inky black in what must have been a trick of the light.

Des's hand shook and he pressed the gun forward again, squeezing off two more shots. The first caused another barrel of salt to erupt, dousing some of the flames that had made their way to it. The second hit The Man in the collar, but somehow did not even result in him losing his stride.

The flames from the boat arched again, obscuring The Man from Des's view. He shot again, through the flames, to the space where The Man had been.

A shadow emerged from the fire, rocking the boat, and eventually coming through it. What emerged wasn't The Man, or any man. It had long teeth and snarling red eyes that glowed with the same intensity and passion as the fire. When the flames kissed its black, tarry skin, it stank like vomit and bile, even as its flesh moved and changed in response to it.

The Creature leaped forward, fingers outstretched, revealing claws.

They both screamed.

Des screamed the last sound he'd ever make.

The Creature screamed: "Black Womb lives!"

CHAPTER ONE

Soft notes drifted through the house like the hum of bees, just loud enough to be audible but not loud enough for Tash to discern where they were coming from. The steady tick of hands counting down time cut above the music, and louder still than that was the rumble of an engine coming up the drive. Her reading glasses were perched precariously on the bridge of her nose and she glanced up over them to look at the clock on the wall. It was well past curfew, making Nick almost four hours late for dinner.

She got up from her seat and straightened, her billowing shawl falling around her like water. In one smooth motion, she plucked her glasses off and slipped them into the collar of her shirt. She crossed the room and with two fingers pried a small gap open in the blinds covering the window. She peered through the gap to confirm it was indeed Nick's blue beater pulling up toward the house. Seeing the peeling paint and rust spots, she breathed a sigh of relief, her face relaxing slightly before she fixed it into a stern scowl.

She made her way toward the front door, then exited the study and stood at the entrance to the foyer with her arms crossed. She could hear Nick's door close, then his feet hitting each step as he climbed the stairs to the porch. She tensed and steeled herself as she heard his key in the door, watching as he turned the knob and inched it open. His head poked around the door, his face hopeful at first but his expression falling as soon as he saw Tash standing there.

"Shit," he muttered, wincing and stepping through the door. Kelly was behind him, her blonde hair entering the house before she did, swept up in the breeze that blew in, having finally found a weak point in its architecture after having pounded at it all evening.

"Close the door behind you. You're letting a chill in the house," Tash said, crossly.

Kelly's cheeks flushed and her feet set into place as though bearing down to defend her territory, but Nick nodded, shutting the door gently as he slipped his shoes off.

"Look," he started, his voice sheepish as he struggled to meet Tash's eye. "I'm really sorry-"

"Eleven thirty, Nick," Tash cut him off. "You're due back here eleven thirty. I don't ask you to follow many rules, but I do ask you to respect everyone else and at least show up on time. I told you when you got that car you couldn't be running all over creation. I have rules for a reason."

"It was the car," Kelly interjected, her voice in the range between pleading and indignation that only young women of a certain age were capable of. "We would've been here sooner. It stalled and-"

"And you couldn't call? Or answer your phone? Is that broken too?" Tash interjected.

"I tried, I'm sorry. I didn't have service on the road, and I had to flag someone down to help me jump the thing."

"That's convenient. It took almost two hours for you to get a jump and you couldn't pull over when you had service again to let me know so I could stop worrying?"

"We panicked," Nick said, before Kelly could give voice to the rebuttal he knew was on the edge of her tongue. She always had some snappy line lifted right from an early-90s sarcastic sitcom character on the tip of her tongue, and they always made him laugh. They perched there like soldiers on the end of a tiny pink diving board, ready to leap forward at the slightest sign of provocation. As much as he loved to watch her put them to work at the theatre jockeys or when they were out and about in town, seeing her and Tash exchange barbs again was not something he had been looking forward to seeing. "I just wanted to get home quickly and getting it working again took longer than I thought it would. I didn't think-"

"You certainly didn't," Tash frowned, stepping forward, her manufactured icy demeanor falling away. "I've been worried sick."

She reached out and turned his head, seeing the grease smear that ran along his cheek, and tisked. Her eyes fell further down onto the nape of his neck and found a lipstick smear there, the same bubble-gum pink shade that was currently pressed onto Kelly's lips. She looked from the smear to Kelly, who did not have a retort, colour rising to her cheeks. She turned back to Nick: "Electrical trouble, was it?"

Nick blushed sheepishly. He reached up and pushed the sleeve of his shirt against the nape of his neck, dislodging the stain.

"Go get cleaned up. Your dinner is in the microwave and I know you have homework to do," she instructed.

They began to move past her toward the kitchen when the house phone began to ring.

"Hear that?" she called after them mockingly as she stepped down the hall toward the phone. "Proof positive the phone is working on our end."

She kept an old rotary phone at the base of the stairs that led up to their dorm rooms, sitting on a desk that looked like it would be for a receptionist but which was pressed tight to the wall next to a bookcase, leaving no room for someone to sit behind and 'receive.' She liked the way it looked there, though, covered in pen marks and with its curly cord kinked up from being twisted absentmindedly. It looked well-used, as all the best things were, in her opinion.

It rang again, and from somewhere down the hall Iseulte called out, "Should I get that?"

"I've got it!" Tash yelled back, reaching the phone and clearing her throat before she picked it up.

"Heeeeello," she said into the receiver, and then after a moment. "This is she. May I ask who's calling?"

Tash stiffened, glancing around to make sure the kids weren't nearby.

Kelly opened the microwave door, revealing the

steamy, cheesy baked potatoes within. There were two of them, orbiting in a lopsided curve around the edge of the clear glass plate that stayed at the bottom of the oven. She hadn't put in a plate of her own, and now there was cheese congealing and adhering the potato to the plate. She licked her fingers and reached it.

Nick eyed her from the island in the centre of the kitchen, where he was eating from a healthy mound of corned beef hash. "That's too hot," he said, watching as steam rose from the piping hot vegetables.

She turned to him, narrowed her eyes, then stuck out her tongue defiantly. She reached in and grabbed one of the potatoes by the tips of her fingers. They sank in past the soft flesh easily, surrounding her digits with the scalding hot mess that was the meat of the potato.

"Fuck!" she screamed, drawing back her hand quickly. The potato came with her, stuck to her finger for a moment, before it dislodged and momentum took it out of the oven and toppled it to the floor where it exploded with the grace and poise of gelatin on concrete.

Nick laughed so hard that his food got caught in his throat. If it were possible for mashed potato to shoot from a man's nose, he would have in that moment. He slapped the table once, then raised his hand to his mouth to stop from losing any food. "I told you!"

"Shut up," she chided. She was cradling her injured hand in the other, blowing on it gingerly.

He frowned, then reached over and turned on the faucet. He stepped around the island and gently took her by the wrist.

She pulled away slightly, a reflex.

"It's okay," he soothed, his voice suddenly gentle. She let him take her burned hand and he guided it toward the running water, uncurling her fingers as he did so. They were red and swollen at their tips with watery blisters. He hissed. "Oh jeez, look what you've done to yourself."

"What?"

"It looks bad. I should get some Bactene." He opened the drawer beneath the sink, examined its content a moment, then closed it again. Frowning, he guided her hand up the water.

She hissed.

"I know," he said. He let me go and stepped away from her. "Keep that there though, I'll be right back with some."

He left the kitchen and jogged through the hall at a steady trot, winding through the ether of the corridor until he found what appeared to be a linen closet. When he opened it, it was packed with gauze instead of towels, and the third shelf from the top was lined with painkillers. He grabbed the bottle of Bactene and an anti-inflammatory with one deft motion of his fingers, then shut the door again.

Tash was standing behind the door, next to the desk the rotary phone sat on. She hadn't been hiding there, just standing, her arms clasped about herself as though she were cold. The phone receiver dangled from her hand by its cord, entwined through her slender fingers.

She was as white as freshly pressed paper.

"Tash?" Nick asked, gently pressing the closet door closed until it clicked.

She looked up as though she hadn't noticed him there,

then saw the medicine bottles in his hand. "Everything alright?"

"Kelly burned herself."

She tisked. "Is she okay?"

"Yeah, is everything okay with you?" He stepped forward, his voice taking on the same tones of parental concern hers had a few minutes before.

"Hm? Yeah. Yes." She put the phone back onto its receiver and opened the closet door. She found a jar of petroleum jelly almost without looking she knew the layout of it so well. She unscrewed the top, made sure there was some inside, then screwed it back and started back towards the kitchen with Nick.

As she walked, she reached into her pocket and produced her cell phone. It was a flip phone in the style that was common before the widespread use of touch screens, the kind that most people now associated with burner phones, although Nick knew she'd had that one for well over half a year. She flipped the screen up and started to text with her thumb as she walked.

'Come in,' she typed, then pressed send. A small animation of a metal mailbox came up, an envelope pushing in and out of the box until the phone made a soft whooshing sound and the screen went black again. She kept the phone visible as they walked, waiting to see if it would light back up with a return message, but it remained dark.

"Who was on the phone?" he asked, his voice lowered although he wasn't sure why.

She did not answer. She opened the door to the kitchen. Kelly still had her right hand running under the cold water of the faucet. With her left she was holding a fork of corned beef hash between Nick's plate and her face. There was significantly less of it than there had been when he'd left for the medicine.

While she was applying the petroleum jelly and wrapping the wound, Tash checked her phone three times and was denied a return message each time.

Nick closed the door to Kelly's room quietly, pressing his hand against the frame and pulling taut until they met with a single, subtle, click. Sound travelled in this house, he knew that all too well. The slightest creak of the floorboards or latching of a lock past 2am and he'd have to put up with that impenetrable stare that Tash always employed all during breakfast. Never judging, never punishing, just... knowing. And letting you know that she knew. And somehow, that embarrassment was worse than anything else she could do.

He stepped lightly along the edges of the hardwood floors closest to the wall, where the boards were newest and least likely to bend or moan. His hands splayed out to either side like a trapeze walker's baton, pantomiming those stepping quietly that he'd seen on television without really realizing he was doing it. The house was quiet for the moment, making every sound shatter through that quiet like ripples across a still pond.

Gunfire rang out, muffled but clear, and Nick's back was suddenly ramrod straight.

It was real gunfire; he'd known that right away. He'd been around enough to know the difference. Real gunfire had a pop and a presence that the blanks used on television did not. But while it was real, it also wasn't live. It was muffled and lower in volume than real in-house gunfire would be, and it wasn't echoing the same way.

He raised an eyebrow, then stepped forward towards the top of the stairs without caring if he was heard or not. He made his way down, the front door and foyer coming into view as he came around the bend in the stairs from the top floor. As he came around the last rung of steps, three more shots rang out: each similar, each with the same muffled unrealism that almost hid the deadly reality they represented.

He came around the corner into the living room and saw the back of Tash's head illuminating by the glow of the television all around it. The glow was the bright orange of fire. The colour arced and waned the way only real fire did, making the glow of the television in the dark room broad with the orange spectrum. There was no sound or background music, just that ephemeral glow coming out from behind Tash's skull as she blocked his view of the screen, her head and shoulders all that was visible above the swell of the couch.

"What is that?" he asked, stepping from the foyer into the media room.

Tash lunged forward, surprised by his sudden company. She thrust her right hand forward, aiming the previously unseen remote at it, and paused the playback quickly. A black bar formed across the top of the screen, with white text proclaiming that the video was playing from a jumbled, scrambled URL. "What're you doing up?" she asked, turning and trying to compose herself. She was as white as balance again, all the colour gone from her cheeks even under the intense scrutiny of his vision. Some of it had returned as they'd eaten and treated Kelly's burn, and by the time they'd gone upstairs she had been back to herself, but now she was ghostly and gaunt again.

"It's nothing. Something I was sent." She spoke without confidence, finding it hard to take her eyes off the screen and face him.

The image on the screen was blurred by bad photography and compression, and was obscured by smoke, but parts of it were still very clear. There were two men standing across from each other, separated by a docked boat. There were flames all around: the boat was on fire, the pier was on fire, the large stack of cash splayed out over the hull of the boat was on fire, and, if Nick squinted, the *man* on the right of the frame appeared to be on fire as well. The aflame man was in mid-stride, the direction his position implied for him putting him into a lunge at the other man within three frames.

Nick narrowed his milky white eyes, trying to take in as much of the visual information as he could.

There was a shadow near the top of the screen, a huddled mass of black, that it took Nick several seconds to recognize as a body. "What am I looking at here?" he asked, shaking his head imperceptibly.

Tash frowned. "I was sent some footage from out of Los Angeles. Some of it hit the news last month... some of it hasn't hit anywhere, yet."

"Footage of what?"

"Someone with powers."

He turned to her, sharply. "Pardon?"

She frowned, her mouth warbling back and forth as she debated whether or not to tell him more. "Murders. Someone with powers in Los Angeles, committing murders. The one that hit the media, it would have just slid away... but it's been linked to an ongoing serial case, so that's -- so it's not going away. There's still most people claiming the footage is doctored, so that's good... but I don't think it is. It doesn't look doctored to me, and the people who sent it to me can't find evidence of any CG wizardry."

Nick nodded to the frozen image. "Play it back, my eyes'll catch it if anything's fishy."

Tash paused, holding the remote aloft as if considering his course of action, for a moment. "No," she said, finally. She took a moment, nodded to herself, then nodded with more definiteness. "No, I don't want you involved in this."

He winced. "I'm not involved. I'm viewing a video file for programming artifacts. That's... that's not 'getting involved.'"

She paused, hesitated again, then played the video from the beginning.

It started with the man on the left firing his gun, that same familiar crack that Nick had heard from the top of the stairs. The same instant as the sound the man on the right's shoulder exploded in a spastic display of gore, splaying out to decorate the unseen wall behind him.

"Jesus," Nick breathed.

"Wait for it," Tash said, not taking her eyes off the screen.

The shot man did not fall over. He stepped forward

on a shaky foot, the blood pluming making his clothes glisten in the light of the blooming fire. The man on the left pressed the gun forward again and squeezed off two more shots. The first missed, but the second hit the shot man in the collar.

Somehow it did not even result in him breaking his stride.

The flames from the boat arched and another shot happened, grazing the man's cheek. But somewhere between the frames the man's cheek had changed from the same tanned hue of most in Los Angeles to a sort of ephemeral, black darkness.

It had happened so quickly that Nick had barely noticed it begin, and when the last shot brought his attention to the man's face he jumped. "What?"

When the shot man emerged from the fire, he had long teeth that came down too far, his jaw unhinged like a snake's. He snarled and at once his eyes -- buried in the shadow of his brow until now -- were large and red. He leaped forward, continuing the forward motion he'd started when Tash had paused the video: when his hands were outstretched and came to sharp points, and they both screamed. The man with the gun screamed in terror, but the shot man screamed with something that sounded -- almost -- like words.

Garbled words, words that sounded like those spoken while underwater or holding back bile, but words all the same. When the words completed, the shot man was on the shooter, pulling his fingers across the man's chest and revealing them, through consequence, to be sharp, long claws.

Tash paused the video again.

"Is that the end of it?" Nick asked, swallowing.

She sighed. "No."

He nodded. "Show me the rest of it?"

She shook her head. "That I will certainly not do."

He squinted, leaning forward against the back of the couch as he studied the frame she'd ended the video on. At that point, the man who'd been shot was all black, made of oily shadows that caught the light from the fire and bent it in strange directions along his musculature. His back looked as though it were bare, he noticed, made of the blackness. "What did he say at the end?"

"I'm not sure."

"He said something. Rewind it?"

Tash paused and sighed, then reluctantly obliged. The video skipped back fifteen seconds and then began to play again. The man leaped forward, and as he did, he said something so violent and guttural that it struggled to be heard over the roaring of the fire and the yelling of the man with the gun.

"Blekwoundhives," Nick repeated, trying to mimic what little of the man's mouth movements he saw. The video played longer than it had the last time, despite Tash's efforts to stop it, and Nick saw something red and long that was meant to stay inside the shooter tumble into the open air. He winced. "Did he live?"

Tash shook her head. "He did not."

Nick shook his head. "Blekwoundhives."

"It's clearer in the other file," Tash frowned. She pressed the menu button on her remote, navigated to the second file in the folder -- of which there were only two

-- and pressed play.

The audio was scratchy and nasally, with the sort of whines and interruptions that usually came over dollarstore two-way radios. The shot was again from security footage and was a wide shot of a hallway. There were cars parked along one side of the screen, and along the other was a solid wall of concrete. The Shane logo was stenciled along the far edge of the wall.

Nick narrowed his eyes, moving around from behind the couch and sitting next to Tash.

For a long moment there was nothing in the frame, the only thing moving the timestamp in the lower right of the screen. Suddenly there was a woman in the doorway at the far right of the frame, walking forward towards the camera. Her shoes clicked along the pavement as she made her way along the row of cars, closer and closer to the camera. There was nothing else in the frame and she was halfway across it, the video halfway to completion. Suddenly, a part of the shadow between cars reached out and found her, striking her in the back of the head.

Nick winced when he saw the way the woman hit the concrete.

The shadow raised, dark and black and looming. It was fully black, as if the dark noise at the edges of the video had come to life and was haunting their feed. It stood above her, watching the woman as she moved.

She was still moving, half of her just out of frame as she writhed, trying to find the leverage to get back up. Her knee kept slipping, blood already making its way past her hairline and into her face and disorienting her.

The shadow creature bent like a cat, its sharp hands

grabbing her and forcing her around, its feet on either side of her, pinning her. There was a scream when she was spun around to face it. The shadow creature grabbed her and shook her, slamming the back of her head against the pavement again and again until she stopped making sounds and stopped moving.

It brought its hand up to her slender neck and pulled, each of its four fingers making a separate slice that combined to form one long cut that ran from ear to ear.

"Jesus," Nick said under his breath.

Blood spilled out as her head leaned back, growing in a steady pool that leaked back into the frame, making its way toward the drain that the floors all sloped towards.

The creature tilted back its head to reveal two large, cat-like red eyes. It opened its mouth and revealed it to be full of massive serrated teeth.

The creature grabbed her by either side of her shirt, thrust back its head, and bellowed: "Black Womb lives."

Nick jolted to his feet, so suddenly that it took Tash aback. "Black Womb lives."

She nodded.

"That... that thing just said Black Womb lives." He motioned to the screen, frozen on the last frame of the shadow-creature drawing back to strike at the still form of the woman again. The light of the room on the screen was muted, a stark contrast to the fiery hell of the first, and the brightest spots the camera picked up with the silky gleam off the creature's wet back. He turned from the screen, to Tash, and then back again. "When was this?"

"Recently."

He swallowed. "The week I left my hometown, Coral

Beach... that same week, someone was killed there. A lot of people were killed there, people I knew. Friends. That was on the wall behind one of them. Black Womb lives, it was written on the wall in blood."

Tash nodded, leaning forward and looking at the black mass of flesh crouched in the corner of the screen. The colour of her cheeks fought itself, alternating between hot and red and a sallow white. She stared at it as if she expected it to defy the laws of video playback and turn to look at her.

"Did you... did you know about this thing when you pulled me out?"

She turned to him, taking a moment to tear her eyes from the screen. All maternity had gone from her gaze and she looked at him, perhaps for the first time, as someone on equal footing as her. "No," she said finally, with definitive weight to it. "We'd gotten a tip that something was up there. When I got there and found you, I'd assumed you were it." She turned to the screen again. "You weren't."

Nick held his breath, turning back to the screen. On Tash's command the video switched back to the pier fire, with the boat full of barrels of cash ablaze in its middle.

She froze the frame as the man who'd been shot was about to lunge, just before he turned into the scaly black creature, almost where it had been when he'd entered the room. The face was blurred and darkened by shadow, caught between frames of the video. "Do you recognize him?" she asked.

He squinted, stepping closer to the screen. After a long moment, he said. "No. Not offhand. It's not unfamiliar, but... you know."

She nodded.

"You going to LA to look into this?"

She nodded.

"I'm going with you."

She turned to him sharply. "I told you, you're not --"

"I'm going with you," he said, without debate.

"Someone needs to watch the other students."

"Iseulte can do that. Iseulte *loves* that."

She let out a breath.

"I can help."

She paused, her upper lip bending slightly, then finally nodded again.

CHAPTER TWO

Morgana's was an upscale restaurant just shy of the Hollywood Boulevard in Los Angeles. It stood tall and wide, taking up a third of a city block with its thick, black brick exterior and iron-rimmed windows, also black. Atop it was a large crystal letter X that caught the sunlight during the day and sent it shimmering down to the street below. Tonight, it caught the light of the full moon, turning it into a whirling oblong.

Underneath the iron window was a table for two that was on permanent reservation. No matter how busy the restaurant got, the table was set and clean, and was never occupied by anyone save for one man, who now sat there finishing the last of a fine cut of lamb and a glass of '95 Chateau Margaux. There were uneaten stalks of asparagus littered about the plate, drenched in the blood that had leaked from the rare meat. There had been mashed potatoes in garlic sauce and baby carrots, though they had been eaten. Stephen Fields placed a healthy strip of meat into his mouth. It squirted moisture into his cheeks when he bit into it, then fell apart with ease and was succulent.

He washed it down with wine so expensive that most men would never even lay eyes on the bottle.

The woman that sat across from him was twenty-seven but looked much younger. She had bright red hair, pale cheeks, and wore a black dress with a plunging neckline.

"How's your steak?" he asked, once the last remnants of his had slid down his throat.

She paused and looked down at the plate. Her vegetables were gone, save for a scant line of mashed potatoes that had been stained red with the blood of the rare steak he'd ordered. The steak was untouched -- sliced into easily digestible sections with neither of them being digested. Her wine was also untouched, the glass free from the bright red of her lipstick.

She frowned, then cast her eyes back to his expectant gaze, and forced a thin smile. "It's wonderful," she said. Her voice was sultry, like silk. She didn't just smile and speak, she spoke *with* her smile, and if the evidence of her deception wasn't clear on the plate before her, he might have believed it. She looked at him when she lied: directly in the eyes, and yet somehow past them.

He stared at her for a long moment, the red rims around his eyes sagging along with his cheeks as his smile lowered. It made his face look like a mask that didn't fit quite right, revealing the second, more sinister skin underneath.

She shifted uncomfortably, bringing her shoulders back flush against the cushion of her chair. This had the effect of pushing the plunging neckline of that dress -- which wasn't hers -- forward in a way she hadn't intended, drawing his attention briefly. She was wearing a pendant that was hers, a small faux jade bobble that sat comfortably between her meager breasts.

"I hope you can lie better than that," he said. His lips barely moved when he said that -- she'd noticed that already. Orders and repercussions were not barked or screamed, they were said quietly and not at all bombastic. His proclamations were a part of the act, but those quiet moments -- hidden by the barest movements of his lips -- were who he really was.

She wasn't sure how to take his statement. Her smile faltered a little at first, then returned. She nodded.

He cocked his head forward. "Eat your steak."

She turned toward the large bay window that looked out onto the Los Angeles street, and to the people walking past it. Her gaze lingered on them for an uncomfortably long moment as she picked up her fork, rested it gingerly between her thumb and middle finger, then paused. Again, her smile wavered.

"Eat your steak," he said, again with the barest motion of his lips. "It cost more than you did."

She stiffened, her frown growing to the point that it drew lines along either side of her mouth, and he noticed.

A large man with a barreled chest and close-cropped hair along his ears entered the room through the kitchen and surveyed the restaurant.

"I don't like... I don't eat meat," she said finally, sheepishly.

He maneuvered his mouth, his tongue travelling the entire perimeter of his teeth. He placed down his own fork and made a pyramid out of his hands, elbows against the table, then aimed the tip of that pyramid at her as though it were a spear. "There may be several things you do tonight that you don't like, but you'll like them. I'll be convinced that you like them." He paused and she held back a shudder. The pyramid retracted from being directed at her, rising again to the ceiling. "Eat your steak."

She nodded, then swallowed. She plunged the fork into the most outer chunk of meat, cold with the time she'd spent eating her vegetables.

The man with the barrel chest stepped over to Field's table covertly, striding up alongside it rather than approaching it head-on. He cast one furtive glance toward the window and the streets from over the top of his glasses, then looked to Fields without a word.

"Chase?" Fields asked, wiping his red-tinted lips with a napkin embroidered with his initials.

Chase breathed a sigh through his nose, then leaned down and spoke into Fields' ear.

"What?" Fields snapped. "All of it?"

Chase leaned forward and whispered again, nodding.

Fields wiped his mouth a second time, though it was clean. He did so with animation and force, then pushed the napkin away and onto his plate with a snarl. "Get the fire out and run the river. See if there's anything we can salvage." He rose from his seat and pulled his jacket taut.

His escort stood up as well, keeping her dress down and happily backing up away from her steak. Chase reached out and touched her on the shoulder, his massive, calloused hands cupping the tender flesh of her in its entirety and holding her in place.

"No, let her come," Fields said, turning and motioning toward them both with two fingers. "I'll need something after this."

Chase frowned and took his hand off of her shoulder. She nodded and looked at him, in the eye from her two feet of height detriment, possibly the first real look she'd given another man in months. She swallowed a dry mouth, then nodded.

The window came forward, sending shards of glass everywhere.

"Jesus!" Chase bellowed, turning away from the debris. A trash can -- full to the brim with trash -- finished its arc through the pane and connected with his shoulder, sending him forward onto one knee. Diners screamed and started to yell past Fields, scattering in one direction or another searching for the exits they hadn't paid attention to upon entering.

Fields stood straight, his smooth chin raised high as the wind swept in through the pane, catching his receding hair and pushing it back in the hot updraft. He stood with his feet firmly planted as Xander Drew stepped through the broken stalagmites of glass that jutted up from the pane's steel edge.

He watched as Chase tried to rise off his knee, then lashed out with one swift kick to the back of the shin, sending him fully to the floor. The escort screamed and backed up a pace, saw that Fields was no longer watching her, and ran for the exit with the rest of the diners. Xander turned his attention towards Fields, locking eyes with him. "Hello, Motherfucker," he said in a voice that was meant to be low and intimidating... but which he couldn't help but let the barest hints of a smile into.

Fields stepped back a pace.

The back doors to the kitchen opened and three men came out, guns drawn. They looked and acted like secret service members -- but were just more men like Chase, on Fields' payroll, admittedly at a higher rate than most. One still had sauce smeared across the left side of his pale face from being raised from his meal.

Chase swore, looking up from his spot on the floor to where the escort -- Candice -- had been, and finding nothing but vacant air. He looked up to the men with the guns, then sucked in a painful breath through nostrils that were draining and flaring. He stopped, his eyes going wide at the moist, dank trash all around him.

Xander took his lighter out of his pocket and flicked it once, producing a long, arcing flame that bent back in the hot Los Angeles draft and singed his fingertips. He turned back to Fields and smiled in the glow of the light and looked as though he were about to say something definitive.

"Fire!" Chase yelled at the men, as he reached for his own weapon and arose.

Xander dropped the lighter onto a large pile of trash, the kerosene that soaked it igniting. In a flash it spread out, onto the trash and the pools of stank fluid that had bled out from it like a shockwave, finding its way towards the lush curtains of *Morgana's* and sending them into flames.

The flame pushed back with such force that it sent the can -- still half full of the soaked debris -- rocketing backward like a bomb. It struck the edge of the shattered window and spewed hot refuse as it spiraled, spitting it onto

Chase's pant leg and catching it there as he rolled away.

Fields raised his arm and backed away, several of his men caught in the draft. One started to fire, and once again Xander's shoulder exploded in a mass of heat and rendered flesh -- and before Fields' eyes, it was knit back together. He stared in awe, stepping back to the wall. His man fired another shot as the other two checked their rounds, and in an instant Xander was on him. A moment later, he was unconscious in the growing flames.

A wall of fresh fire stood between Fields and Xander, and in the look between them both men knew it was only a barrier for one of them.

"The fuck are you?" he asked, his lips barely moving again despite his awe. His throat stung from gas and fumes.

Xander stepped forward, the flames lapping at his knees as they spread. "You ever hear of a Black Womb?" he asked, in a tone that was somehow serious and not at once.

Fields shook his head slowly, trying to recall if -- and where -- he'd heard that before. For the briefest of moments -- perhaps the first in his adult life -- there was no anger in him. Just fear and wonder as he stepped back from the spreading flame engulfing his favorite restaurant.

Xander smiled.

A second of the men stepped back into the hall, his coat off and burning in the corner. He was holding a wet napkin over his face, brought his gun up and shot again. The shot was quick and caught Xander in the ribs, sending bone and meat into his shirt. He turned and grabbed at the man, squeezing his trigger arm before he could re-lease another shot.

Chase grabbed Fields by the shirt-collar in a way he never had before and shook him. "Come on!" he bellowed, unafraid to let *his* voice raise to its fullest potential.

It shook Fields out of his prone state and back to real-ity. He coughed, then with a second tug from Chase, both men fled through the window Xander had smashed in.

Xander turned back from the shooter and screamed, so loud that it was heard above the roaring of the increas-ing flame. It was an ethereal scream, something neither Chase nor Fields had ever heard before -- not fear but not anger either. It was like the rage of the titans: a sound man had never been meant to hear.

Chase pushed Fields into the open back door of a car and opened the front door himself. He ordered the driver to drive the second his foot was inside, and the car sped down the boulevard with the door flapping from the in-ertia and Chase riding it, gripping the open sunroof for balance.

Xander stepped out into the street and watched the car speed away with unblinking eyes, his coat still awash in flames and fire as *Morgana's* burned itself to the ground behind him.

Chase slammed the car door as the driver revved the engine up to fifty, passing three cars by swerving into the opposing lane before ducking back into their own. He hissed through ground teeth, reaching a hand up to the right side of his face and feeling the sharp snap of burned skin.

"Fuck!" Fields yelled, taking off his jacket. It was smoldering and melting, the fibers sticking to the fabric of his shirt. They pulled and then snapped as he threw the jacket into the corner, smoke and kerosene stench still rising from it. He turned and looked out the shaded back window, watching as *Morgana's* faded into a horizon of smoke and ash. "What the fuck was that?"

Chase grabbed an embroidered handkerchief from the centre console and used it to grasp a handful of ice from the champagne well, quickly pressing it to his face in short, quick swirls to bring down the swelling. He hissed again.

"Where are we going?" the driver asked, struggling to keep his composure.

"Just drive," Chase snapped. "He's been hitting us for weeks, but not like this. He's been skittering around the edges but... fuck."

"It's gotta be the Russians. They're making a bid. Or the Checs. Could be the --"

"Due respect sir, I think you're underestimating the people you've pissed off over the years."

Fields' head snapped up as though he were about to rebuke, but the sharp pain in his neck and the still-swelling burn that Chase was tending to made him rethink it, quickly. He nodded. "Get us to Yellow," he said, his lips back to the nearly inanimate uncanny valley posture.

Chase grabbed the radio and made the order. He paused and listened to the response as Fields turned and looked out the back of the car again. Though they'd gone miles, he still scanned the sidewalks for the man that had come closer to him with ill intent than any man had in nearly a decade. Chase turned back to Fields, swallowing. "Yellow's gone, sir."

Again Fields' head snapped up. "What?" He spoke as though he were being talked back to and rebuffed... not as though what he was being told were true.

"Safehouse Yellow. It's gone. Firebombed twenty minutes ago." He paused. "So has Burgundy and Green."

For the third time, the colour left Fields' cheeks. "How long has this fucker been on me?"

Chase winced. "We haven't used Green in six months. At least that long." He paused, then gave the driver directions.

Fields spent the rest of the ride looking out his windows.

CHAPTER THREE

Stanford University, California

The cafeteria was large and open. There was a half faux wall made of brick and glass dividing the kitchen and the line to it from the rest of the seating area.

Tash sat at a table far from the rest, across an expanse of hall that was meant to allow for ease of foot traffic but instead divided one row of tables from all others, making them rarely used -- and therefore, often clean. She was a tall, lanky woman with dark black pixie cut hair that clung to her scalp as though it were wet, even though it was not. Her eyes were large and dark and distracted from the lines on either side of her mouth, making her age hard to determine and leaving more people to -- incorrectly -- assume she was in her late thirties and well-kept for that age. She was wearing a Stanford hoodie of a style long passed that most of the students who noticed it mistook for a knock-off.

To her left was Nick. He was drinking an off-brand soda he'd gotten while in the line and intermittently casting his steely blue eyes toward the chicken sandwich he'd selected from a spinner. It had been overpriced and was a disappointment. Across from him and to Tash's right was Kelly. She had a single cup of coffee on a saucer in front of her and seemed to take sips only to punctuate thoughts that neither of the others were privy to. Twice now Tash or Nick had said something that had made her eyebrows raise, but rather than responding, she had paused long enough to formulate her rebuttal, then taken a sip.

Despite himself, Nick found it impressive. He smiled at her from across the table, and she smirked back at him from over her cup.

In front of Tash was a tiny cup of espresso, sending steam wafting up into her chin, and a small plate next to it that held a fluffy, buttery croissant that she'd only eaten one crusty corner of.

"The air's dry here," Kelly said, turning away from the both of them and scanning the crowd. Everyone was wearing shorts and shirts without sleeves and she found her eyes darting from one slice of exposed flesh to another. Her eyes finally landed on a plump girl, improbably dressed in both a fluffy pink sweater and spanks. She was playing a game on her phone while an uneaten bowl of oatmeal cooled in front of her. Kelly watched her, pushing her hair back away from her face so that her view was unobstructed.

"It's California," Tash said, her voice motherly and somehow still matter-of-fact. "It's always dry here."

"Well, thanks ever so for bringing us then," she drawled, taking a sip of her coffee. Her face shone blue briefly when she brought the cup to it, making her flesh appear to be something soft and supple. "You say what you want about Georgia, but we'd never let half our state burn while we watered our lawn."

Nick looked at her and smirked. "Same back home. West Coast is a different world."

"You're from Maine!" she laughed, flicking her fingers to dismiss the thought. "The last time you had a dry spell, the Red Claws were on top!"

"Hey," he said, trying to sound indignant but unable to muster the ability to.

"Is for horses," she said, reaching over and pinching his plate between her thumb and forefinger and dragging it over to her side of the table without asking. She smiled as she picked up his chicken sandwich and took a bite... before the smile slowly faded from her lips and was replaced by a sneer. "Fuck's sake, *everything's* dry here."

"This isn't a social visit," Tash said finally, more curtly than she would have liked.

Kelly and Nick exchanged a concerned look across the table. It was only now that they noticed how straight Tash was sitting, her back and legs at a ninety-degree angle. Her head was arched, not sloped or slouched in the slightest, and she was scanning the crowd around them with the anxiety of a meerkat. She went from one side of the room to the other, scanning each face individually, then moving back the way she'd come again.

"What's going on?" Nick asked, cupping his hand around his soda without having any.

"We got a tip from one of my contacts," she said, reluctantly taking her eyes off the crowd and pulling her phone out. She turned it on with a flick of her finger and opened her messenger app. There were five conversations with pending messages, but she ignored the top three and pressed the fourth. The contact had no name, just a series of numbers too short to have been a phone number.

The only message in the thread read: Black XX / L.A. / 4 DOA.

"Is it from Victor?" Nick asked.

"If it had been from Victor, I would have said it was from Victor," she said, turning off her phone and tucking it back into her pocket. "It's from someone else."

"Mind telling us who?" Kelly drawled, raising an eyebrow.

"I do, actually."

Kelly rolled her eyes, and after a moment, took a sip of her coffee. That made three times, and Nick grinned. She smiled when she noticed this, and as far as he was concerned her lips had never looked quite that kissable before.

He reached out his leg to touch hers, and she smiled at him in response.

"Message says Los Angeles, we're five hours from there," Kelly noted, cocking her head toward Tash's pocket. "Three, if you let Nick drive."

"We're here to make sure we need to go to Los Angeles. That the problem isn't *here*," she said. Her gaze had returned to the crowd but was no longer scanning, it was locked on something. "My three o'clock, don't stare. Kelly take a glance, but Nick, tell me what you see."

They both turned.

Sitting on the far side of the cafeteria was a large man, over seven feet with broad shoulders. He was wearing a blazer that was fitted and yet still looked too small for him, in a shade too similar to his ashen albino flesh. He was bald save for small patches of stubble behind both his ears, and there were bumps of flesh that travelled from his eyebrows to the base of his skull in two parallel lines. He was eating a fried tomato sandwich and looked to be oblivious to it, a large folder of papers in front of him holding all his attention.

"Power," Nick said absently, his eyes darting over the scant hints of muscle tone that showed even through the arms of the blazer. He chanced a look at the man's face, trying not to linger too long in case the man met his eye. "Frustration. There are lines around the eyes and the mouth... deep, cut lines from frowning. Power and frustration, not a great combination."

"No," Tash said evenly, taking a second bite of her croissant. She had ordered it heated but had waited until it was cool to eat it. "No, it isn't."

Nick squinted, his eyes finding his way to the manila folder the man was holding, and the writing on it.

"That's enough now, Nick," Tash said. When he didn't turn away, she put her hand on his, snapping him out of his concentration.

He shook his head and turned first to Kelly, who was looking up at him with eyes that were filled with worry. When he met her eye, she turned from him to Tash, her expression neutral but her tone accusatory: "Is that Jona?" she whispered from between clenched teeth. "Did you put us in a room with Jona?"

Nick looked from Kelly to Tash disbelievingly.

Tash took a sip from her espresso cup. "That man is called Jona, yes."

Kelly turned back for a moment, unable to stop herself.

She had never been so scared of a man grading papers before.

Jona's office was small and long, made even smaller by the bookcases that took a foot off the width of the room on either side. The stacks were piled high with the sort of dusty navy and beige texts that anyone would come to expect from a professorial office -- texts that had long since shed the splashes of colour and vibrancy of their dust jackets and had revealed themselves to be the same dry, boring texts as those that had come before it.

The door to the office was open. Jona liked it that way -- he'd worked in countries where the only door in a structure was the exterior door, and all other barriers were maintained only through personal respect and acceptance of boundaries. Even in those places, had there been the option of a door, he would have preferred to have left it open... It provided a sense of willingness to help that he wanted to portray to his student body that he knew his physique did not aid with.

Tash stood with her toes along the invisible barrier at the doorway, peering in at Jona as he wrote a fraction atop a collection of papers and then placed them top-down atop a large pile, before moving on to the next in the stack. He looked up briefly before he started to read, stopped, then did a double-take and locked eyes with her.

"Tasha," he said warmly, putting down his page and motioning her in. "To what do I owe the pleasure?"

Tash looked down at her feet, her toes standing perfectly along the metal ridge that slid under the door when it was shut. It divided the hall from the office, even the rectangular tiles moving differently inside. In the hall they were straight and perpendicular, while in the office they were slightly askew. The effect was nauseating, giving the straight lines and ninety-degree angles of the office the appearance of being tilted without actually being so… an optical illusion that reflected the reality of the situation deftly.

She took a deep breath through clenched lips so that he wouldn't notice, then placed one foot in front of the other and entered the room. Even the atmosphere inside was different, the humidity hitting her as though she had stepped into a brick wall.

She paused, briefly, when the wall of heat passed through her, and he smiled.

"Forgive me, it can be hard to get used to." He smiled, then gestured up to the Spider Plants that grew in spidery twigs outside the confines of the pots that lined the book-shelves. "But the Spider Plant thrives in the heat and the damp where it came from… as do I."

Tash nodded, coming to a stop with her hands folded along the back of the chair opposite Jona, but not taking it. They stood like that for a long moment: her hovering above him. Her height should have made it a powerful dichotomy, but his own body was so tall that it nearly closed the gap between them. It was only up close that it was clear how oversized his desk was to accommodate him, squeezed into the room in such a tight fit that it must have been assembled within rather than carried in whole. Even knowing that, she could not see the seams where the desk had come apart, nor was it immediately apparent how Jona easily got in and out from around his seat at it.

"I'm heading into Los Angeles," she said matter-of-factly. All her fingers formed straight little bullets along the back of the chair, her thumbs hidden behind.

"It's nice this time of year," Jona nodded, puffing out his lower lip contemplatively. "You should try *Morgana's*. Their steak is excellent, I'm told, but they do a broccoli and bacon risotto that is simply heaven."

"It's not a social visit," she said. Her voice was already showing the borders of her patience, fraying along the edges of itself. She fought back the urge to sneer, hating herself for coming loose so quickly. "One of mine is missing, I've gotten a tip and I'm checking to see if it's related."

"One of yours?" Jona asked, the ridges where his eyebrows would have been rising. "Has anyone called out an Amber Alert?"

Tash lowered her eyes at him. "One of Victor's, actually. You may have met him. Theo?"

"I know him by reputation," Jona replied. He moved the paper he'd begun to correct when she had come in to the blank space in front of her, a tacit implication that the conversation was grating on him. He looked down at the paper, read the first line, then looked up again. "Is there a reason you're bringing this to my attention?"

"I wanted to make sure I wasn't wasting my time... that you didn't have anything to do with it."

He looked at her for a long moment with a slack jaw, then slowly a smile spread over his lips. He held it for a long time, just staring at her.

"I'm sorry, I'm not sure if I should take that as an ad-mission or not."

"The fact that you think of me in such nefarious terms amuses me. As though I sit here behind this cheap desk and just..." he made circular motions with his hands over the papers on his desk, as if collecting the ephemeral na-ture of his thoughts. "Plan and plot, like some sort of Bond villain."

"Oh, I'm not saying you're a Bond villain," Tash said with a hushed tone, shaking her head. "Bond villains get other people to do their dirty work."

Again he smiled, this time showing off long rows of white teeth. He'd spent considerable money on them, she knew that, because she had seen him while missing two front teeth on several occasions. Even so they looked nat-ural, only that sharp eye tooth looking a touch too long. "If you're speaking about my anthropological endeavors, you'll never see me following in the footsteps of Frazer or Tylor, that's true. But you can check with the AAA, I log all my expeditions."

"You logged New York?"

His smile wavered slightly, receding half an inch on either side. "I did," he said finally, and unconvincingly.

Tash smiled, just out of one side of her mouth.

"I do have a lot to do, Tasha." He reshuffled the pa-pers on his desk as he spoke without looking at them, as if pantomiming work. "I don't know anything about your missing teammate or anything else. This may shock you and Victor, but I don't spend all my time thinking about what you two get up to."

She nodded. "Checking out something else, too. Something a tipster sent me."

"No need to be coy with me. The students aren't around... what did he have to say? Simon he goes by now, isn't it?"

She stiffened. "There've been murders in L.A. Something with... strange abilities. I can honestly say I haven't seen anything like it before. It was caught on video taking out a shipyard. You... ever hear of a thing called a Black Womb?"

He thought a moment, running his tongue along the inside of his mouth. "No," he said finally, and with finality. "No, I haven't."

Tash nodded. She backed up three steps to exit the room without turning her back on him, then continued down the hall.

Jona continued reading the paper he'd been submitted for a moment, then put it down and cursed.

CHAPTER FOUR

Los Angeles, California

Nick flicked through the channels while sitting on the edge of his hotel room bed. Kelly was behind him, lying with her hair splayed out across firm pillows, her arms stretched to cover as much room as possible with her meager form. Her bed was a few feet away, divided only by a table that was affixed to the floor with bolts. The blankets on it were clean and undisturbed, as flat as a sheet of paper.

Nick flicked past the Weather Channel, then a twenty-four-hour news channel, then a channel that showed nothing but retro cartoons.

"You know there's a channel guide, right?" Kelly asked, leaning her head up until her chin touched her clavicle and she could see him. "Like a legit channel that is a guide. You can just go there and it'll show you what's on now. On every channel. And what will be on, every channel."

"I know," he said, continuing to press the 'next' button on the large remote over and over again. He wasn't staying on each channel long enough to even see what it was really, except for vaguely iconic images. One channel had a weird quality to the film that made him recognize the show as a BBC program, although he didn't know which one. Another had slapdash animation like the old Hanna Barbera cartoons, although he didn't stay on the channel long enough to tell if it was a legitimate H&B cartoon or just another program aping its unique style.

She continued to watch him for a moment, the constant and imprecise nature of the way he turned the channels making it hard to follow. The second her mind started to latch on and make connections about a thing it was gone, and as it happened more and more her brow became knitted in the centre of her face. Finally, she sat up, pressing her hands against the bed and sliding her tailbone back until it rested against his pillow and she was in a sitting position. "I give up, what are you doing?"

He turned back to her, unsure of what she was talking about, then smiled. She was running her hands through her hair on either side of her head, teasing out the static that the bedspread had imbued it with until it was again framing her face like blonde curtains. "Sorry. We didn't have all these channels when I grew up."

She smiled and brought her knees up to her breasts. She was wearing jeans that were tight to her slender form and he wondered, not for the first time, how she could manage to move with such freedom in such restrictive clothing. She pushed her hair back behind her ear on one side and said, "We grew up in the same time, and I had a shit ton of channels. Don't try and sound older than you are."

"My parents didn't have cable," he explained. "All we watched were free streaming and torrents. Which is fine… but there was no, like, *channels* to flip through."

"Really?" she giggled, scrunching her nose in the way she did that he found irresistibly cute. "My dad never used to download anything, he bought into those ads that said it was the same as stealing a car. He caught me downloading a pop song once and tanned me so hard I couldn't sit for a week."

Nick winced, then mental image of someone laying hands on Kelly causing a tight bother in the centre of his chest. His eyebrows curled upward in pity, which she noticed and ignored.

"We had satellite though," she continued. "He loved that damn satellite because he had a generator and if the power went out, we could still have TV. The house could be losing its roof from a hurricane but if he had a case of beer and twenty sports channels to choose between, he did not care."

Nick nodded. She didn't talk about her family life before they found each other often, and he was never sure if that was because she didn't like to think about it or if it was because she thought he didn't. On the few times he did get a new detail, they were inevitably added to a file in his mind: a long list of tidbits and anecdotes that, when combined together, formed the jumbled yarn-ball of experience that was Kelly Saunders.

She pulled herself closer to him, disrupting the sheets and blankets even more than they already were. She was seated in the middle of the bed now, and she reached behind her and repositioned the pillows so that they were still behind her propping her up. When she was comfortable, she turned back to him, her chin resting on her knees and forming a crest and dimple in the supple flesh of her jaw. "Tell me more about where you're from," she said. She used the same tone she would have as a child when requesting to hear her favorite story again.

He met her eye with a skeptical look. "Coral Beach? Nothing to tell."

She did not move or change her expression.

He smiled, hit mute on the television, then turned toward her. "Maine is... different."

"From what?"

"From *everything*. There's something about living near the ocean that just changes people. Seeing something that big every other day, it just puts things into perspective. You're... small, and the world knows you're small, and you can tell because you're next to this big thing that's calm and soothing but if you get too close it will swallow you whole without even thinking about it."

She smiled. "It sounds pretty."

"It is," he said, with an air of reminiscent nostalgia in his voice. "Maine small towns are bizarre. The part where I'm from, it doesn't really have small towns. It has small *populations*, but the towns are like tiny cities. In the fall people come up from New York and down from Canada to Cape Cod, and if they can't get to Cape Cod, they go to the surrounding towns. They come to see the leaves change and for fall cookouts and festivals. It's all about fall. But like, you need to have all the amenities that city-folk are used to, so you end up with small towns not big enough to have malls that have malls, or not big enough to have theatres that have theatres. The businesses take the hit nine months out of the year because for three months they'll make their mint."

"I think that sounds nice," she said, her cheeks rising into her vision. "You get your small-town vibe but you still get to go to the movies when you want to. I bet the theatre is almost empty most of the time, like having your own private viewing."

Nick nodded. "During really slow months, they don't even show all day, you go online and book when you want to watch something, and they open for that. They're an appointment-only theatre for three months."

She snorted and laughed.

His smile faded a little. He looked off toward the heater that was under the window to their room, which looked out onto nothing but stone and concrete. "It's not all good. A lot of kids get very... bitter, towards the people coming in. It's xenophobia times ten, outsiders are *literally* coming into your town. Into your home, if your parents register on Air B&B." He paused, thought for a moment, then nodded as though he were coming to some realization for the first time. "There's really two types of people in that town: people who realize that the town basically can exist because of tourism since the mine closed and are grateful, and people who hate the outsiders coming in." He thought another moment. "And some of that bitterness is from false paternity, I think."

She raised an eyebrow.

He frowned, thinking of how to word what he was thinking. "There's a lot of young girls that get pregnant there, but not a lot of men who got them pregnant. Most kids there are born somewhere between May and July, because their mothers got pregnant during the tourist season, while men were in from away. There's a generation of kids without fathers there because their fathers came from outside for a good time, then left when the vacation was over like there was no responsibility left behind."

She winced, then nodded. She moved so that her cheek was resting on her knee instead of her chin, her golden hair tumbling over the crest of her leg. "Tell me about *your* father."

He stopped and stared at her for a moment, then turned and looked at the glow of the city as it filtered in through the misshaped window. Hotel windows were tiny and hard to open because it discouraged suicide via them, he'd heard once. He thought he might have heard it from his father while on a family vacation. He smirked, with melancholy. "I didn't really know him."

A concerned look found its way to her face, and she opened her mouth to speak without knowing what to say.

"Not like that," he said with a slight laugh, cutting off her apology. "He wasn't absent. I just... never knew him." He paused, his brow furrowing, as if trying to find something that would answer her question to his satisfaction. "He wasn't a drinker, but he drank in moderation. I don't think he ever stepped out on my mom, but I don't know anything about how they met or... anything they did before me. I just... don't really have anything."

She touched his arm, the warm cup of her palm gently caressing the tender flesh of his inner bicep. When she touched him, there was a spark between them that lit the area around them blue for an instant, and though it stung he didn't pull away. He'd become used to it, the electricity of her. "I'm sorry I brought it up."

"No," he smiled. "It's really fine. I just never really... thought about it. I don't even know where he stands on things. I guess I assume he's progressive because I feel like I am, but he never talked about it, so I guess I don't really know." He put his hand on the bed to prop himself up and leaned closer to her as his voice became more engaged and animated. "Does that... How can I know who I am if I don't know who he was?"

She pressed her head forward and kissed him with passion and force. She brought her fluttering fingers up to either side of his face and held him by the ears to pull him forward even as she pushed him away with her lips. The same electric sparks danced between their lips like fairies, and when she was done, she lowered her hands to either side of his collar and gently pushed him away. "I know who you are. You're a good man."

He smiled, light-headed for a moment. "I'm seventeen. I'm not even a man."

"Oooh no," she grinned, moving one leg over him until she straddled his legs. "I've known men. I've known more bad men then I'd care to count." She placed a finger on his lip, both to quiet his objection and to point to him. "You, Nick Carry, are a good man. Or you will be, if you prefer."

He smiled at her.

She reached out toward him gingerly, tracing the air around his ocular orbits and just barely caressing his high cheekbones. When she looked at him again it was with a serene calmness that was rare on her. "Take them out," she said, her voice wet with the fragility of the request.

He paused, wincing.

"Please?"

He reached up and pressed a thumb and forefinger to either of his eyes, gently. When he pulled them back there was a small circular disc affixed to each finger, stuck with nothing but moisture. He looked at her now with eyes that were milky white and without pupils, his real eyes, and he held out his contacts to her.

She took them from him and leaned over him to place them on the nightstand between their two beds, her hair falling over him and brushing his face with their fruit-scented tips. When they were away, she moved back, her body suddenly only capable of smooth motions like liquid, and she took his face in her hands again.

"A good man, who sees me," she said, staring into the flecks of white and gray that made up his sclera.

She kissed him again, her hair falling around him until it surrounded him.

CHAPTER FIVE

Fields pushed his way into the bathroom of his safe-house, the buttons of his silk shirt snapping as he peeled it off. It fell to the floor as though it weighed more than it did, half landing on the toilet before tumbling off that as well. Once it was on the floor, his red-rimmed eyes fell upon the bright red burns of seared, shiny flesh that spiraled out from his chest hair onto his arm. The affected skin looked plastic and unreal, as though he'd been stitched together by an uncanny valley-esque model.

His chest sank more than it did in his memory, sagging. It looked more like the chest of the young woman he'd had on his arm at the restaurant than the firm barrel of Chase's chest, aside from the hair.

He brought his hand up gingerly to the raw flesh, skittering along its edges and taking away the peeling bits of burnt skin and melted fiber. When his thumb skated too close, it sent a pain of electric shrill through his system. He cursed loudly, slammed his closed fist down against the rim of the sink, then cursed loudly again.

Chase appeared in the too-thin, gray-rimmed doorway of the bathroom. "Boss?"

"Get me eyes on him," Fields barked. He pressed his hand to the wound, which only made it hurt more, than ripped open the drawer to his right and began ravaging it for ointment. He brushed aside several large bandages, allowing them to spill onto the floor and roll across the corroded base of the toilet. This was Safehouse Red, and everything was claustrophobic here. There was no natural light, and the ceilings all seemed too low. It made his chest itch, but he wasn't able to scratch it without irritating his wound.

"Eyes on who?"

"The Spook!" Fields said, turning his whole body toward him. "The fire-starter. Burning Man. Whatever the fuck you want to call him, I want eyes on him. He's not playing coy anymore: well, that works both ways. He's making big moves; he'll be easier to find." He found a large tube of cooling ointment and pried its cap off with his teeth. He squeezed out fully half the tube into his opposite hand, then smeared it all over the burned flesh.

Chase frowned. "You want me to take a look at that?"

"You looked at it in the damn car."

"Well, we're in the safehouse, now."

"Not much bigger than a damn car," he huffed, looking around the too-tight bathroom. He backed up a pace and found that before his stride was even complete his heel had come up against the tub. He turned and looked at its stained, brown-rimmed surface with a disdainful sneer. "Can we get a woman in to look after this place? I feel like I'm in the Styx."

"I wouldn't have anyone in until we find out how

badly we're compromised, sir."

Fields turned again at the dissent, curled his lip... then let out a long sigh, his shoulders falling. "Yeah, I got it." He turned to the mirror again, and all at once red found its way to his cheeks. "You know how long it's been since I had a fresh scar?"

Chase turned to look out into the bedroom area of the house. The walls were gray in places, and unpainted in others, the drywall showing through. "I'd guess six years at least."

"Eight," he corrected, his lips barely moving. His free, un-ointmented hand found its way to a thin scar that ran its way between the lower two ribs of his left side. "Martoc tagged me while we were negotiating territory. The fucker." He stifled a bitter laugh. "He got right up in my grill about it, too. Nose to nose. Could've done me in, but I don't think he was trying to. He was trying to be tough, not take over." He paused, long and hard, looking into the beads of his own eyes. "What happened to him?"

"I buried him in the foundation of the new Arts building on Cline."

Fields nodded contemplatively. "His people got more territory, though. Give him that."

"All due respect, sir, this guy isn't looking for territory."

"No," Fields said, bringing his hand up to one of his bushy eyebrows and tracing its edge. "No, he isn't."

"I think we should consider calling in Mr. Smart."

At that, Fields' eyes got wide, at first staring forward into his reflection. His hand fell from his burn, letting ointment sloth off and drain down his chest and onto his pants and the sink. He turned to Chase, his mouth more open than either man had ever seen it previously. "You must be out of your damn mind to say that to me."

"We need to get this situation under control before the Cartel gets involved." Chase stepped forward, finally stepping over the divide into the washroom proper. He uncrossed his hands and let them slide into his pockets. "He's dealt with men like this before. Obsessed men."

"He stopped me from expanding into San Bernardi-no."

"You're who I was talking about," Chase frowned.

Fields turned to him, his eyes turning red. "Is this what I've got to deal with from you now, this shit? Some punk takes a pot shot at me and now you think it's a good idea to run off at the mouth." He snarled, picked up a glass soap dispenser, and pulled back as though he were about to put it through the wall-length mirror. He paused, huffed, then extended a finger towards Chase. "It's not."

"Men like that need to be dealt with, sir. Swiftly. Men like that are like cancer: once they're in, they do too much damage, and it doesn't matter if you get them out. Damage is done. So to deal with someone like that -- someone *obsessed* -- you need a surgeon."

Fields turned back to the mirror again. "What's got this guy hitting me now? What's his play?"

Chase pursed his lips, waited for something further, then turned to leave.

"Don't call Smart," Fields said under his breath, just as Chase was leaving eyeshot. "Be like... kerosene. My world's already burning, Chase."

Chase nodded, then stepped out into the hall of the

small, cramped safehouse.

Fields stared forward for a long moment before he tried to collect the ointment that had fallen in great globs along the edge of the sink. His burn had begun to radiate heat again. His fingers slipped twice, he cursed, then brought his fist through his reflection in the mirror, scattering silver plate in all directions.

CHAPTER SIX

Tash stood in front of a long row of cars, staring at a large section of the pavement the lay beneath them. It was vacant now, but in her mind's eye she could see shadowed figures interacting with one another in the moonlight. They were atop one another in a way that -- in another circumstance -- could be mistaken for the silhouettes of lovers but was not.

Kelly and Nick stood behind her, leaned against the bumper of an old Chevy that, judging by the puddle of oil and fluid beneath it, had been there for months.

"We're in a parking garage," Kelly said, pursing her lips together until they resembled a mannequin smile. "An office parking garage. You do so spoil us."

Tash turned and looked at them both over her shoulder.

Nick sighed, giving Kelly a sidelong glance to which she scrunched her nose at him.

"We've got a meeting upstairs," Tash said, absently. "You're assistants. Try and act the part."

Nick followed her gaze low, to that five-foot segment

of floor in front of him.

"So, what are we doing in the here, the very much downstairs, then?" Kelly asked, blue light casting shadows from her fingertips every time she strummed her fingers against the hood of the Chevy.

She sighed, then cocked her head toward the open pavement before them. "I want you to look at that. Really look, the way only you can."

Nick paused, then did as she asked. He squinted at first but only at first -- it was natural to squint from the concentration, but it restricted the light that could come in. He opened his eyes to their extreme, letting all the light in that he could.

Slowly, more than just the pavement came into view. There was an oblong white stain, ragged at the edges and with scant spurts that came from it.

"Bleach," he said, his voice having become faraway.

As he stared, flecks of black came into view just outside the radius of the white stain. As more and more light entered through his retinas, he saw that they weren't just black, but in fact a deep, dark red that just appeared black in the harsh light of the parking garage.

"Blood," he said with disgust, as though he could somehow taste it.

Tash nodded.

He blinked twice, turning to her. "Is this where it happened?"

At the car, Kelly stiffened.

Tash took out her phone and pressed play on it, handing it to him. He stepped over to Kelly as the video on the screen started, until she was watching from over his shoulder with her hair falling over it.

The audio was scratchy and popped every few seconds despite there being nothing loud happening on the screen. The shot was from security footage and was a wide shot of a hallway. There were cars parked along one side of the screen, and along the other was a solid wall of concrete. A corporate logo was stenciled along the far edge of the wall, and just below it was a beaten old Chevy that looked as though it had been there for months.

Kelly raised her hands off the hood of the car, as though it had suddenly become untouchable.

For a long moment there was nothing in the frame, the only evidence that the video hadn't paused the continuing progress bar. It was already a quarter of the way through the clip. Whatever was going to happen was going to happen quickly, and Nick could feel his pulse quicken as he watched, his eyes taking in more and more of the subtle shadows and contrasts in the light than Kelly's were.

Suddenly there was a snap of the frame and the timestamp in the lower right moved five seconds forward. A woman appeared on the screen in the doorway at the far right of the frame, walking forward towards the camera. Her shoes clicked along the pavement as she made her way along the row of cars, closer and closer to the camera.

Nick and Kelly both looked up as one, past Tash to a spot on the wall they hadn't noticed before. There was a small half-sphere against a pillar of concrete there, and inside it, a small blinking red light. They turned back.

There was nothing else in the frame and she was halfway to the camera, the video halfway to completion. Suddenly, there was a part of the shadows next to the Chevy. From the shadow there was an arm that reached out and found her, striking her in the back of the head.

Kelly's eyes went wide.

The shadow raised, dark and black and looming. It was fully black, as if the dark noise at the edges of the video had come to life and was haunting their feed. It stood above her, watching the woman as she moved.

She was still moving, half of her just out of frame as she writhed, trying to find the leverage to get back up. Her knee kept slipping, blood already making its way past her hairline and into her face and disorienting her.

The shadow creature's sharp hands grabbed the woman and forced her around, its feet on either side of her, pinning her to the same splotch of concrete where Nick had been staring, only moments ago. She screamed and the creature was on her again, slamming the back of her head against the pavement again and again until she stopped making sounds and stopped moving.

It brought its hand up to her slender neck and pulled. Blood spilled out as her head leaned back, growing in a steady pool that leaked back into the frame. It tilted back its head to reveal two large cat-like red eyes. It opened its mouth and revealed it to be full of massive, serrated teeth.

The creature grabbed the woman by either side of her shirt, thrust back its head, and bellowed: "Black Womb lives."

The video stopped.

Kelly looked down to the shadow at the right of the car she was sitting on, then immediately propelled herself to her feet. Her hands shook as though they had touched something putrid. She turned to face the Chevy and backed up until she was behind Tash, so that she could address them both at the same time. "What the Jesus fuck?" she huffed, refusing to take her eyes off the car. She hugged her arms, then the touch seemed foreign to her, so she jolted her hands away from herself again. "I mean, what the Jesus fuck?"

Nick stepped away from the Chevy but turned toward the shadow at its side, rather than away from it. He stared at it for a long moment. "There's nothing fishy here. No doors or compartments or... whatever." He paused.

"Could he have been in the car?" Tash asked, stepping forward.

Nick eyed it. There was a trash bag in the backseat that was overflowing with blankets. The cushions were stained, but other than that the car was bare and non-descript. "No," he said with finality. "It hasn't been used in longer than the bleach has been there. There's no disruption or distortion to the dust or the mud from a door opening... no. He didn't come from the car."

"Is there a reason you're calling that thing a *he*?" Kelly said. She had backed up to the point that she was under the camera, her back against the concrete pillar that propped up the garage.

"The other video," Tash said, sliding her finger across her phone. "Here, you can --"

"No thanks, actually," Kelly snapped, raising both her hands and blotting out her vision of Tash. "I'm quite good, really."

"He was blending in with the shadows," Nick said,

squinting. "Harsh light like this, that's... difficult. Even if it was night, even if she was preoccupied..." he paused. "I could see him before you two could on the video, I think. I saw him full form in the shadow, right when the arm came out, but even in this light... that's a hard sell."

She nodded.

"We saw the claws. And the... whatever he turned into. If there's this now... have you ever met anyone with two powers? Let alone three?"

She pursed her lips, saying nothing.

He reached up to his eyes. "Maybe I can --"

Tash's hand snapped forward, grabbing him by the crook of the arm. "Don't."

"Maybe with the lenses out I can--"

"Remember how we saw the murder." She turned toward the camera covertly, tilting her head in its direction. "Trust isn't big on the list of things I have for them."

Kelly stepped back from the pillar it was on, uncomfortable no matter where she stood.

Nick furrowed his brow, then nodded. The camera once again produced a blink of red light, as if it were winking at them.

Arthur Shane was a tall man who was going bald, a fact made more obvious by the wall-wide plate windows behind him that looked out onto the Los Angeles skyline. The view popped out and the light came in, reflected off the towers of steel and glass and returning to make a halo of shimmering light along the crown of his head. It was offset by long cheeks that looked to have gotten used to scowling, but were now curled up in a widow's smile.

"The police are doing everything they can, but they're... limited. Resources are stretched thin, as you can imagine."

Tash nodded, making a note on her legal pad. There were more unsolved homicides in Los Angeles every day than there were officers trained to deal with them: an average of eight per hundred thousand, in a city of millions. And that wasn't even counting the suburbs. "That tends to be why people hire a private firm, yes. Have you considered that before today?"

"We have two, currently. One was contracted out by our law firm, the other... the other we hired ourselves. I hired myself, actually. There comes a point when you just... can't *not*."

She nodded again. In the seat next to her, Nick was staring at the wall of photos and awards to their left. Many had Arthur in them, and as they got closer and closer to the centre of the wall, he had more and more hair. Next to him in almost all the photos was a younger woman with a smile that pressed her cheeks up into her eyes and a shock of purple running through her hair. Despite his hair, the photos featured them both in the same position, as if photoshopped: shaking hands, cutting ribbons, accepting awards. Smile at the camera, click click click, again over here. Snap snap pop. Tash moved her elbow out imperceptibly, touching it against his rib. He stopped, his eyes snapping forward into pleasant eye contract with Arthur.

"Can we ask what they've found?" Tash asked, smiled perfectly.

Arthur gave her a long, serious gaze, weighing her. After a long moment of this, he nodded. "At first, they'd never seen anything like it, but the more they scratched the surface... there was precedent for it. There were some tales from out in the midwest, things that looked like... well, that looked like this thing. And there've been more since in Pica Rivera."

Tash made a note.

"But figuring out why someone's been attacking us, in general? Your guess is as good as mine."

"I somehow doubt that, actually," Tash said under her breath.

"Pardon?"

"I mean only that: people are paranoid. People walk past a dark alley and think someone's in there that's going to get them. But in the real world... nobody is that interesting. Nobody is coming to get you because nobody cares enough to come get you. Yet, imaginations go wild. Every spouse of a homicide victim has a list of ten people they think might have done it, if you give them long enough to come up with it. And you... you've had plenty of time."

He nodded solemnly. "Yes, that's true. Months."

"*Years*," Tash stressed, taking a slip of paper from behind her notepad and handing it to him. It was a full-page article reporting on the attack of a young woman at a private school. The headline across the top read: Port Haven Under Attack.

Arthur looked at it sidelong for a tense, drawn stretch of time, then shrugged with it and batted it back towards her. "I'm not sure what I'm to make of this."

"The girl in the article, the one that was attacked. She lives, but she was one of your employees. Or, ex-employees, at the time. And it wasn't the first time she'd been attacked, there was at least twice more. One attack ended in a collateral fatality." She handed him another slip of paper, this one smaller. It was a police report, screenshotted and printed with low resolution, the blacks from the letters bleeding out onto the surrounding white.

Arthur picked up the page, watching it flutter in his unsteady hand. "This is deeply distressing."

Nick squinted at him, looking past the printout of the article to the man reading it. His pores were open despite the coolness of the AC climate control in the office.

"You think this... this thing had something to do with this?"

"Actually, as far as we can figure, he was across the country when this happened," Tash drawled, her mouth warbling. She caught Arthur's gaze when he looked up, shocked. "As far as anything can be known, at this point."

He nodded. "You are... good. You're good, I'll give you that." He stiffened. "How much do you need for a retainer?"

Tash paused. "Five thousand should do nicely."

Nick turned to her, his eyebrow cocked.

"We'll set the terms for what constitutes a success," she continued. "If the bare minimum isn't reached, you'll receive eighty percent of the retainer back within twenty-four hours. If the maximum for success is reached..." she paused, eyeing him. "I wouldn't ask more than a half million."

Again, Shane bristled, then nodded. He reached over the table and extended a sweaty palm to her. She took it, pumping it twice curtly.

There was a knock at the door and it opened without response, a sharply dressed twenty-something woman with thick-rimmed glasses and a purple streak in her hair leaning in.

"Erika?" Arthur asked, starting to stand.

"Can someone tell me what this girl's doing here?" Erika asked, cocking her head back towards the hall, where Kelly was unloading sodas from a malfunctioning vending machine.

Tash sighed.

"We're doing contract work now?" Nick asked, snapping the cheque from Shane out of Tash's hand. He examined it. Even though it was, he assumed, a reasonable amount of money, it was more than he'd ever seen stated in one place. It felt heavy somehow, despite only being a double-thick sheet of paper.

They walked through the glass doors of the Shane building foyer and out into the heat of the Los Angeles sun. Nick blocked his eyes as it happened, the intensity of the rays surprising him every time. He cursed, squinting.

Kelly took a pair of sunglasses out of his breast pocket and handed them to him. He placed them on even as she brought his hand to her mouth and kissed it.

Tash smirked. "Clearly not. We'll continue our investigation and if anything leads back to Shane, they won't question us poking around... but when the time comes, we'll politely apologize and refund his eighty percent. Hell, we'll refund the whole five thousand if he kicks up a stink, just to keep him from fishing around too much." She smiled at him. "What did you see in there?"

He turned to her, then licked his lips. "He was nervous."

"That's normal."

"Very nervous. He was surprised by some of it, but not all. His carotid artery really started to pump out of his neck a few times. Like, hardcore. And he was sweating. Something in there surprised him." He paused. "The attacks from years back frightened him. Was that... was that Abby?"

Kelly looked up, her attention snapping forward at the mention of the name.

Tash nodded. "Anything else?"

Nick thought for a moment, then shook his head.

"I'm sorry, are we... are we saying this ties back to us somehow? To one of us?" Kelly asked, pushing herself between the two of them.

Tash turned back to the building, the tall monolith standing like a jagged spike into the LA skyline. "I'm not ruling anything out, yet."

CHAPTER SEVEN

Xander knelt on the floor of his apartment, his hands splayed out before him. They dripped with blood that ran down from the back of his head and bare back, making small pits and pats as they hit the floor.

"Hurgh," he coughed. It was loud and haggard. It was the cough of a smoker whose lungs had rebelled long ago and were acting out in protest, the cough of a miner. The cough of someone who had let a flu run rampant through their system for far too long and were now paying the price for it.

He wriggled his fingers in front of his own face, testing how they moved.

There was a sound from the kitchen and he spun around, making the same haggard, growling cough he had a moment before. He could see nothing there, just the empty void of space. He lowered his arms, let his fingers fall into loose fists, then knelt back down again.

He took several deep, long breaths, then brought his hands back up into his line of sight and wriggled his blood-stained fingers.

"Come on," he said. "Work, you fuckers."

Outside, the afternoon sun beat in through his open window.

The elevator doors opened with an audible ping, revealing the vast-yet-cramped department that was Homicide 12.

The Homicide division of any city was busy, but this was a completely new level of confusion. The room was a living, breathing entity under the always-hot sun, moving and pulsing with excitement and energy and need. The walls seemed to expand and contract with the heat, as though it were actually breathing.

There was a large window by her door, the blinds of which were always shut. The rest of the office was a massive floor with glass walls on all sides, making the halls around it and the Los Angeles sky constantly visible. Thirty-something desks were arranged around the room like Tetris blocks, all the same make but a few were painted a different colour from the average ones. Most were damaged or scraped, and all were covered in case files, family photos, or both.

Tash stepped onto the floor just as the doors were starting to close again. She surveyed the floor to one side, then the other, nodding. "You two hang back," she said curtly, as Nick and Kelly flanked her position.

Nick made an annoyed face. "Why's that then?

"Lying to Shane is one thing. These are LAPD Homicide. It's not a stretch to say these are the last people you want being suspicious of you, and there's no better way to get on their radar that way than lying to their face and getting caught in it. Better to mitigate risk."

"You saying I'm not a liar on that caliber?" Kelly chimed, turning back after watching a woman be brought in in handcuffs.

"That is exactly what I'm saying, yes." Tash took the few steps past the main hallway as though she belonged there, her shoulders back and standing taller and taller the more she moved in. There was a woman at her desk just to Tash's left that was bathed in sunlight from the bay window, so much so that her shoulders were burnt. She was yelling at an automated VDN on the other end of a phone call as she pushed through a large stack of papers on her desk.

She turned right and there were two desks that were almost in line with one another, one forward slightly more than the other. The one to the left was clean and precise, the officer behind it eating a slider while he typed, hunting and pecking the entire time. He looked up from his work at her briefly, his eyes sunken into a skull that were struggling to hold onto the extra flesh that a desk position had wrought him, and after a sustained moment of eye contact turned back.

The desk on the right was cluttered with files and file folders, so much so that the wireless keyboard was propped on a small stack to get it to the desired ergonomic height of its user. The man who sat behind it was twirling a red pen between long, deft fingers. He had shaggy brown hair and the sort of dark circles under the eyes that only came when sleepless night became a rule rather than an exception. His cheeks were sunken, but his brown suede jacket hid the broad shoulders of someone who knew how to handle themselves in a fight.

"I'm looking for an agent named Duncan Taggart?" Tash asked, motioning between the two men but clearly leaning towards the man on the right.

Duncan glanced side-on at the officer eating the sandwich, whose ears had perked up. "If you think Hazer could make Agent than the Bureau's reputation has gone downhill more than I thought."

Detective Hazer turned away with a disgruntled frown.

Tash smiled, extending her hand fully. "Pleasure to meet you."

He eyed the hand a moment, then smiled and took it, pumped it twice, then released. "What can I do for you...?"

"Natasha," she smirked, tilting her head to one side. "Tash though, please. I'm here because I've been hired by Arthur Shane to investigate the homicides within his company. I was hoping I could chat with you, have a little professional courtesy."

Duncan sighed, running his hands over his face and suddenly looking even more tired than he had. He leaned forward on his chair, hitting his elbows off his desk. "Another PI firm hired by Shane. That's... that's terrific. That's totally what we want, doesn't gum shit up at all."

Tash smiled her perfectly pleasing customer-service smile. "You are the Agent-In-Charge of the case, correct? The liaison between Homicide 12 and the FBI?"

"Yeah, that I am," Duncan drawled, scratching the hair behind his ear. "Although the way people keep lining up to do the job, I'm starting to think I'm not enjoying it as much as I should."

"I didn't mean to offend you."

"You didn't," Duncan scowled, waving the thought away with a fluttering brush of his hand. "It's just been a day. Week... *Month*." He paused and reached for his coffee cup, realized it was empty, then set it back down and sighed. He turned and motioned to Tash: "You want a coffee? We can walk and talk."

Tash nodded, and Duncan placed both palms onto the arms of his chair and pushed himself up. He wasn't as tall as her, she now realized, but he stepped the swagger of someone who owned the room, marching out from behind his desk the way someone would step from room to room in their own home.

He stepped out past Hazer and the woman on the phone, who had since hung up and was now sorting through files on her computer. Tash followed as he stepped through the glass doors that led out of Homicide 12, then down the hall. He entered the first door on the right, a small kitchenette with a single counter that housed three separate coffee pots. He lifted the one labeled Dark Roast and eyed her. She nodded, and he poured three cups. He took a long glug from his, refilled it, then handed Tash hers. The mug had the LAPD seal emblazoned on it.

"Thank you," Tash nodded, taking a tentative sip of the hot coffee. Her eyes widened slightly. "It's good."

"I know the stereotype is to have one of those vending machines where the cup falls down, but Sergeant Lake wasn't having it. We spend enough time trying to stay awake, we need good coffee." He took another long swig, cutting the contents of the cup down by ninety percent even as it barreled steam out over his cheeks, then refilled it again. He turned to her: "What's the angle you're coming at this from?"

Tash squinted. After a pregnant pause, she answered, "The Laura Bennett murder, the tapes. The whole thing is different from the rest of them, so I'm picking it apart."

Duncan cursed softly, sniffed back hard, then nodded. "Yeah, that makes sense to do."

She narrowed her eyes at his reaction. She didn't know him well, but his motions were well telegraphed. His torso was aimed away from her, his eyes cast down into his rapidly emptying cup of coffee. "The body was moved, right? It was the only time the body was moved?"

He nodded.

"She was moved from the Shane building -- the garage -- to Bezos Place?"

Duncan sighed. He downed the rest of his coffee, refilled his mug again, then took it and the third mug and stepped toward Tash. She moved to one side and let him pass, then followed him back out into the hall, and back into the main habitat of Homicide 12. Instead of going back to his desk he made a beeline for the female detective sorting through paperwork that Tash had passed on the way in. He held the spare mug out to her, gripping it by the lid and aiming the handle toward her. "Janet."

Janet looked up from her work, then smiled and took the cup with a grateful nod. "Thanks. I'm past my ears. Another one..." she lowered her voice without realizing it, "of Fields' places was hit last night. And there's been three ATM heists, and two home invasions gone bad. Things are starting to really get nuts."

Tash turned her head, listening without trying to look as though she were listening.

Duncan nodded. "You need company running through things later, let me know."

She nodded, and he stepped back to his desk, motioning for Tash to take the seat opposite him. She remained standing. "I wouldn't worry about the Laura Bennett murder," he said, with as little emotion in his voice as he could restrain.

He seemed like the type to be boisterous. He had the look of the sort of man who all-too-easily fell into sarcasm, without even realizing he was doing it. He was fighting now to restrain himself, to keep his voice level and even and to not adlib commentary or marginalia, and she could see it.

"I'm not... worried about it," she stressed, almost smiling. She was trying to draw him out of his professionalism, subtly. "It's done. But if you're trying to catch a killer, ignoring the one time that killer was caught on tape would be a bad move."

Duncan frowned. He turned on his computer monitor, avoiding her gaze after the comment.

She smirked. "Have you found the first attack yet?"

"Yeah," he huffed. "A lawyer name of --"

"No no, there was one before that. *Years* before that, with a victim that lived. I just finished briefing Arthur Shane about it." She withdrew a folded piece of paper from her pocket and held it in the air between them like a treat. "If you want it."

Duncan squinted. "I'm not here for quid pro quo."

She laid the piece of paper down in front of him and

slid it across the stack of papers, then let it go. "Of course not. It's yours. I just... need help. This one," she motioned to the paper, "makes sense. Most of them make sense. I can't figure them out, but they make sense. The Laura Bennett thing makes no sense. It's like I'm putting together a jigsaw puzzle and there's a piece that legit fits nowhere."

He frowned, picking up the paper and unfolding it. He looked over it briefly, then added it to the top of the stack underneath his keyboard. He ran his fingers over his face, then through his hair. He licked his lips, both preparing for and delaying speech. "When that happens to me, I usually assume the piece is from another jigsaw puzzle."

Tash straightened slightly. Her eyes widened at first, then narrowed. "Are you... are you insinuating that Laura Bennett's death is unrelated to the Shane Murders?"

"I'm not saying anything," he said, his hands in the air. "But when there's a piece that doesn't fit, and you take it out and suddenly everything fits... you take the piece out. Every time. As messy as it seems, as much as it denies Occam's Razor... it's the nature of the job. And yeah, it'll make things sticky when it comes time for a trial, but that's the job of a prosecutor." He motioned to the paperwork in from of him. "I have the job of an agent, and that's to look at those pieces and see how they fit."

Tash nodded. She turned and looked at the people sitting and waiting outside the bullpen, watching the back of their heads through the glass wall for a long moment. When she turned back, she licked her lips, choosing her words carefully. "There was crossover with the Bennett murder to another case... yes? Because of where she was dragged to?"

"And a few other linking parts, but yes. It was linked to two ongoing cases, and I'm not entirely sure it actually has something to do with both." Some of the sarcasm that she recognized as his nature came out on the word *entirely*, and she recognized with finality that he was actually *quite* sure that the Bennett murder had nothing to do with the Shane Murders. More sure than he should have been, given the circumstances.

"The other case involved... Victor Murdock, if I recall correctly? Several deaths, including Murdock himself?"

Duncan frowned, his eyes bulging for a moment. "Yeah, there were assaults at first, then a second degree. He actually went down for the second degree, but then a, ah..." he paused, swallowing. "Lawyer fucked us, and he got out. And things went sideways, as things often do when you let a bad guy who has been escalating out of lockup."

"And things escalated."

"Yeah," he said, mouth warbling. "I was there for some of it, sorry. It was a mess. The case is still technically open, but with Murdock dead..."

She nodded, flicking her tongue against the back of her teeth. She picked up her mug and took a long drink of her coffee. "If he's dead... do we have a lead on who killed him?"

Duncan turned his head, only slightly, finally making full eye contact with her and looking directly at her. For the first time since the conversation had begun, she had his full, undivided attention, and she could see it. He picked up his mug again, but only to move it away from himself. "You've been hired to work the Shane case," he said, bluntly.

She nodded.

"I tell you that Laura Bennett has nothing to do with that case, but instead of not pulling on that thread anymore... you follow her to the new case." He leaned forward touching his face and cocking his head at her.

She stepped back a pace from his desk. "I'm just trying to figure this out."

"Yeah no I see that. Natasha. Hired by Shane as a PI." He squinted, then smirked. "Pieces of puzzles not fitting, right?"

She pursed her lips.

Hazer looked up from his desk at the exchange, and from behind her Tash heard the sound of Janet rising to her feet. She was aware, suddenly, that there were eyes upon her.

"I think it's okay if you go," Duncan said, nodding towards the door.

Tash nodded slowly, then turned and made her way past the glass entrance to Homicide 12.

Nick sat on the edge of the picnic table with Kelly just below him, her head nestled between his thighs. He was squinting against the glare of the Los Angeles evening sun.

"This must be murder on your eyes," Kelly said, holding up her hand to shade her own.

"You get used to it."

They watched as a man at a street vendor bartered over the price of a chili cheese hotdog, the man behind the grill punctuating every sentence by pointing to a sign scrawled in chalk. It proclaimed that the dogs were two for ten, and they were arguing over whether or not that should mean that one was five.

"She's been in there a while," she said, straining to see over her shoulder to the entrance of LAPD12.

"I'm sure it takes time."

Kelly's hair fell over Nick's waist as she turned from the scene out into the street, where thousands of people walked on either side of the road as if their motions were pre-programmed. When they all moved together like that, they became one flowing motion, one unit, like a million cups of water forming together into one rushing waterfall. The only thing that stood out were the outliers: joggers and cyclists going faster than the normal flow of traffic. People going the wrong way down a street. Deliverymen carrying far too much and going slower than those around them.

She sat up, reached for her drink alongside him, and took a long slurp. "I've never been to LA before," she said suddenly, watching the people as they moved to and fro.

"Yeah?"

"Yeah. It just seemed... I dunno. Beyond me. It's so huge. Like, incomprehensibly so. But it's not really. It's like you get here and you can't see it all at once. You can only see it in chunks, so it just becomes: city. And so much of it I've seen before in movies and TV and stuff, it's hard for it not to all seem..."

"Familiar?" he guessed.

"*Uncanny*," she clarified. She paused, looking past the glut of people in the distance to the row of buildings behind them: businesses and boutiques whose doors were open and whose neon signs flashed the same. "Do you think we'll get a chance to look around while we're here?"

Nick smiled, lifted her hand, and gently kissed one of her fingers. "We'll make time."

She hummed, then turned and found her chili dog with deft fingers, maneuvering it around Nick until it was in front of her. The steam that had poured from it when they'd purchased it had subsided, and the grated cheese that had melted on top had become a solid layer. She slid it forward in its cardboard tube, tried and failed not to get the chili onto her fingers, and took a bite.

"Is it good?" Nick asked, watching her in his peripheral vision as he looked around the park at the people on its margins.

She nodded, lifting it into the air. "You sure you don't want some?"

"I will absolutely pass," he laughed, raising his hand to be between the dog and his mouth. "I don't put much weight into things my dad said about the city, but not eating street-vendor food is one I'm going to plunk into the Common Sense column."

She laughed at him, a bubbling laugh that started in her gut and erupted, like baking soda with vinegar added to it. She laughed at him in the way only a partner could, when they'd moved past the point of trying to offend each other and into the realm of 'look at what this insane person is like.' She laughed so hard that she almost dropped the cardboard sleeve the hotdog was on, and his hand swept out to catch it before it could fall.

"I'm glad someone's having a good time," Tash said, stepping up behind them.

Kelly stood immediately, getting up off of Nick's lap, her laughter subsiding gradually. She took the hotdog back from Nick with one deft motion. "You were in there a while."

Tash nodded.

"What was that about?" Nick asked, raising an eyebrow critically. "Your pores are open."

Tash huffed, even as Kelly put her hand on her shoulder, jolting her with static electricity. "We're not looking for the Shane Killer."

CHAPTER EIGHT

The club pounded, the walls reverberating with tense, salty-hot excitement. The lights were low, and the sheen of the sun had faded, leaving only the cool respite of shadow and neon to bring the night sky to life.

Xander laid down his tall glass of beer as patrons bumped and grinded all around him, their hair flickering about as they moved in pace to the movement. He glared across it, looking for inconsistencies, people who stood out from the motion of the crowd as threats. Several men moved not in time with the beat, and there was a large man with thickly gauged ears whose wide frame was guarding a winding stairwell that didn't move at all. They were like muscle groups that refused to move with the rest: standing out not for what they were doing, but for what they weren't doing.

"You want another?" the bartender asked, taking the empty glass from him and leaning over to hear above the thumb and drone of the music.

"No," Xander said, still eyeing the broad man guarding the stairwell. He turned back. "Wait, yes. A whiskey sour, actually."

The bartender nodded and leaned back. He was wearing a polo shirt made of light green chainmail and had matching earrings. He was tanned and his jaw was square. He looked like the sort that would make very good tips in this lifestyle, and the jar tucked under the lip of the bar confirmed it.

Xander shifted uncomfortably, maneuvering his arm around the bulge of his jacket pocket. Three more people joined the bar to get drinks, but he was the only one sitting at it. For everyone else the bar was a waystation on the path back to the dance floor.

The bartender brought Xander his drink and Xander gave him a twenty, then waved off the change. The man's eyebrows bobbed but he did not object, shoving the bills into the jar beneath the bar with two fingers.

Someone on his right laughed heartily and sipped a Cherry Coke, and without warning Xander felt a sharp pang in his side. He gritted his teeth and pushed through it.

"You okay?" the bartender asked, a look of genuine concern playing over his face.

"I'll be fine," Xander glowered. He took a sip of his drink, then looked at it disappointedly. "You got anything stronger than this?"

The bartender squinted at him, leaned forward, and cocked his head to the far wall. "That's the strongest we got tonight," he said, then in a lower tone: "Cops are here."

Xander turned, and just as the man had said, against the far wall opposite the stairs was a circle of three dancers wearing conservative shirts. They were dancing out of synch and only minimally, and even though there were only three of them -- two men and one woman -- they stayed together.

"I cannot believe I didn't spot that," Xander hummed, smiling genuinely. He turned back to the bartender. "You've got quite an eye on you...?"

"Eddie."

"Eddie," Xander smirked, raised his glass in a salute, then downed the remainder of his whiskey sour. He pushed the glass forward and smiled. "Can I give you a tip?"

"Eight bucks was already quite a tip," Eddie laughed.

All humor left Xander's face. "Take your money and then take your break early."

Eddie started to laugh, but the stony expression on Xander's face made it catch in his throat before he could escape. "What're you...?"

"Now." Xander stood up, pushing himself off from the bar. "Take your break. Now." He turned and faded into the crowd of dancers before Eddie could ask again.

Eddie flipped his towel to the floor of the bar, grabbed his tip, and flagged over his replacement.

The music blared, so loud that it could be heard easily above the roar of roughly two hundred people dancing and jumping and talking. The sound found its way deep into Xander's chest and made a home there, the solid thumb of the bass affecting even his step. He moved in tune with it, marching toward the large man with the gauged ears.

As he stepped through the crowd, his eye caught a

young girl walked around it from the peripheral of his eye. She was coming from the washroom alongside the bar and made her way around the glut of people towards the stairs and nobody bothered her, save for a few turned heads.

She was dressed as though she were old enough to be at the club but wasn't by at least six years. Her hair was cut short and she wore large hoop earrings and looked as though she'd stepped out of an eighties movie, but her cheeks were still soft and plump with baby fat and she walked in heels like someone unfamiliar with the act. She pushed past one dancer who tried to talk to her and made her way to the stairs, the bouncer moving to one side and letting her up without a word.

Xander watched her as she ascended the stairs and arrived at the balcony that looked over the club. It was edged with a broad sectional couch that had three men on it and a large glass table in front of them, with nearly a dozen girls walking about. He called them girls, because a glance told him that was what they were, and he felt heat rise into his cheeks. The girl walked to the edge of the balcony and looked over onto the crowd, before being joined from behind by a tall man with a thin face and a red rose pinned to his lapel. He turned her head towards him and brought her into a kiss.

Xander glowered, turning back to the police, still pantomiming dance at the far end of the club. He sneered, then made his way past the dancing crowd and up to the guard.

The man easily stood a foot taller than Xander and was standing on the lowest stair of the case to boot; combined, the effect made Xander only come up to his chest. His arms were folded. Xander turned to step around him just as the girl had, but the man blocked his path.

Xander huffed, feigning annoyance. "I've got a message to deliver."

"Yeah?" said the man sarcastically. He had a slight British accent, and not one that was well practiced. "Send a text."

"Not really the kind of thing you can say with words."

The guard lowered his eyes, then cocked his head toward the balcony. "Who's it for then?"

Xander withdrew his lighter from his pants pocket and plucked a pack of cigarettes from his coat, but did not take one out. He began to flick the flint of the lighter preemptively. "Stephen Fields."

The guard stopped, his hands unlocking with the momentary shock of hearing the name he'd just heard.

"I love that you people treat that like Voldemort," Xander laughed, pressing the lighter again and making only the charade of sparks. "It's precious, really."

The guard shifted uncomfortably, then looked up at the balcony. One of the men who'd been sitting there had made his way over to watch from over the ledge, and was doing so with the casual interest of someone who saw the earmarks of a conflict but didn't know what was actually being said. He turned back, his voice suddenly drier and deeper than it had been: "What's the message?"

Xander smiled, finally sparking his lighter into a flame. "You are."

He opened his jacket and revealed a large, leaking

canister of charcoal lighter fluid.

The guard stepped back and started to yell, even as Xander pushed it forward and splayed it all across the bottom of the stairs. He dropped his lighter and it caught, a trail of flame moving back through the crowd and back to the bar, making a jagged lightning-strike through the dancefloor. People screamed and ran as Xander's jacket caught aflame and he stepped through it, up the stairs towards the men that were drawing their guns.

Fields threw the ashtray at the wall and it slammed in, making a long, cigar-shaped dent in it before falling and breaking the glass end table beneath. He huffed, grinding his teeth audibly as his hands clenched and unclenched. "Is any of it salvageable?"

Chase frowned, half inside the safehouse bedroom and half outside of it. He hesitated.

Fields turned his head toward him slowly, as though even the delay in answering were unheard of. "Is there anything left of the club?"

"The structure's there, but that's not the problem. There were... it was a security night. There were cops we owned there, Vice low-rankers."

Fields narrowed his eyes. "What're you telling me?"

"The guy... Burning Man... he pushed about ten kilos of coke over the edge of the balcony, sent it raining down onto the crowd while everyone was scrambling for the exits. Our cops were there, but a hundred witnesses, too. They couldn't hide it."

Fields sat down on the edge of the bed and rubbed his

eyes, letting out a long, haggard sigh. "I'm going to fucking kill this fucker," he said under his breath. "I want... I
need him gone. We need a price tag on him so big it'll have
everyone's grandmother taking out their piece, and..."

"We don't know who he is. You can't hire a hit on
someone you don't know," Chase drawled. "And that's
not why I'm here."

Fields looked up from his hands, his jaw slackening.

"The Cartel is here to see you."

Fields' face lost some of the colour that had been burning up into his cheeks, nodded resolutely, then got up and
straightened his suit. He sniffed back hard, regarded himself in the mirror, then nodded. "Bring them in."

Chase nodded curtly and stepped back out of the door,
reemerging a moment later with two tanned men with
slicked back hair and matching gray suits, different only
in their height and the colour of their ties. The shorter of
the two wore a green tie, the taller a pastel pink.

"Milagros!" Fields exclaimed heartily, with a pasted-
on smile as he gripped the hand of the tall man in the pink
tie. He clapped the man on the arm with a healthy palm,
then turned and did the same to the shorter man, bringing him in for a brief embrace. "Hector! It's been too long!
What brings you into my city?"

Milagros raised his bushy eyebrows, pointing his forehead forward and laughing. "Your city? That's rich, Stephen. Your city. If it was your city, perhaps we wouldn't
be here. And you wouldn't be," he gestured around the
cramped circumference of the safehouse, "here."

Fields laughed the amicable, friendly laugh of someone whose boss has told an off-colour joke at an office

party, touching Milagros' arm again. This time, Milagros pulled away. "What do you mean, here?" he smiled. "We have safehouses for a reason, otherwise we wouldn't have them. These things happen. If the business was easy, everyone would do it, yes?"

"Everyone doesn't do it because we fuck the ones who try," Hector corrected. His drawl was more acute than his brother's, each word forming together into one long strain that only the practiced ear could distinguish between.

"Come on, guys," Fields laughed nervously, taking on a Brooklyn effect for a moment with his hands turned out in front of him. "You're here for a few days and things are bad. There are dips and valleys. It's going to get taken care of."

"We have been here for three months, Stephen," Hector corrected again, leaning in. His mouth barely moved when he spoke, like a ventriloquist. He rarely blinked, and the effect of those two mannerisms was unnerving.

"Three months," Milagros chimed. "For three months we have watched this man peck along the edges of your business, scraping things away. Shaving away our profits, our *money*." He said the last with emphasis, thumping his chest and then stepping closer to Fields. "And we wait for you to notice, but you count your share and you sit in your restaurants and you fuck your women and you smile and laugh while this man shaves at the edges of you."

Fields licked his lips. His palms faced each of the men and he backed up a pace, eyes cast downward. He took a moment, then produced his car-salesman smile again. "You're right. Of course! But the guy, he wasn't looking for territory. He's a... waddaya call it, he's a vigilante. They tend to deal with themselves. But you're right, I didn't pay it as much attention as I should and now --"

"I wish it had been someone looking for territory," Hector interrupted. He made eye contact for a long, slow moment. "Because then we would do business with him, and not you."

The smile left Fields' face again and this time he made no effort to replace it. He ran his tongue along the inside of his teeth and nodded.

At the doorway, Chase tilted his head and tisked.

"So you come here just to break balls, is that it?" Fields said, raising his voice. "Because that helps things, it really does. I'm so glad you sat on the sidelines for three months. Heaven forbid you get your hands dirty."

Hector pushed up his mustache and stepped away, walking to the side of the bed and wagging his finger in the air, but did not say anything, fuming silently.

Milagros stepped forward, and Fields backed up, the small of his back wedging against the writing desk. "We have you," he said, softly annunciating every word, "so that we need not *get* our hands dirty. We put up with your bullshit and your fucking and your Frank Sinatra shit because you keep us from getting down in the mud." He held up both his palms. "And yet here we are. In your filthy fucking city. Dirty."

Fields paused a moment, looking between the two empty hands. He nodded.

Milagros stepped back a pace.

"You get your house in order," Hector said, turning his waving finger and jolting it at Fields. "From now on, we don't take a percentage anymore, we take off the top.

A set amount. You can absorb the losses from this... vigilante, then."

Fields straightened. "Pardon fucking me?"

Milagros raised his chin.

"We've been doing this together ten years. Ten years and not one hiccup! Now there's one thing and all of a sudden your cut isn't good enough for you?"

"We want our money, Stephen," Hector reiterated. He reached into his jacket and took out a single cigarette, lit it, and took a sharp drag. "That's all we want."

"There's a ship five miles off the coast," Milagros said, his voice calm. "It has product on it, for your flesh trade."

"Product you are not to touch," Hector interjected.

"It's been there for days with no safe harbor to come in to. You are to see to it that it makes it to land and that things continue to run, smoothly." He paused. "Or this man will be the least of your worries."

Fields laughed, brought both hands to his face, and wiped his mouth. "Fuck you," he said finally.

Milagros' eyebrows bobbed again. "Pardon?"

"I said fuck you. You want your girls brought in, I'll bring your girls in. And your drugs. But you get the cut of it I say," he thumped his chest. "This is my town. You get paid what I say, when I say it. And if you don't like it, you can come back with a gun and I'll bury you with the rats you keep on about."

Milagros nodded, pointed to Fields, then turned and looked at his brother. They both turned and stepped to Chase without a word, who opened the door for them. "The girls come in, Stephen," Hector said, as they stepped out into the hall. "They come in or we'll need someone else to get fucked."

Chase shut the door calmly behind them, locking it with a scant *click*. He turned, clasping both hands in front of his waist, then cleared his throat. "I wouldn't be doing my job if I didn't tell you that threatening them was a bad idea."

"You're not doing your job at all," Fields spat. He turned and pushed his knuckles into the veneer of his table. He let out a long breath. "Call in Mr. Smart."

Chase stopped, wincing. "Are you --"

"Call him," Fields snapped, then opened the desk drawer and produced a bottle of vodka.

CHAPTER NINE

Tash spread her paper out over the floor of her hotel room, dispersing it until every square inch of the plush carpet between her bed and the television was covered in paper files. Nick and Kelly watched her do it, watched the way the paper spilled from one manila folder and cascaded with the pages from another, crumpling and fighting against their staples and paperclips, like playing cards hastily shoved together.

"This is all of it," she said, motioning to the sea of paper before putting her hands on her hips. "This is everything we could find on the Murdock case and their victims. Everything that's public and a few things that aren't. All of it."

Kelly raised her eyebrows, looking from Tash to the pile and then back again, as if the older woman had lost her mind. "That's a lot."

"Not really," Nick mumbled, squatting down to look over the pages assembled. "Not when you're talking about -- how many victims?" he asked, looking up at Tash.

"Five murder victims, if we're including Murdock.

Which I don't." Her voice dripped with contempt at the man's name. "And before that close to a dozen assaults. That was how they tried to put him away the first time, for the assaults."

Nick nodded.

"None of this makes sense as a whole," she huffed, making a broad circle with her arms as though she were trying to form a globe the entire story could fit into. "Laura Bennett didn't fit in with the Shane Murders, that's fair. So maybe she belongs over here, with Murdock's victims." She reached down and grabbed up the sheet she had on Bennett. "It fits over here, but the attack on the shipyard doesn't. It seems like no matter how far I step back, none of it... none of it *fits*."

Nick nodded, picked up one of the files closest to him, and started to leaf through it.

Kelly read over his shoulder for a moment, then turned back to Tash. "Why were people being targeted?"

Tash sighed. She ran a hand through her hair. "Near as I can figure, when I step back from it enough, these were hate crimes. They started as assaults and got... they got worse. It's hard to pin it down because he's dead, and that's basically when you stop getting answers in a case like this, but I think he was targeting members of the church whose lifestyle he didn't agree with. First trying to get them out, then... well, then."

"Lifestyle?"

"Members of the LGBTQ community, from what I'm gathering," Tash sighed. "I've seen it before, but from what I got of the public notes, the police didn't make the connection."

Kelly winced, looking back at the file Nick was flipping through with pity.

"The hate crimes don't fit the fire at the pier, though," Nick nodded, putting down the file on Fabian Mitchells and picking up another.

"No, they do not," Tash drawled. "And even some of the rest... they only fit if you *make* them fit. There are three deaths that fit and some that... that don't." She paused. "Thomas Horton, a retired cop that worked for the LAPD. Same division we were just at. He gets killed while Murdock was behind bars, but the same way the first murder was."

"That's bizarre."

"Yes. Then there's the lawyer. The lawyer was the one who got Murdock off after the cop was killed, made the case that they'd had the wrong guy all along. She doesn't fit into any of this at all, except in her link to Murdock. There's just..." she frowned. "There's too many pieces to this that don't fit, and too many others that only fit if you make them fit."

Nick nodded. "The lawyer?"

Tash sighed, plucked one specific envelope out of the pile, then handed it to him. He laid down the file on Thomas Horton, putting them back in a semblance of order that Tash had displaced. He took the new file and opened it gingerly.

He paused.

"Maybe we need to come at this the other way," Kelly offered, stepping out from behind Nick and around the pile of paper until she was next to Tash. She kept a wide berth from the folders, as though the pages were made of lava. "Instead of trying to figure out how these murders connect with everything else, find out what's up with everything else first. The fire at the docks, figure out what's up there and link it back."

Tash nodded. She sat on the edge of the bed, looking down at the stack. "There's three parts to a murder. There's motive, weapon, and opportunity. The more murders you have, the easier motive should be. But this... this is muddled. This is messed up."

Kelly furrowed her nose. "You talk like you've done this before."

"Guys," Nick interjected, raising a finger. "I think... I think I might have something." He turned around the folder on the lawyer he'd been given. Pinned to the top were two photos, one of her bio from her law firm. The other was a head-and-shoulders shot from her autopsy, her skin sallow and gray, red hair looking like it was deep black in the harsh light. The name at the top of the page read Megan Greene in large Courier font. "She's from Coral Beach."

Tash turned to him suddenly, as if not quite believing what he was saying. "What?"

"The lawyer. The one... Murdock's lawyer. She was from Coral Beach. Maine. I went to school with her cousin."

Tash stood up and stepped over the pile of papers. She held out her hand and Nick gave her the file. "You're sure?"

"You can check but... yeah. Yeah, I'm sure. You know what I'm like with faces."

Tash withdrew her cell phone from her breast pocket

and started to press buttons with one thumb, even as she scanned down through the file on Megan Greene.

"What're you doing?" Kelly asked.

"Getting everything I can on her. Court filings with keywords linked to the case, all of it." She watched as the message sent, waited to see that it was received, then turned back to the file. "She was called in specifically for the case. That was why she was in the city, some hotshot who'd made her name on cases like this."

"Hate crimes?" Kelly balked.

"Wrongful convictions," Tash corrected. "Which they thought Murdock was, remember."

Nick looked into the blank distance between the two women, staring into nothingness. "There's no way this is a coincidence, is there?" he asked sullenly.

Tash frowned, then shook her head. "The odds are bad on that, yeah."

Kelly winced, noticing the faraway look in his eyes. She'd seen it before on him, but rarely, and on others, often. It was the face of a young man on the verge of crisis thoughts. She maneuvered her way back to his side of the pile, placed a steady hand on his shoulder, then kissed him.

Tash's phone chimed, and all three looked up. She fished it back out of her pocket and looked at the screen.

"Did you find anything?" Kelly asked.

Tash turned the phone towards them. There was a text alert comprised of one word, followed by two attached files. The word: MOTHERLODE.

CHAPTER TEN

The attached files had been court transcripts. She'd sent them each to Nick and Kelly, and then to her tablet, and now each sat reading through the documents in hushed silence.

Nick's hand was covering his mouth, and he was struggling to keep from tearing up. He was reading a court transcript one line at a time. The wetness in his eyes did nothing to impede his vision, as much as he wished in this case that it would.

Kelly put a hand on his knee. "What's wrong?"

"Nothing," Nick breathed, sucking in air through clogged nostrils and composing himself. "Sorry. It's just... ah, I knew this kid."

Tash looked up.

"This file, it's, ah... it's about this kid named Jaden Mal. He lived not far from me, he was a lot younger though. I didn't... I didn't really know him. But I saw him like, at least once a week. You know how small towns are."

Tash nodded.

"He'd ah... he'd accused a priest of molesting him. I

knew the priest too, God damn it." He paused. Kelly put down her phone and squeezed his knee, moving in toward him to read his document with him. He nodded. "The lawyer, Greene. She was defending the priest. She got him off with it. They think -- they thought Jaden was having trouble at home, that he was making it up. They institutionalized him."

Kelly winced.

"Sorry," Nick huffed, composing himself again. He almost laughed, even though he found none of this funny at all. "It's... weird. You keep your hometown in amber, you know? You keep it perfectly preserved, but --"

"It's not," Tash finished for him. "I know. Believe me, I know."

Nick scrolled down the page, finding highlighted text.

"That's the spot that triggered the search result," Kelly chimed, pointing.

Nick nodded, bringing up the highlighted text until it was fully in view.

He read aloud, "**Jaden Mal**: The Boogy Man. He told me I had to tell the truth. I should tell the truth.

"**Anthony Jones (prosecution):** Uh-huh, and... who is this 'Boogy Man'?

"**Jaden Mal**: It was black... and slimy, and it had scales and black blood. And it had red eyes and a red mouth with lots of teeth and it came into my room last night after I went to bed and told me I had to tell the truth."

Kelly sat up, the hair of her arms on end. She picked up her phone again and started scrolling back up through her document.

Nick stared at the words on the screen. "Black scales, red eyes and teeth... that's... what was on the video, right? That was the thing that killed Laura Bennett and attacked the pier?"

Tash nodded slowly. "Let me bring up the rest of that file."

"I got it," Kelly snapped, thrusting her finger into the air. "I know where I've seen that, it's in the other file." She scrolled until she was near the bottom of her selection as well, then pinch-zoomed on a passage. "Mine's from a murder trial.

"**Megan Greene (defense)**: Mr. Genblade--

"**Adam Genblade (defendant):** Please, Adam.

"**Megan Greene:** Adam, do you know the man seated behind me?

"**Adam Genblade**: His name is Xander Drew."

"Xander Drew?" Nick said, scrunching his nose. "I know Xander Drew."

Kelly made eye contact with him, then kept reading:

"**Megan Greene:** Correct. And how do you know him?

"**Adam Genblade:** We studied together.

"**Megan Greene**: Really? Where?

"**Adam Genblade**: At the Church of Smoke and Mirrors, of course.

"**Megan Greene**: But how do you know him, really?

"**Adam Genblade**: He is the Black Womb.

"**Megan Greene**: Of course he is. And what is that exactly?

"**Adam Genblade:** A manifestation of a genetic disorder which resulted from meticulous breeding for decades by Engen's top scientific minds.

"**Megan Greene**: What does it look like?

"**Adam Genblade:** It covers your body in a dark, black film with red eyes and mouth."

The room was quiet.

Tash licked her lips. "You knew this man?" she asked. She switched her phone back to text view with a few deft motions as she spoke.

Nick nodded. "He was... he's a little older than me. We had a lot of friends in common, but we weren't friends." He paused for a beat. "He didn't really have friends."

She texted: 'Get me everything you can on Xander Drew' with both thumbs, giving it her fullest attention. When it was done, she scrolled back through her apps, finally landing on the media player and opening the file from the fire at the pier. "But you knew this guy. Knew him to see him, could pick him out of a lineup?"

Nick squinted, nodding. "I'd know him if I saw him, yeah. He was good friends with... with someone I was very tight with. Someone I loved."

Kelly turned to him, and again squeezed his knee.

"Yes, I'd know him to see him. You know what I'm like for faces."

Tash turned her phone screen to him, revealing the blurred image of the arsonist from the pier fire, before he'd stepped through the smoke as the scaly, black creature. It was smudged by smoke and distortion, and the obscured lighting of the surrounding fire. "Is this him?"

Nick stared at it: the sunken cheeks, much thinner than they had been. The dark hair. The chiseled, tense eyeline. "Yeah," he said, his voice suddenly dry. The phone chimed with a notification. "Yeah, that's him."

"How sure are you?" Tash asked, pulling the phone back.

He moved his mouth around his face, letting his gaze fall from her to the files that lay between them. "Eighty percent," he said finally, raising one shoulder.

Kelly turned, locking eyes with Tash. "That's good enough for me."

"Me too," Tash nodded curtly. She paused. "Especially since he's in LA."

They both looked up at her as one.

"He was listed as a missing person, and months ago an FBI Agent who'd started out in Maine tracked him out here." She swallowed, then looked back at the pile of paper between she, Nick, and Kelly. She bent down and started gathering it up, arranging it into piles. "New plan," she said softly.

CHAPTER ELEVEN

Nick stood on the balcony, looking out over the Los Angeles night. It was hard for him to call it night -- there were so many lights that it shone like day, so bright that he hadn't been able to sleep. There was a scant breeze on the air, but it wasn't enough to keep him cool, as even the evening here was hotter than the peak of summer in his home.

His lenses were out and he looked out over the city with his natural, milk-white eyes as people scattered along the street three floors below. They yelled at and cat-called each other, but mostly they ignored each other.

At once Kelly was behind him, her arms shocking him with static on their approach as she wrapped them around him. She hugged him tight, her cheek smooshing into the grit of his shoulder, and he could feel the weight of her chest press into him. She kissed him, then lay her head down on him like a pillow. "Trouble sleeping?"

"It's the city," he said, looking past his arms to the concrete below. "It's too bright."

She waited, continuing to hold him and hold herself

into him.

"I was thinking about home," he said, more honestly.

She nodded. "This guy, the one we're looking for, with the weird name?"

"Xander."

"Xander. He's from there, too?"

"Yeah."

They paused, her hair moving in the scant breeze that came off the street and getting tangled in the ebbs and wanes of his bare shoulders. "You said you had someone in common? Someone you loved?"

He let out a deep breath through both nostrils, then turned around to face her. She hugged into him still, pressing her cheek against the meager mound of his pectoral muscle. He kissed the top of her head. "There wasn't much to like about Coral Beach, let alone love... but she was good. She was a good person, though she'd punch you in the kidneys if you ever said it to her face." He smiled. "You would have liked her. She was popular, but not... cheerleader popular, you know? She dated a lot, but always seemed in control of it. I dunno, she was just one of those, 'Do what I want and don't have to answer for it' type of people."

She hummed, picking up to look at him, resting her chin on the valley of his chest. "She sounds absolutely horrible."

He laughed. "Yeah, yeah, that's fair. Come to think of it, you two probably *wouldn't* have gotten along."

She smiled. "You have a type; I'm seeing that now." She picked herself up onto her toes and kissed him, long and lovingly on the mouth, then let herself fall back to chest level and hugged into his chest again. They stayed that way for a long time, swaying slightly in the breeze and holding one another.

He brought his hands up and cradled the back of her head and her shoulder.

"Why do you keep referring to her in the past tense?" she asked finally, continuing to hold him.

He stopped swaying with her. "She died," he said finally, pushing the words out. "Not long after I left town." He swallowed.

She nodded, waited a moment, then added: "She was murdered?"

"...Yeah."

"Around the same time as the Black Womb stuff?"

He pursed his lips, then nodded, unable to say it.

She broke off their embrace and took his face in her hands again, pulling him into a kiss that ended in another embrace. She took him by the hand and brought him back to their room.

CHAPTER TWELVE

Mr. Smart was a tall man. Unnaturally so, coming up on seven feet, with shoulders so broad and thick that he looked like he could have fit a full-grown man atop either. His hair was stark white, slicked back and gelled down into a sharp widow's peak that sprawled into tendrils down his back like a mane. His eyes were sunken and his cheekbones sharp. He looked old but not wrinkled, even though Fields knew he was neither.

He sat wearing a solid black suit and white tie as stark as his hair, both of which must have been customized to fit his massive, lurch-like frame. He sat behind a round table meant for two and drank from a pastel orange mug, both of which looked like a doll's tea-set when used by him.

The Jitterbug coffee shop buzzed around him with natural light coming in from the street, diffused by its brick interior. There were paintings on the wall hanging from uneven perches that were for sale, though none of them were particularly good. Fields stood in the entrance to the shop hesitantly, flicking his appointment card back and forth between his fingers as he watched the scene play out before him, like a student play mashing Norman Rockwell and Tim Burton.

"You should sit if you're going to sit," Smart said loudly, motioning to the chair across from himself with his mug.

Fields hesitated, grinding his molars, then stepped forward past a barista bussing empty mugs and pulled out the chair. It squealed against the tile floor and he sat down, leaning forward with his chest pressed against the mesh band table. "You wanna tell me what the fuck that was about? Chase said you were discreet."

Smart moved his hand from the cup's edge, dismissively. "You think standing like a spook in the door of a coffee shop is discreet?" He motioned to Fields. "You think leaning over and whispering at me is discreet? Who taught you discreet? You don't know the word."

Fields bit his tongue, then leaned back on the uncomfortable chair and straightened his suit with a sharp tug at its bottom.

The barista stepped over to them, bouncing as she stepped and smiling from ear to ear, white teeth behind blood red lips. "Hi, what can I get you?"

"Nothing," Fields snapped, not turning to look at her but instead keeping his gaze affixed to Mr. Smart. "Leave."

"He'll have a dark roast coffee, black," Smart said passively, turning to smile at the young woman with a grin that was ghoulish, but somehow kind at the same time. "And a pastry of some kind. Something with frosting."

The barista nodded politely and stepped away.

"I don't drink dark roast," Fields started to say, but Smart moved his hand again. It was a small move, less than a quarter inch, and only two fingers: but somehow it said a lot behind it.

"You'll have the dark roast, and you'll drink it black," Smart reiterated. He sipped his coffee. "And you'll learn it's also not discreet to sit in a coffee house with someone and not order a coffee. Nor is it polite."

Fields licked his lips, smiled wanly, then laughed. "This is a joke, right?" The barista brought over his mug of dark roast and an éclair, setting both down in front of him before stepping away again. He nudged the mug away from him, sloshing some of the liquid. "This is a gag?"

Smart sipped his coffee again, his large, meaty hands holding it gingerly on either side. "You're being attacked."

Fields paused, glanced around the room, then nodded.

"Do you know what you did to cause this attack?"

He sighed, his brows elevating and his anger fading for the first time since the Cartel had ventured into his hotel room. "I don't. At first, I thought it was the Russians, but now I... I don't know. Some pissed off father, maybe? Angry his little girl is turning tricks? I just --"

"No," Smart said, bluntly. "Not what you did to someone else, what you did to yourself. The mistake you made that made you vulnerable in this way: do you know it?"

"Hey, why don't you just --"

"You buy women and then you bring them to restaurants. You put them in dresses more expensive than they were and you parade them out in front of politicians and actors and you smile and you shake hands and you treat the woman like filth in front of them." His accent slipped on the word filth, somewhere between Creole and Boston, but Fields could not place which. His cheeks were drooping, becoming more and more serious, showing the red rim of their meat beneath the tear ducts. He leaned forward, ever so slightly. "That's how you've failed. That's why you're open. You've forgotten how to get a woman to fuck you because she wants to fuck you. You've forgotten how to behave."

Fields laughed. "I'm gonna take you and fuck you if you don't shut the fuck --"

"*You exist*," Smart stressed, "partially in the open and partially in the shadows. You belong to neither, and it's made you weak. You do your dirty deeds, but it's not enough to do them in the dark, you needed to be in the light at expensive places. You needed to be seen in the sun, and that's where he struck at you. And now he's brought fire to the dark and there's nowhere left to hide, but you can't avail of the light. Those policemen, senators, actors... they can't help you; you can't turn to them. You coveted them but now you're stuck in the bed you've made: half in the dark and half in the light, about to be cleaved in two by the dawn."

Fields swallowed. He took a drink of the dark roast, winced, then set it back down. When he spoke again his voice was low, almost inaudible. "I need someone to help me with this guy. He's put the pressure on, and I need it off. I don't... if you're not the guy, just tell me, and I'll step off. I don't need your shit."

"I took the job when I agreed to meet with you," Smart

droned, peering out from out the ridge of his mug with those sunken, dark-rimmed eyes of his. He looked like a Death's Head. "I will deal with this man, and I will deal with him my way, without question. But: there will be pressure."

Fields tilted his head.

"You said you needed the pressure off. I am telling you: there will be pressure. It will get worse. Like lancing a boil, the pain will reach a fever pitch and then, suddenly, it will be gone. And when it goes the relief from that pressure will seem like ecstasy."

Fields sucked in his cheeks, nodded, then extended his rough-hewn hand across the table. Smart took it, pumping once and then letting go.

CHAPTER THIRTEEN

The elevator door chimed at LAPD12's second floor, opening into its Homicide division. Tash stepped out of it before the doors were even done closing, marching into the brightly lit sheen of stainless steel and glass that lined each edge of it. Her expression was stern and resolute, her mouth a tiny pucker in the middle of her face.

Nick and Kelly stepped out behind her, jogging to keep up as she pushed her way into the hall of Tetris-block desks. "You sure this is the way you want to play this?" Kelly hissed under her breath, turning and eyeing the uniformed policemen all around them. That many in one place still set her teeth on edge, even though she told herself it shouldn't.

Tash did not answer. She looked right to where Duncan and Hazer's desks were, then turned back and eyed Janet behind her desk, picking up her phone and only just starting to dial, and marched over to it. "You said crime was up," Tash snapped.

Janet froze, then put the phone back on its cradle. "I'm sorry?"

"I was here yesterday. You said crime was up. Heists. Home invasions. Violent crime. You said it was getting out of control."

"Hi, sorry," Kelly smiled, stammering. "Do we need an appointment, or?"

"Crime is up," Janet nodded. She arose from her desk, placing her fingers down onto it to balance herself. "Violent crime especially. Most of it's being handled by Vice, but a lot of it's getting kicked up to here. Why... what do you know?"

"It's being handled by your Vice department because it's gang related?"

"Allegedly."

"It's people fighting to fill the vacuum left by Stephen Fields?"

The room went silent, suddenly. There had been clamor and bustle, the sound of people chatting and arguing and getting through their day: all of it stopped, and all eyes turned toward the discussion happening at Janet Nesbit's desk. Tash turned and eyed the lot of them, standing with their mouths open and eyes wide. Duncan Taggart wasn't at his desk, but Bill Hazer was stammering as though he'd heard the name of the devil himself. He set down the cola he'd been drinking and picked up his phone.

Tash turned back to Janet, glowering. "You're all afraid of him."

Janet's cheeks flushed red. "Hey --"

"You are. You've let him run rampant, and now he's everywhere. He's eaten away at what you are like a cancer, and now there's more of his cells left than yours. And someone's finally sick of it and is trying to burn it down, but it's in too deep now. Its burning everything down with it."

Janet winced.

"That's what's happening, isn't it?"

Kelly turned to Nick, who was staring at Janet and watching her every motion, unblinking. He watched her weapon, clipped at her hip, as if expecting it to make a move all on its own. "Hey," she said, stepping out alongside Tash. "Let's just... let's just, okay?"

"Is there something I can do to help you?" Janet said, sighing.

"I'm looking for this guy," Tash said. She reached into her breast pocket and for a moment Janet flinched, then relaxed again when she produced her cell phone. She tabbed open to a picture of Xander Drew, then handed Janet the phone. It was a picture from his youth, before his move to Los Angeles, a school photo.

Janet squinted at it. "That's... we've had an APB out on this man for months." She paused. "He's wanted for arson. Among other things."

Nick cocked his head. "He burn down a Fields building?"

The room, which had started to chatter again, hushed itself for a second time. Nick frowned.

Kelly turned and stepped back out into the hall.

"I can't say," Janet said, finally. "But if I could say, I'd probably say yes. Yeah."

Tash chuckled wryly to herself, looking over the bullpen again before turning back to Janet. "You've done this to yourself, you know. This level of corruption... it can't abide. Someone will always come to carve it out." Nick placed a gentle hand on the crook of her arm, and she stopped. She sighed. "Anything you can give me on this man, I'd appreciate," she said, clipping each word.

Janet snorted, ran a finger across her chin, then sat back down and pulled up her active files.

Nick stepped out into the hall where Kelly stood, leaned against the glass wall of the meeting room. "You mind telling me what that was about?"

She winced, turning back over her shoulder and looking past him. Tash was leaned over Janet's desk now to look at her screen, both of them pointing to it and talking inaudibly. "All those people, and she says one name and they just... stop."

Nick nodded. "It's gross, I know."

"It's not gross," she said. "It's a *cult*."

He balked, turning back to see what she was seeing and leaning against the wall next to her.

"When I was living with Gavin... when all of us were living with Gavin, we weren't hidden. We weren't in some sewer or a gutted-out hospital or something. We had a big house right on the street. A little ways off the beaten path, sure: but on the street."

Nick nodded.

Kelly shook her head, almost in disbelief. "That was part of what made it seem normal, the world acting like it was normal. Every day cars would drive by, mail would come, pizza would get delivered... people saw us. People looked out their windows and saw how we were living, and they didn't point, they didn't yell, they didn't call the police. They kept... their mouths... *shut*."

She turned to face the bullpen head on, her arms crossed. Nick put a hand on her shoulder but did not speak.

"Everyone was in that cult. Not just the people who lived in that house, *everyone*. The Pizza-Boy, the Mailman, and the Grandma with her kids in the back that drove past every Sunday on her way to church. The whole fucking town of Atlanta was in that cult." She paused. "A Cult of Silence."

He leaned over, kissing her on top of her thinly haired head. "Not you."

"Not *you*," she clarified, then cocked her head towards the bullpen. "But them. Every last one of them. It's the same thing, Nick. It's a Cult of Silence. Everyone walks by this... this gang lord every day, everyone knows, and everyone just... they just..."

"Keep their mouths shut," he finished, under his breath.

"*Exactly*," she hissed. "And they let this happen."

Nick nodded, and they both watched the Homicide division of the LAPD12 work while Tash got the information she needed.

Four men looked at Fields from where they sat, each of them surrounded by plumes of cigarette smoke. Two sat, one squat, and the other stood. All four wore black and jeans -- the type that went with everything. One had a large belt buckle in the shape of Colorado. Fields had never seen a belt buckle in the shape of Colorado before, and wouldn't have been able to recognize it apart from the other squarish states if not for the word 'Colorado' raised across it. That man's thumbs were tucked behind the silver, his fingers splayed out over either side of his crotch. His cigarette dangled from his lips and he let the ash from it fall to the motel room floor.

All of them had shaved heads, and most had tattoos that ran up their necks and behind their ears. Two were of swastikas, one was a large stylistic numeral 1488 with spikes and horns from each of the numbers.

"The fuck is this?" Fields spat, turning around to face Chase and Smart.

Smart blocked the door that led out to the parking lot with the entirety of his frame. His expression was grim and sour, but he said nothing.

"I'm not," Fields looked over his shoulder, aware suddenly that he was being watched and listened to. He lowered his voice. "I've spent a lot of time and energy over the years to not have to be in a room with people just like this."

Smart smiled.

Chase looked over Fields at the crew assembled, put a hand on Fields' shoulder, then stepped in front of him to block between the two.

"I've worked for you five years," the largest of the men said, stroking a blond handlebar mustache. "You ain't seen me, but you've taken my cash. So, don't act like you're big shit in small water."

Chase broadened his shoulders, brought his hands together slowly, and began cracking his knuckles.

"This isn't going to work," Fields said, his voice resolute. "I can't be seen with people like this, I just... It'd ruin me." He turned back to the men who'd been waiting on him. "I'm sorry." He stepped towards the door.

"Why can't you be seen with these men?" Smart asked softly and politely, not moving from the exit.

Fields winced.

"It is because of your public face. This, this is what I mean. You want to exist in both worlds, but you cannot. You cannot do what needs to be done to make the shadows safe while still keeping the image of yourself in the light." He leaned forward, lowering his voice. "If you try to do this, you will fail."

Fields pursed his lips, sighed, then turned back around to face the assembled men.

"Boss," Chase started, even as Fields stepped past him.

Fields stepped into the plume of smoke and held out his hand. The man with the Colorado belt buckle smiled and produced a pack of cigarettes from under his shirt sleeve and handed it to him. He lit it, took a stiff drag, then leaned back against the mini fridge.

"I'm stuck in a middle," he said, puffing out a cloudy blue smoke. "On the one side, I've got this guy: do-gooder, rival, whatever. Burning Man. He's been taking a torch to my operations." He took another puff, then waved the cigarette around, making tendrils and circles with the smoke. "On the other, I've got the Cartel breathing down my neck."

The man with the handlebar mustache cursed and said a racial slur.

Fields looked up past the smoke at him, then continued. "It's two sides of a vice. One of these things has to go. Now despite what you might have heard, I'm no lover of the Cartel." The men chuckled. In the corner, Chase stiffened. "But, I don't fancy taking them on with five guys and a shiny belt buckle." He motioned with the smoke, "No offense, 'Rado."

The man with the Colorado belt buckle grinned with yellowed, corn-kernel teeth.

"So, we've gotta take out this guy. Whatever it costs." He threw a look at Chase, who sighed, then nodded. "Whatever it takes. It's gotta get done, and it's gotta get done fast. The Cartel ain't been paid and if we don't deal with the Burning Man side of the vice, they might make the choice about which side we're fighting for us." He took another puff and finished the cigarette.

The man with the mustache stepped back and found an ashtray and brought it to Fields with a smile. Fields paused, dosed the ember, then let the man take the tray back away. The corner of Fields' mouth twitched into a grin, and at his side Chase shook his head.

"Cartel has a ship off the coast, loaded with girls. It can't stay there long, and they need it to come in."

Smart stepped in from the door, his dark eyebrows perked with interest.

"So, we've got to deal with this guy and deal with him fast so we can get the boat in and get the gravy train flowing again."

"The boat," Smart drawled, extending the A-sound to its longest ebb. "You didn't mention a boat." He smiled to his men, then men smiled back and nodded.

"Yeah, there's a boat." Fields waved a hand dismissively. "There's always a boat. This one's fuller than most, granted. This guy, Burning Man, he started his gig by picking away at my sex trade. We've needed to get in new girls to keep the money flowing. I'd let it in, but he just hit one of my piers. Motherfucker burned seven mil on me. I don't know what he knows, and I don't have the resources right now to get a new pier. Unless you got one."

Smart smiled his ghoulish, death's head smile. "I think you should let that boat in." He looked at the men again, and they laughed. "To your pier, preferably."

Fields squinted, thrusting up his hands in frustration. "The guy... someone talked, and now I don't know what piers Burning Man is watching. If I bring the boat in, he could --"

Fields stopped himself, a wry grin playing over his thin lips. He shook a finger at Smart, nodding.

Chase stiffened. He stepped forward as if to object, then swallowed.

"I'll make the call," Fields nodded.

"Please," Smart said, puckering his lips. "Allow me."

CHAPTER FOURTEEN

Tash projected a map of Los Angeles onto the wall of her hotel room using a small cardboard cube with a lens attached, her smartphone slid into the back. It looked like a bastard blend of high and low tech: and was. The effect was a jarring disappointment: a jittering, blurry mess along the salmon pink wall.

"This is *madness*," she huffed, flicking a full pack of pink Post-It notes back and forth between her fingers. She paced back and forth in front of the projection, her shadow blotting out most of the east side when she did.

Nick and Kelly watched from her spare bed, behind the projector. Kelly was eating from a kilogram bag of peanut M&Ms, laying on her stomach with her feet in the air, as though she had turned up for a Friday night movie and stayed anyway. Nick sat with one leg tucked beneath the other on the edge of the bed, and occasionally took a handful of the sweets.

"He's hit three places in the last few days," she said, scribbling on the Post-It with a ballpoint pen.

Her phone chimed and a text alert overtook the projection: 'Victor - Things hairy here, how there.'

"Sorry," she tisked. She took the phone out of the projector and the room went dark until she dismissed the notification and replaced it. "Like I said, madness. There's been a fire at a club downtown that the vice cops say he was using to funnel drugs and money through." She wrote 'club' on the Post-It and slapped it on the wall at the corresponding address downtown. "Before that he burned down a restaurant off of Hollywood Boulevard." She wrote the restaurant name and placed it on the wall as well. "And then there's the pier." She wrote pier on a note, then stuck it down at the waterfront on the far western edge of the projection.

"He's busy," Nick said softly, looking from sticky-note to sticky-note.

"Are we... sure we wanna fuck with this guy?" Kelly asked, hesitantly.

Tash frowned, then continued. "Weeks before that, we have the Laura Bennett murder, Megan Greene, Victor Murdock, Thomas Horton." She picked up a second packet of yellow Post-Its and unwrapped them from their cellophane. She wrote the name 'Bennett' across it and stuck it on the headquarters of Shane International's Los Angeles branch. She paused then pointed at it all four of her fingers, as though she were saluting it. "That has nothing to do with Fields, near as I can tell. The police... the LAPD aren't even dialed into it being linked into the rest of the case, but it's important."

Nick squinted.

She picked up the pink pad again and wrote a four-letter word on it, the characters so tall that even Kelly could see them despite the glare from the projector. She peeled it off and stuck it at a cul-de-sac called Cedarwood Plaza. "A few months ago, he robs a bank."

Kelly stopped chewing suddenly, her hand falling onto her bag of M&Ms. "A bank. He... he robbed a bank."

"He robbed a bank."

"Like, went in, took the money, shot the place up, robbed a bank."

Tash raised a finger. "That's part of my point, actually. He didn't shoot the place up. No deaths."

"But he robbed a bank," Nick said. "Why's this in pink?"

Tash smiled. "Glad you're paying attention. Vice thinks its Fields' bank."

Nick raised his hands, shocked. "He has a bank? He has a bank. How much money does this motherfucker have? How much crime is running through him?"

"Lots," she sighed, flipping the notes and looking back at the map. "Most of it, from what I can see. Not all of it, but... yeah, lots. Billions, possibly."

Nick ran his hands through his hair, tugged at it, then waved her forward. "Okay, he robbed a mob bank. Then?"

"Then there's nothing, for months. There's petty stuff here and there, but nothing probative. Then all of a sudden, a few months before the bank heist: bam." She scribbled the word FIRE in bold letters on the pink Post-It and slapped it against the wall. "Arson. The original arson, the one the LAPD want him for. He lit a brothel owned by Fields on fire, burned the whole thing to the ground, and tortured a pimp. Damn near scared him to death."

"I'm filled with pity," Kelly snarled.

"But no deaths," Tash said, raising her finger again. "It was on Homicide's radar because there had been prostitutes being burned, and they thought it was linked." She pulled a sheet of paper from a file on her nightstand and held it up. It showed Xander Drew sitting across from a man in silhouette, each on either end of an interrogation table. "They actually had him in on impersonating a police officer, but whatever. He burned that brothel to the ground, but there'd been a tip to the police beforehand. It was empty when it burned: no deaths. And!" She raised the same finger, then pulled the picture back up, pointing to the man in silhouette. "That man is Thomas Horton." She motioned back to the yellow Post-It.

Nick looked at the pattern of Post-Its, most of them clustered along the west side of the city. "And then?"

Tash shrugged. "And then nothing. Not a damn thing. Nothing for months until he's back in Coral Beach and shows up in Megan Greene's court transcripts."

Nick shook his head in surprise.

"Do you see it?" Tash said, pointing to each of the notes with her saluted hand. "Early days, no deaths. No deaths. Then all of a sudden, bam." She tapped the yellow BENNETT Post-Its. "Four dead, just like that. And all of a sudden there's deaths at every turn. Deaths at the pier, deaths at the restaurant... Fields men, sure. But dead Fields men."

Kelly stared at the pink Post-It with the word BANK scrawled across it.

"He's escalating," Nick said solemnly.

"He's *triggered*," Tash stressed, tapping the yellow

Post-It again. "Guys like this, there's always a trigger. The *obsessive* type. Something sets them off and off they shoot. It can be simple, like, BTK's kids moved out. It can be anything. But I guarantee you, in this case: it's here." She tapped the wall again.

Kelly sat up. She backed herself away from the edge of the bed until she was at its opposite edge.

"Something here set this guy off and set him off bad. He was driven before, but now he's *obsessed*. Narrowly focused, no time for decent. Before he had one hand on the wheel, and now there's none. That sound like the guy you knew?"

Nick narrowed his eyes. He remembered Xander walking home after Sara Johnson: not with her, but after her. He remembered him every day, the jagged looks he would give Sara's boyfriends. The bitterness behind them. "It does, actually." He licked his lips. "So, we're thinking it was Greene, or Horton? The ones he had a connection with?"

Tash nodded. "That makes the most sense, yeah. Yeah for sure." She paused. "The timeline on Greene puts her after Bennett, so my money's on Horton. There was some connection with him, and when he was killed things went really wrong."

Kelly looked up finally, tearing her eyes away from the BANK Post-It and making contact with Tash. "Do you think it was Fields?"

Tash raised an eyebrow.

"He was a cop, right? And he was looking into things on his off time? Too much of a stretch to think he got close to something?"

Tash winced, tapping her pen against her lip, and looking at the map. "Maybe... maybe. Yeah. I like it."

The phone chimed again, and a notification took up the majority of the screen. Unlike the text from Victor, there was no name attached, and the body of the text was garbled. Tash walked to the cardboard projector and plucked the phone out of it again.

"What the fuck was that?" Nick asked. "You getting spam alerts now?"

Tash shook her head. "It's my contact." She paused, reading the message. Her eyes widened.

"What is it?" Kelly asked, leaning forward.

"He um... he set alerts at all the docks that Fields has been suspected of using, set it up to alert of suspicious activity." She paused. "They just scheduled a new docking in. For tonight."

Kelly got off the bed, her eyes darting back to the bold blue words: BANK.

Xander sat in his steaming tub, his arms on either side of it, breathing deeply. The lights were on overhead and he stared into them almost unblinkingly.

There was a chime next to him.

He reached for his burner phone but missed, hitting it to the floor. He cursed, then leaned over the edge, his wet hair dribbling as steam rose from the water and off his reddened form. He stared over the edge of the tub for a long moment, then cursed again.

He breathed in until his lungs could take no more, then held it, and closed his eyes. He let out the breath through his mouth in a long, slow rhythm, feeling the tickle of condensation navigate the pores of his ribcage.

When he opened his eyes again, he reached for the phone, plucked it off of his bathroom floor, and turned its screen toward him.

'WHITE - Santa Monica Pier. Tonight. Replenishing the ranks. Solid tip.'

Xander coughed deep in his throat. He rose from the water and stepped out.

CHAPTER FIFTEEN

The far south side of the San Diego Pier was as black as pitch, the neon shine of the Ferris wheel and fairgrounds a distant distraction on the horizon. Its bright, vibrant sheen only served to make the shadows of the far beach more shadowed by comparison, the gray dunes of sand evaporating into the inky void of the sea.

"Do you see anything?" Tash asked. She unlocked her phone, switched between three open apps, then tucked it into her breast pocket with the camera facing out. She clasped the button flap over it, careful not to obscure the view of the lens.

The three of them sat hunched at the edge of the bluffs, the rocky edge that fell sharply to the sand below. They crouched until they could be confused with the uneven formations of rock, Kelly flat on her stomach.

Nick stared into the void, to a space where Tash couldn't tell where the sea ended and the sky began.

"Nick?"

"They're there," Nick said, his voice hushed. "There's a ship half a mile out, running without lights on. Its heading into shore." He blinked, then turned back toward the Shelby Pier. It had closed operation hours ago at dusk, but as Nick looked upon the black, he saw movement. "There's a man at the pier... no, two. They're waiting near the docking doors." He paused. "One of them has a massive gun."

"Define massive."

"It's an AR-15."

"Fuck my life," she huffed, keeping her volume low. "Any sign of Xander?"

Nick squinted, running his eyes along the edges of the coast that were in shadow even to him, searching of some hint of motion. He shook his head. "Negative."

Kelly shuffled forward, bringing her gloved hands up to shield her eyes from the glare of the carnival rides. She looked deep into the shadows of the horizon, trying to see some hint of what he saw. "Do you see the girls?"

Nick took a breath, then licked his suddenly dry lips. "Yeah. Yeah, I see the girls." He stopped. "Not many, but there are some on the deck." His lip curled.

Kelly turned to Tash. "What do we do if he doesn't show up?"

Tash turned to her. "Pardon?"

"If Xander doesn't show up to raid the place -- what do we do about the girls?"

Tash narrowed her eyes, then bit her lip.

"They're coming in," Nick said, his voice hushed.

Chase stood on the edge of the darkened pier, the toes of his shoes protruding over the edge. He looked down between his feet into the water below, the stark blackness of the waves broken only by the curling white of their froth. The boat approached, now almost close enough that they could begin tossing their ropes ashore to anchor. He watched it, a triangle of deep black on the black of the sea, the erect figure of a man standing on the deck in the same position he was in.

It was his shadow self, and they were coming together.

"Hoo-e," the man with the blond handlebar mustache -- Dale -- said excitedly, keeping the muzzle of his AR-15 aimed high. "I just about smell the poon-tang from here, ayuh?" He clapped Chase on the shoulder.

Chase turned to look at him. "If you touch one of those girls, I'll break your hands."

The smile left Dale's face, and he lowered the muzzle of the gun slightly, almost imperceptibly.

"You can't ruin the product," Chase added, turning back to the boat.

Dale laughed and smiled heartily. Chase did not join him.

On the deck of the ship, the shadowed man grabbed a long pile of rope and tossed it ashore.

Beneath Chase's feet, the dock began to move and sway with the motion of the tide, letting out a long series of moans and creaks. Chase could already hear the sound of fear.

He tied the ship to its post, and began to pull it in.

"He's not coming," Kelly said, her voice almost to its

normal volume now, panic setting into it.

Tash watched the darkness of Shelby Pier, her eyes unblinking. Sweat began to exude itself from her pores and roll down her cheek and nose.

"We have to go in," Kelly hissed again, even rising from her position to squat, ready to move. "We have to go now, before they get off the boat. If they get off the boat, they could get away with any number of them." She started to peel off her gloves.

"Wait," Nick snapped, reaching out and putting his hand on hers without looking. He paused, squinting as though that could somehow sharpen the image he was seeing or zoom it in. "I see him."

Tash turned to him. "You're sure?"

"Yeah," he said with a sullen sigh. "Yeah, I'm sure."

The metal plank extended from the hull of the ship, bouncing and clattering on its rivets as it descended, the loudest sound that had shattered through the calm night air in hours. It slammed against the dock, rope rails jittering back and forth like an untrustworthy rope bridge.

Before the plank had even finished its descent, the shadowed man on the deck had pushed the first girl onto it and started her walking down. She stumbled and then caught her foot along the metal lip stair, the jarring motion bringing forth a fresh crop of sobs from a throat that had become accustomed to them. Her face was soaked and puffy with tears, and her arms spotted with large, oval bruises.

She was no older than nine.

"Christ," Chase cursed, removing his gun from its holster and looking left and right along the edge of the shore.

Before the girl was even a third of the way down the plank, three more had been forced onto it behind her, the rusted metal bending and bucking with their footsteps. Two were platinum blonde and looked not much older than the first, their features matching so much that they were almost indistinguishable. One was crying the wide, open-mouthed wails that only a child could. The other -- the older -- was resolute. As they got closer, Chase could see that the taller of the two was at least fifteen.

The first stepped off the plank and stepped until she was between and before Chase and Dale. She held her arms tight against herself, making herself as small as she could. Her eyes were cast down at the wood of the dock and the roaring shore beyond.

Dale reached out and took the girl's chin between his thumb and forefinger, tilting it up and grinning to the extent of his handlebar mustache.

The motion drew a look of ire from Chase. "What'd I say?"

"Aw calm your bitchin'," Dale drawled, laughing. "I'm just seeing what we got here." He examined her, then spat the same racial slur he had at the motel.

Chase's nostrils flared.

There were more than a dozen on the dock and the plank now, with a waning but steady stream still being led down. The later were older, some old enough that they wouldn't have been carded, Chase guessed. The final two were sixteen at the least, but he assumed seventeen.

Dale let the girl go, and her face shot back down to the floorboards as if on a weight. Her eyes went wide.

Kelly ripped off the last of her leather gloves, letting them fall to the rocks at her feet. Her hands glowed a slight blue in the pitch black of the night, and she wriggled her newly freed fingers, generating sparks of static between them.

Next to her, Tash withdrew a handgun from her go-bag and then discarded the bag behind her.

Nick shot her a surprised look. "A gun? You?"

"Desperate times," she whispered in response. She felt the gun -- felt its weight in her palm for a long moment, took a deep breath, then nodded and extended her grip around the weapon. "We can't wait anymore."

Nick nodded, stood to his full height, then stopped. His face lost its colour, and Tash could see it in the glow from Kelly's hands.

"What?"

Nick cocked his head toward the bottom of the rock face below, where the bluffs met the beach. In the new light, there was the scant hint of motion. At once there was more than a hint, and the silhouettes of four men emerged from the shadows, making their way towards Shelby Pier.

Tash's eyes went wide.

Three of the men had round headed silhouettes. The fourth -- the one if front -- had a long mane that bounced behind him like a cape. It was so white it glowed even in the low light of the shore.

"What's happening?" Kelly whispered.

"I think someone had the same idea we did," Tash answered, staring forward and watching the men progress.

As they watched, the men approaching the pier produced the long, erect shadows of guns, each the same size and shape as the one Dale had held.

Nick jumped forward without a word, quickly skidding his way down the steep edge of the rockface.

CHAPTER SIXTEEN

"Get them into the vans," Chase growled, turning back from the docks. The girls were trying, all of them. Each one was only a whimper, but together they were a cacophony of mewling white noise. "And get them to be quiet, for God's sake."

Dale pushed the girl the furthest to the front with a sudden, firm shove to the shoulder blade that sent her rocking forward. She stared at the floor, her eyes wide, as if trying to see it in the black.

Chase stepped into the darkened back on the pier. Once again it swayed and groaned, the damp boards extruding a long, mournful growl. He paused, then turned back to the girls, and the sea beyond it.

It had calmed, nary a wave or strong motion of the tide inside.

He squinted, stepping forward.

The boards of the pier erupted beneath him in an explosion of dust and splinters, forced up into the atmosphere by a mass of black shadow. He fell back and raised his gun, but while he was still in mid-fall, he felt two firm, sharp pressures against his chest. His mind raced to catch up, and an instant after he thought that the shadows had grabbed him, he was pulled beneath the pier, lancing his arm against the jagged wood.

He screamed. He was under the pier with a shadow now, a shadow with glowing red eyes. As he watched, it grew a mouth and long, jagged teeth. It roared, then pushed Chase back with such force that his legs fell out from beneath him. Before he could scream again or raise his weapon, he was completely submerged in the seawater and being held down.

From above, the sound of automatic weapon fire rang out like thunder, followed by the shrill screams of a dozen children. The creature's face turned, then its head, craning up at an unnatural angle as hot lead rained down through the floorboards all around them, splintering the wooden floor and the beams and sending splinters in all directions.

The creature let go of Chase and he emerged from the water, gasping with want for air. It crouched and then leapt, emerging through the same crack in the floor it had hauled Chase through and landing in a crouch in front of both Dale and the children.

He was behind them, using them as a shield, his gun aimed forward with the precision of ex-military. The muzzle quivered only slightly.

The creature stood to its full height, lanky and slender, its eyes catching all of the meager ambient light and retro-reflecting it back as deep red. "I wouldn't," it said, its voice raspy and almost not understandable.

The door at the back of the pier slammed open, and

before the creature could turn, the dark of its shadows were alight with automatic weapons fire. Bullets streaked through the air from Smart's gun, his white hair sprayed back.

A lantern on the wall exploded in a shower of polarized glass, sending sparks of blue electricity shimmering in its wake. Three more punched holes in the walls of the pier. Two embedded themselves into the creature's shoulder, exploding out the other side of it in a splay of inky black ooze and sending it hurtling to the floor, clutching its arm with its clawed hand.

"Fuck!" it cursed, its voice suddenly clear. When it turned back to face Smart, it was Xander's face that glowered, the lines on either side of his face forming deep ditches as he ground through the pain.

The children screamed, and more bullets came.

Smart stepped into the room fully, flanked by his three skinhead followers. He lowered his AR-15 until it was level with Xander's face and smiled. "Fields sends his love."

Xander sneered and pushed forward, connecting his wounded shoulder with Smart's gut even as more bullets came. He slammed Smart's gun arm high, and the bullets shattered through the ceiling, punching a maw of holes before the muzzle stopped flashing.

He wrapped his hands around Smart's neck and squeezed, the ghoulish man's eyes bulging in his gaunt, grey head. His men aimed their guns and fired, a section of flesh on Xander's ribs peeling away. The shots went in and out, grazing Smart, who screamed for them to stop.

Smart dropped his gun and raised his thick, long fingers to Xander's neck and pressed his bony thumbs deep into his Adam's apple.

"Bet you break first," Xander smirked, chuckling.

"Hoo-e," came Dale's siren call from the edge of the room.

Xander turned. Half of the girls had gone, but Dale stood on the edge of the pier with those that remained. His assault rifle was pressed directly into the back of a young girl with olive skin, her eyes big and white and locked with his.

He stopped. The other three had taken aim at the children as well, arranged in a line like a firing squad.

Blood arose to Xander's cheeks even as the wounds on his shoulder and side stopped ebbing blood. He released his grip on Mr. Smart, brought his hands high, and backed up from him. He kept his eyes on Dale. "You do that, I'm going to peel you like an orange."

"You talk like you weren't gonna do that anyway," Dale grinned, poking his chin out toward Xander. "This was gonna go this way the second you decided to step into it. You know it." He smiled. Both his eye teeth were missing. "I seen the look of you before."

Xander moved to step forward, then stumbled.

All eyes widened.

"Not now," he said, softly, and forced himself to his feet.

"Boy, I am not gonna count to three," Dale yelled, pushing the gun further into the girl's head, "I am not gonna count to one; you will stand the fuck down or I will blow this child's head off, you understand me?"

Dale's knee erupted in a gory splatter of blood and bone. He screamed, jolted to the side, and fell, striking his back against the sharp edge of the pier. He toppled over the edge and splashed into the water as the second gunman's kneecap exploded, then the third's. The fourth, the man with the large swastika tattoo covering his neck and head, stepped out of the pier and shot into the dark.

Smart scrambled to his feet and reached for his weapon, but Xander stepped between the two. Smart glared up at him... and saw no glint of recognition in return.

Slowly, Smart smiled and rose to his feet.

"Run!" Xander barked in the direction of the children. The last of them scattered.

"Where'd you lean to shoot like that?" Nick yelled, plugging his ears as Tash brought the smoking gun around to aim it anew.

"You don't know where I've been," she said, her face devoid of emotion.

Children ran along the edge of the shoreline, and a bald man with a large swastika tattoo emerged from the back entrance of the pier. He brought his gun up to eye-level, propped it against his shoulder, and opened fire.

"No!" Kelly screamed, tackling him to the ground with all the force her slender from could manage.

He cursed and tried to bring his gun around, its length a hazard in close quarters.

She brought her hands high and they erupted in blue and purple sparks, then brought both down hard on his head and chest. He seized, then fell flat against the sand.

"Jesus!" Nick screamed.

"He'll live," Kelly spat, standing quickly to get her

body off of his. "It's more than he deserves." She turned to the shoreline. "The kids?"

"I don't see it being an issue," Tash said, nodding towards the bluffs. The blue and red light of police cherries lit up the formally black night sky.

"Where is he?" Nick yelled, spinning around. "Where's Xander?"

He scanned the darkness in the opposite direction the children were running, and found a shadow running haphazardly across the shoreline toward the neon of San Diego Pier. "No!" he yelled, taking off across the sand after him at top speed.

"Nick, no!" Tash bellowed. He did not stop, and both she and Kelly bolted after him.

Nick was about to overtake Xander, when he saw the twist of ribs and stopped short. Xander spun, and narrowly missed bringing his fist around into the side of Nick's face. He did so with a grunt of exertion, the motion continuing along and pulling at the tendons of his arm.

Xander pushed forward again, swinging at Nick. He pulled back then lunged forward, clipping Xander in the jaw with a quick jab.

Xander edged back, his feet in the tide up to his ankles.

"Stop," Nick commanded, his voice firm and almost not his own. "Stop it, Xander."

Xander's eyes went wide and he pushed forward again. Nick saw the start of the motion and stepped aside. Xander turned in mid-motion, extended his leg, and swept

Nick's out from under him.

Nick fell into the surf, and in an instant Xander was on him, his hands around his neck and pressing him beneath the foamy, churning tide.

Nick grabbed at his face and tried to scream. Bubbles came out, and water rushed in.

Without a word, Xander bit his lip and tightened his grip.

CHAPTER SEVENTEEN

"No!" Tash screamed, her voice full of fear for the first time since Kelly had known her. She grabbed him by the shoulder and pulled to force him off of Nick, but he didn't budge. She pulled again and he spun, connected his elbow with her central plexus, and sent her back into the wet sand.

She reached for her gun.

"Stop it!" Kelly screamed. There were tears on her cheeks and she pounded at Xander's back as he turned back to Nick, reapplying the pressure on his windpipe.

Kelly pulled her arm back and her hand erupted with blue charge, then jumped onto Xander's back and brought her hand around and over his shoulder. She connected with his chest and released the full charge, and they both shot back to the beach.

Nick pulled himself up out of the water, gasping for air in deep, whooping gusts.

Kelly rolled onto Xander, straddling him, and pulled back her arms again. They both sparked blue, so bright that they lit up her fingernails with neon. It sparked from her eyes, and her hair stood on end.

"Kelly!" Tash barked, scrambling to her feet and aiming her weapon at them both.

"Fuckers!" Xander bellowed. He flailed his arm, striking wildly and connecting hard with Kelly's cheek. He grabbed her by both shoulders as if he'd just found her and flipped them both, rolling until he was on top and the back of her head was pushed into the sand.

He pulled back to strike, his hand ejecting blood as claws shot out.

Kelly brought her hands high and connected with both of his cheeks and released her full charge.

The entire beach flashed bright blue and there was a clap like thunder. For a moment everyone was blinded. When their sight returned, Kelly was standing and holding her arm gingerly, hissing.

Xander was on the ground in a nest of melted glass.

"Don't do that again," Tash said, her voice motherly again as she touched Kelly's arm.

Nick stepped forward and they embraced, then kissed. All his hair stood on end.

Tash leveled her weapon to where Xander lay, steam rising from all around him. She kicked him and he turned over, his chest rising and falling rapidly. His eyes were open, and he stared up into the black of the night sky.

She loomed over him, looking down. His face twitched and he moved his arm, slowly, with a long groan escaping his lips. But he stared up at the sky and did not respond to the gun leveled at him.

"Is he alive?" Kelly asked, genuine concern in her tone.

Nick nodded before Tash could answer, his vision allowing him to see the steady movements of Xander's chest.

"He's conscious," Tash clarified, keeping her gun pointed at him.

Kelly stiffened.

"I think..." Tash winced. "I think he's blind."

CHAPTER EIGHTEEN

Xander breathed heavily, glaring into the lens of Tash's camera phone as she took his picture. He was shirtless and handcuffed to the iron bar of the heater on the far side of her hotel room with handcuffs, so tight that they dug into his wrists when he pulled against them. It did not stop him from pulling against them.

Kelly and Nick stood behind and to either side of Tash, watching as the man pulled against his restraints. His mouth was dirty and unkempt from his fall at the dock. There was blood mixed with it, but no wound for it to have come from from what they could see.

He looked in their general direction but not at any one of them in particular, his gaze unfocused, as though he were hearing where they were in the room as opposed to seeing it.

"He's definitely blind," Nick said under his breath, with a tinge of sympathy in his voice despite his efforts to fight it. He recalled the feeling of sightlessness, and wouldn't have wished it on anyone. Now that he was face to face with the man, he recognized him even less than he had in the pictures. When he'd seen the photo on Tash's

phone, he remembered saying that he'd been eighty percent certain that that man had been Xander Drew. Now
that he was face to face with him, his form toned yet emaci-
ated, his eyes staring blankly but with hate -- he wouldn't
have been able to say he was more than forty percent sure.

"What are we doing with him?"

"I've sent a message to Victor," Tash replied, hitting
send on the picture even as she spoke. "He's getting on
the first plane out here."

"And then what do we do?"

Tash paused for a long, tense moment. "We'll figure
that out then."

Nick and Kelly looked at each other.

In his corner, Xander began to laugh.

Chase huffed, his cheeks distended and shaking. There
was noise and neon all around him, the sort of shimmering light that came with a fever dream. He leaned against
the side of a ring toss tent, and was shocked that it buckled in away from him.

Oblongs of red blood soaked their way into his shirt,
pushing the boundaries of their domain a little more with
each passing minute. They'd almost made their way to his
buttons and would soon overtake them, and he struggled
to hide this beneath his blazer.

A child looked up at him. Her skin and hair were dark,
making her wide eyes pop in the evening. She was staring
at him, and in his ruined state, it took him a moment to
realize that it was not one of the children he'd loaded off
the boat.

He winced, touching his side, and the girl stepped

away from him.

"Get out," yelled the man behind the ring toss booth, leaning around to see what was collapsing his tent in. "You, drunk. Get out!"

Chase ground his teeth, then pushed off and kept walking. People pushed past him, knocking against him from one side, then the other, as if he were tumbling from rail to rail on the highway. But he wasn't; he was stepping straight. He knew it.

Groggily, he reached into his pocket and produced his phone. It refused to turn on, waterlogged. He cursed.

"This is almost too easy," came a voice from behind him.

He turned.

Detective Janet Nesbit stood at the edge of the planks of floor that led back to the beach, her gun drawn but not raised. She was flanked by two uniformed officers. Her hair billowed in the breeze off the water and caught the neon lights of the Ferris wheel, changing from green to purple to red in quick succession.

Chase grinned. He turned as if to confront her, twisted unsteadily on his heels, and connected with the floor.

"Chase Madison, you have the right to remain silent."

"You know who I am?" he glowered, lowering his voice. His eyes became shadowed and he glared through her, as though his stare could slice past her like butter.

Janet stopped, lowering the Miranda card she'd been reading from. "Yeah. Turns out that doesn't matter so much when you're caught trafficking kids."

He glared, then sighed. Before her eyes, he deflated like a balloon, and the cuffs were on him.

CHAPTER NINETEEN

Xander pulled against his handcuffs until they sliced into the flesh of both his wrists, their chain scraping against the solid steel of the heater they were looped around. He felt it grind in tune with his teeth, pulled until his arms drew blood, then relented and laughed. He turned back to Tash, who sat on the other side of the room on a rolling office chair, one leg tucked under the other. Her phone was next to her on her desk, and next to it a handgun. She had a battered Robert Jordon paperback dangling in her hands.

"Your sight is back," she said bluntly, as he made eye contact with her.

"You know if I wanted to get out of this, I'd get out, right?" he said, ignoring her. "Like I could get out of this... now. So, you can save us both a lot of trouble and just *fuck off* with this," he bit, snapping his restraints against the pipe again to annunciate the last parts of the sentence.

Tash picked the gun up off the desk, lolled it in his general direction, then laid it back down. "I'll take my chances on that."

He laughed again, without humor. It was rueful and spiteful and annoyed.

She watched him. He squirmed, trying to find a comfortable position and unable to do so, each time ending up squatting so that his calves were strained and his back was against the inactive heater. She raised her book, read a few lines, then shut it again and laid it down on the desk on the opposite side of the gun as her phone, until they formed a strange tableau. "You want to get back to Fields."

He turned toward her slowly, picking his head back up until they locked eyes. "You might want to keep that name out of your mouth if you're smart. You're not from this city."

"Mmm, neither are you," she hummed. "Maine. You're far from the nest."

He huffed. "Yeah well... what do you know about it?"

She leaned in, her elbows propping on her knees, and laced her fingers together. "I was there, actually. Once. Right before things really went crazy for you, if I'm not mistaken." She leaned back and picked up a file from the table, retrieving a printed-off newspaper clipping. There was a landscape photo across the top of the article of an alley surrounded by police tape, the words 'Black Womb Lives' scrawled across the wall of it in red.

He squinted, but did not respond.

"I got a tip from an undercover source that said something was about to go down there. Something bad. I thought I'd found it, so I left... and then this happens while I'm in the air." She said flapping the article back and forth before moving it back onto the desk. "If it's all the same to you, I'd like to know what I missed out on."

He ground his teeth, turned, and slid along the side of the heater until he could see out the window that ran along the side of the hotel room.

She watched him, watched the restraints strain again, and took note that the skin along the edge of the handcuffs was devoid of redness once more.

He looked out the window to the street below, first left and then right and then repeating the action. "Did you get this room in your own name?" he asked, suddenly.

"No," she answered, simply and honestly. "It's through a third party. We're fine."

He rolled his eyes, then made his way back to a less strained pose. "You moved us to the North Side. Nowhere is 'safe,' but this... yeah, this is the least safe."

"I can handle myself, thanks."

He turned to her with spite, examining her for the first time since Nick and Kelly had left the room. She had taut muscles, thin and wiry. Her shoulders were bold, and when she sat, she sat in ways that could easily be risen from. She was ready, even when she was relaxed. She could handle herself, he realized, and the spite in him faded.

She stroked her chin, licked her top lip, then leaned forward again. "How long has the blindness been happening?"

He stiffened. "Months, off and on," he said, after a tense silence. "It's worse now than it has been. It used to just tunnel vision... but yeah, now it knocks me out. Only for a few minutes at a time."

"Except today."

"Yeah, well... your little blonde bombshell in the other

room packs a punch." He moved as though he were about to rub his chest where she'd hit him, but his hand stopped short at the end of its restraint. "Can I ask what happened to my shirt?"

"Why do you think the blindness started?"

"I had just assumed I wasn't made to last this long, honestly," he said, his voice thick with sarcasm. "Seriously though, why am I not wearing my shirt?"

"We were trying to administer first aid," she answered, her voice even and non-combative. "There was blood at the scene, we were trying to find the open wound and treat it."

He snorted. "Good luck with that."

She narrowed her eyes at him. "You have an accelerated amount of use of MG53." Her voice went up at the end as though it were a question, though she'd phrased it as a statement.

"What's that?"

She paused, considering her words. "You heal fast."

"I do, yeah."

"You have powers."

"You're one to talk. That girl, she's a taser."

"You have *powers*. Plural."

Xander stiffened. "I do."

"That doesn't happen." She eyed her phone, considered it for a moment, then turned back. "That's never *supposed* to happen. People with powers, they're one in a million already. People with two doesn't happen."

He shifted.

"And you've got more than two... don't you?" She reached back to the file folder on her desk, and returned with another sheet, this one a full-page printout of a frame of the security footage from the pier. On it Xander was in the full troughs of transformation, his upper half covered in black, gelatinous shadow. He was in mid-leap, about to land a blow on a man firing on him. "I've seen you in less than a shirt."

Xander huffed through his nose and turned, avoiding her gaze. He pulled on the chain of his restraint again.

"People think they have different powers, but they don't. It's the same power used different ways. Nick," she gestured towards the door that adjoined their rooms, "Nick has his sight. He can see more; his eyes take in more light. He sees at more frames per second than we do." She paused, pointing at Xander. "And he moves fast, and people think that's two powers. They think he's a speedster, and he's not. He's just reacting faster because he *sees* more. He can see the tiny fluctuations in your muscles before you move and can anticipate the motion and react to it. But it's all one power." She swallowed, then leaned back on her chair. "You use your hands for a hundred different functions, that doesn't mean you have more than two of them. You... you actually have more than one hand."

"Your point?" he growled, his voice dry.

"... If I went back to that town, in the middle of nowhere, Maine, and I looked around... what would I find?"

"Nothing now."

Tash paused, then nodded regretfully. After a moment she pushed her chair back on its wheels until it was past the bed. She stopped, grabbed a bag from the other side of it, and rolled back. It was black, with a large red heart with white cross emblazoned in its centre with vinyl.

Xander stiffened, backing until the small of his back was against the heater.

"I'd brought first aid, when I thought you'd need it," she explained, unzipping the bag. She withdrew the Velcro sleeve of a blood pressure unit. "If I get close enough to use this... are you going to make me regret it?"

He squinted, then shook his head.

She stepped forward, keeping her eyes on him, and wrapped the sleeve around his wiry bicep. When it was tight, she palmed the black bulb attached to it and began to pump, inflating it. As she did, she brought her opposing hand up, careful to make sure he saw it, and pressed it against his wrist just over the crest of its cuff.

"Claws," he said finally, looking past her to the dull void of the hotel television.

"Pardon?"

"I have claws as well as the healing. Retractable. Enhanced senses." He paused. "You could make an argument they're a result of the healing."

She nodded. "The healing keeps your hearing, your olfactory, everything at peak human." She squinted. "Makes this business with your sight even harder to understand, then."

He huffed. She pumped, watched the gauge, and the sleeve deflated. She clicked her tongue against the roof of her mouth, then started to inflate it again.

"Why are you after Fields?" she asked, tilting her head away from him but keeping her eyes trained on him all the same.

He avoided her gaze.

"If I just looked at what I've dug up, I'd have said you were looking for territory." His head snapped back toward her. She smirked. "But you don't seem the type. You're the driven sort. Obsessed." She glanced back toward her phone. "I've met a few of those."

He turned back to the null space behind her, as she deflated the sleeve and started inflating again.

"Who of yours did he hurt?"

He turned back, meeting her eye. "A kid. I fucked up, and he killed a kid. And when I went to tear him down for it... he didn't know which kid I was talking about." He ground his teeth. "And it was later that *week*. He killed a kid and a week later I called him out on it, and he asked me which one I meant."

Tash winced, then nodded.

Xander slammed the chain of his handcuffs against the heater pipe again. "That's what you're protecting, keeping me in here. The more I dug in, the more I saw it. That shipment of kids we broke up? He needed that for his prostitution ring, because I've been breaking it up." He pulled the chains again. "You want more dead kids, you keep me in here."

She sighed.

"How long does it fucking take to take someone's blood pressure, anyway?"

She grimaced. "I've taken it three times. You're 190 over 150. You heart rate is well over 120 beats per minute."

He lifted his shoulders ambivalently.

"That's... bad. That's extremely bad. Your heart is strained. It's... it's bad." She paused. "And you're at rest right now. I can't fathom what it gets up to."

"I wouldn't call this at rest."

She bobbed her head, pulling off the sleeve and pulling away from him. "That's probably what's causing your vision failure. When it spikes like that. Does it happen when there's action?"

Xander narrowed his eyes, then nodded.

"I'd like to get a blood sample."

"You come near me with anything to do that, I will make your life a living hell."

She paused, then moved back to her chair. She picked up her phone, composed a text, then pressed send. She stared at the screen, waiting to see that it was received, then laid it back down.

Xander looked past her, to the pink and yellow Post-Its on the wall. He squinted.

Tash followed his gaze over her shoulder, then turned back. "It's --"

"I see what it is," he interrupted. "You've been busy."

"You're one to talk. Arson. Torture. Murder. I've known men who've been in the game thirty years who don't have that kind of rap sheet."

His gaze lingered on the only yellow Post-It, and the word BENNETT printed across it in block letters.

"I've met driven men before. Obsessed men. Men who think that the ends justify any means."

"Let me guess, I don't look the type?"

"You look *exactly* the type," she clarified, her eyebrows coming together. "Mindlessly focused on one thing. Just *one thing*, not thinking about the ripple effects. Not thinking about the *damage* one man can do."

Xander scoffed. "You saw what was happening at that pier?"

Tash shut her lips tight until they were a thin line.

"Bringing in kids by the dozen. *Kids*. Herding them like cattle into his sex trade. You know how much it costs to have one of those kids? How much the fucking freaks that buy their time pay? Because I found out. Digging it and beating my way to answers, I found out. You want to know?"

"I'm sure it's a disgustingly high --"

"It's twenty-five bucks," he barked.

She stopped short. "I'm sorry?"

Xander's lip curled, and he laughed without humor again. "Yeah funny, isn't it? That's the model. Sell 'em cheap, but you can pimp them out ten, twenty times a day. I saved one girl, she used to see thirty. *A day*. That's the model, get 'em free and sell 'em cheap until they're used up. Then they disappear. Kids sold to perverts the way fast food is sold to the obese: fast and cheap."

Tash stared at him for a long moment, as if measuring his words. "That's... awful."

He chuckled at her. "I thought so, yeah."

"It doesn't excuse murder."

He snorted. "Talk to me when you've tried everything else." He cocked his head toward the Post-Its on the wall. "You're missing a few things up there."

She turned and eyed the wall where the map had been.

"Easily two dozen hits, maybe thirty. I chipped away at every part of him. First to bring him in, then to hurt him... then last going off, just to get him to notice me." His shoulders sank. "That's how big he is. I put my all, every-thing I had, into getting the gears of his machine to grind to a halt just for a second. To pause. And you know what? He never blinked." He smiled ruefully. "He blinks now. He doesn't just take notice, he *runs*... you know what it's like, to see a man that untouchable break a sweat getting clear of you? It's beautiful."

Tash stared at the map wall while he spoke. She turned back to him, clasping her hands in front of her again. Her phone chimed and she turned toward it, but did not pick it up to answer. "Men like you, *obsessed* men, you think of only the macro. The big picture." She licked her lips. "Have you thought of the people who worked in that res-taurant? Servers, bussers, kitchen staff?"

He turned away from her.

"What about the men you killed at the pier. All of them single, childless were they? Probably not. Statisti-cally, men in those professions get into them because they have pressure points -- they have families, responsibili-ties. They fall on hard times, that's what gets them into that world."

"And that excuses it?" he said, looking to the lights on the street through the window.

"Their kids don't deserve a father? Their wives a hus-band? Even if it's one who's behind bars?"

He laughed, and this time it was an honest laugh. It was the laugh of a man who found something truly, deep-ly, funny. He turned to her, his bloodshot eyes locking with hers. "You sound like a mob wife, you know that?"

Her phone chimed again. She huffed and ignored it, her jaw set. "What?"

"It's okay, he does bad things, but he does them for the family," he sneered, putting on a slightly higher-pitched affect than his normal one. "He's just doing what he needs to. I don't ask questions about his business."

Tash squinted. Her phone chimed again, then began to ring. She huffed and picked it up. "Yes." Her nostrils flared. She stared past the phone at Xander as she listened, then got up from her chair and walked toward the back of the room.

"Your pimp calling?" Xander called after her.

She turned, glaring at him.

"It's okay. He has good reasons."

She burrowed her gaze into him for a long moment, still listening to the voice on the other end of the line, then stepped back into the washroom to take the call.

CHAPTER TWENTY

Nick sat with Tash's gun held tightly in his hand, dangling between his knees. He was leaned forward and backlit, his face a mask of shadow, watching every motion, every twitch that Xander Drew made. He breathed heavily, his shoulders hunching and rising to his ears with every rapid intake through his nostrils, and his mouth was pressed tight together until his lips were nonexistent.

Xander stared out the hotel window, and the blinking lens-flare reds of the traffic below.

"You look older," Nick said, squinting at him.

Xander stared out the window passively.

"Like a lot older than me. You're not though."

"What's that old line? It's not the years, it's the mileage?"

He nodded, his jaw set. He waited a long moment, cast his eyes down and took several long breaths, then raised them again. He set his sights on the throb of the veins at Xander's clavicle, the tautness of the ridge of his mouth. "What happened to Sara?"

Xander's pupils darted to the side of his eye to watch

Nick, but he did not move his head.

Nick watched him, his pulse steady, his pores closed. "Sara... Johnson."

Xander turned to him, squinting. He tilted his head, leaning forward against his restraints for the first time in hours. "Who the fuck are you?"

"Did you... did you not know who I was talking about?"

He sighed, long and loud, then leaned back against the heater.

Nick erupted from the chair as if the action had been hostile. He stood ramrod straight, his arm extending outward, the gun a natural extension of it as he leveled the crosshairs between Xander's eyes. "How do you forget something like that? How do you just... move past it?"

"Kid, I have seen a lot of things," he growled, staring down the barrel of the gun into Nick's milky white eyes. "Things you would not believe. Things I barely believe."

Nick cursed, stepped back, and hit the chair's headrest, sending it sliding back on its wheels. The gun fell low again, and he ran the fingers of his opposite hand through his hair.

Xander tilted his head, watching the younger man pace. "Do I know you?"

"Nick," he said, under his breath. "Nick Carry. We went to high school together."

Xander nodded, slowly. Realization sparked in his eyes and they twitched, imperceptibly to everyone save Nick. "You're what she brought back from Coral Beach. She got that tip and she came looking, and she found... you."

Nick set his jaw.

Xander laughed, fully and honestly. He laughed until tears formed in his eyes and he had to lean uncomfortably to wipe them away in the cuffs. "That is brilliant, you know what? That is... that is a confluence of fucked up. That is perfect."

"It's not funny."

"Yeah, well," he chuckled, winding down from the laugh as if he'd run out of batteries. "I guess you wouldn't think so."

Xander's face was lined with dirt, sand caked on with blood. It ran down the length of his torso in scuttled patches, collecting under his pallid, exposed ribs. He watched Nick over his arm: clean shaven and barely looking like he was able to grow peach-fuzz. His shoulders were squared, and his hair was styled, pushed to one side. He smelled like soap and skin and *clean*, but more than that: he smelled of woman.

Nick stared back at him, assessing Xander as he was assessed. Calling attention to each scar -- rare despite his lifestyle -- and their placement.

Xander's vision ebbed and waned along its edges, like a movie whose projectionist struggled to keep the film in frame. Nick's was clear, able to see every cut, scratch, and grain of sand in perfect clarity.

"You want to know what happened in Coral Beach?" Xander smirked, splaying his hands out and raising them to expose his chest. "Take a long look."

Nick winced, curled his lip, then raised the gun again. "You're gonna tell me what happened, or I'm gonna start putting that healing factor of yours to the test."

"You wouldn't be the first." He leaned forward. "You wouldn't even make my top ten."

Nick paced forward, bringing the gun closer until it nearly touched Xander's forehead. "Did you kill Sara Johnson?"

Xander paused a long moment, meeting Nick's pupilless eyes from either side of the weapon, the steel a blurry void in his blind spot.

Nick winced, pushing the gun forward. It shook and then finally he snatched it away, stepping back to the middle of the room again and letting out a long, loud curse. He spun back suddenly, drew back, and brought the gun down across Xander's cheek and eye orbit, gnashing the flesh in the sharp metal and peeling it back. It caught under the hammer of the gun and drooled down Xander's cheek. "Fucker!"

Xander glared at him, ignoring the blood and stinging, screeching pain. "Feel better?"

Nick huffed and stepped away, then set the gun down on the table.

"That town... it's not like you remember. I know because I remember it that way, too."

Nick turned back to him, squinting and looking for those telltale signs of deceit again: the throbbing at his clavicle, the dance of sweat across the nape of his neck.

"I remember lunch at the arcade, just... walking around town. Sitting. When there was nothing more on your mind than who was fucking, who might be fucking. Just... simple. Everything was simple."

"Really?" Nick laughed sardonically. "Because I remember a skinny incel who chased around the same girl for years despite her not taking an interest."

Xander bit his tongue, clicked it against the back of his teeth, then nodded.

Nick huffed, turning away.

"I could've told when you left, even if I didn't know," Xander said, cocking his head toward him. "You left before the town took off its mask and showed its true face. That's the thing it took me months to get: I thought I was the thing with two faces. The monster. But it's that town. It's all towns." He curled his lip, nodding at Nick. "You got out clean, I can smell it on you. Not me."

"You been back much? Because maybe -- just maybe -- the only thing fucked up about that town was people like *you*."

Xander smirked.

"What's funny?"

He licked his lips, then nodded ruefully. "Not long after I had my eyes opened, I was working this rape case. These guys -- three of them -- they'd got it in their heads to team up and go after girls." Nick winced. "Two would hold her down and the other would -- you know."

Nick stared at him for a long moment, waiting for him to continue. "...And?"

"I found out later -- long after it was done and the fuckers were all behind bars or dead -- that the second victim, people had seen her. I mean, of course they had; it was broad daylight. But there was this one woman, this old lady that had worked at the gas station, she'd been checking her mail and she'd seen it." He paused. "She saw this young girl walking, saw her walk past these three fuckers. These men, old enough to be her father. She saw them cat call her and chase after her. They caught up to her and she saw her try to get away when they surrounded her. She saw everything right up until it got violent... because when she saw them step around to block her from leaving, she'd stopped walking and gone back inside."

Nick's shoulders sank. He turned back and found his way back to the front of the chair, collapsing into it.

"Her name was Greer Donaldson. She ended that day in a coma. She was still in it when I left. You know who I heard that story from?" He snarled. "The woman. The gas station attendant. I was waiting in line and she was chatting with someone and gossiping, and one of the perps came up. The customer didn't believe he'd done it, and the clerk she just... lays this truth on her. I know he did it, because I saw it start once."

"That's... that's sick."

Xander nodded. "They call me the Black Womb, but really it's that place. It's this gross hole of tar that can't birth anything but darkness. You come out pure but it's there, right under the surface. Of everyone."

"That true of Megan Greene?"

Xander stopped short, meeting his gaze. After a moment he spoke: "I don't know," he said, honestly. "And no one ever will."

Nick shook his head.

Xander turned back toward the window, watching the constant stream of lights outside. He stayed quiet for a long, pregnant moment, then turned back. "I don't actually know who killed Sara."

Nick's arms raised, his fingers splayed.

"That thing I turn into, sometimes I can't control it.

Sometimes I can't remember it, especially early days." He paused. "For a long time, I thought it was someone else. Then someone else again... then I thought it was me. I could almost..." he paused, shifting, his voice losing its edge as he found himself transfixed by his own story. His gaze shifted to the shimmering brass of the table knobs, staring into space. "I could almost remember it. And it was a weird comfort. It was a new memory of her, at a time when I didn't think there would be any new memories of her." He swallowed. "Then at some point I became convinced it *hadn't* been me, but I kept the blame. Because everything, the domino effect of it all, that started with me." He met Nick's eye. "On some level, the bartender that keeps feeding the drunk drinks is also responsible when he runs someone over, you know?"

Despite himself, Nick nodded.

"And then there was that day in the gas station, and something just... snapped into place. I'd spent so long living on that balcony where she'd been killed, and for the first time my world view expanded out, to all the houses and yards around. To the street. To the neighbors... and I wondered... who'd seen her on that balcony, the same way that woman had seen Greer Donaldson? Who turned away at the last moment before they saw something they couldn't ignore?" He pursed his lips. "And I realized it could be any of them. I'd lived forever with not knowing and with it narrowed down to three, and suddenly I realized it could have been anyone. The whole town." He swallowed. "That town had killed her."

Nick's face sank.

"That's how you forget. You forget because if you

didn't, you'd go mad."

Nick nodded, sniffed, and tweaked his nose.

Xander softened. "Once you see through it, you can see it everywhere. That town is lousy with it, and here..." he looked out the window again. "I can smell it here, too."

"On Fields?"

"Yeah. And people... people just look the other way."

Nick sighed. "Did you know my father?"

Xander looked at him long and hard. "No."

Nick nodded, then cursed.

CHAPTER TWENTY-ONE

Jimmy Skids sat on the steps of the Chesterton strip mall, his hands strumming against his knee nervously. He had a smattering of uneven, unshaven hair on his face, half of it looking as though it were three days growth and the rest looking like well over a week's. It was not evenly distributed as such, emerging in patterns that were haphazard and strange. One large circle of it grew out of his left cheek, but there was no corresponding pattern on the right.

There was a duffel bag beside him, black and tucked into shadow.

Despite the night being at its very darkest, it was blisteringly hot on the street. Despite the heat, Jimmy wore a large toque with a yin-yang symbol at its crown. It came down long, past his ears and protecting the back of his neck against the elements. He was wearing no jacket, just a black wife-beater with exposed, lanky, hairless arms that were pocked with needle marks.

He ran his fingers together and patted them over his legs, turning from one side of the parking lot to the other as though his head were on a constant swivel. He was jabbering incoherently; the way people did when convincing themselves not to urinate despite great need to do so.

After what seemed like an eternity, a long black car pulled into the strip mall, navigating the speedbump at its mouth poorly, and grinding its bottom against the sidewalk. The car made a long pass along the perimeter of the empty lot, surveying it in its entirety before pulling up next to Jimmy. He stood as it approached, rising and dusting silica dust off his jeans.

The car did not shut off, its high beams pulsing out into the black of night. A large man with tattoos behind his ears and thick sunglasses on stepped out of the vehicle. His suit was black, and he buttoned it as he moved out from around the vehicle, stepping up towards Jimmy. "You Skids?" he asked, though he phrased it more as a statement than a question.

Jimmy nodded. "Where's Chase?"

"He couldn't make the drop. Indisposed." He looked from side to side cautiously, then extended a meaty hand. "I'm Davis."

Jimmy winced, then took it and shook. "I'm supposed to give the drop to Chase."

"Yeah, but he can't come. I'm here for the drop." He bent as if to reach for the duffel bag behind Jimmy.

Jimmy pushed it further back into the shadows with his heel. "The deal is with Chase. That's who the deal is with. Chase gets the money, nobody else. Ever. That's part of the deal."

"Chase will be indisposed for some time."

"We'll keep the money. We won't spend none of it."

"Chase may be indisposed *permanently*."

Jimmy looked startled for a moment, then smirked. "Then maybe we ain't got no deal no more."

Davis looked shocked for a moment, then chuckled to himself. It was the laugh of a man who heard something honestly funny, who was finding himself in the sort of candid situation that people told of at dinner parties and over many drinks. "The deal was never with Chase, you know that."

"Our deal was with Chase," came a third voice suddenly.

Davis stepped back from Jimmy and looked around, finding no one. As if on cue, the glass door to the closed barbershop Jimmy had been sitting in front of opened, and the third man entered the conversation. He had a small patch of hair under thin lips and a green bandana. He wore the sort of plaid shirt a lumberjack would wear. He was carrying a baseball bat, leaned across his shoulders.

Davis backed up again, his hands raised slightly out of habit. "That money..." He licked his lips and laughed again. "You know who that money belongs to. So, give this shit up, because it's dumb."

"Doesn't seem dumb to me," the man with the bat grinned. "You, Jimmy?"

Jimmy shook his head.

Davis turned back to his car and unlatched the door. As soon as he did, the car pulled away in a screech of tires and a sudden putrid smell of burning rubber.

"Hey!" Davis yelled, the passenger-side door flapping twice with the momentum of the thrust before slamming itself closed. His car slammed against the speedbump that led to the main drag again, spraying sparks and oil in its wake.

Davis spun, turning back to Jimmy and the man with the bat. His expression of smugness was gone now, as was any bemused laughter he'd uttered. His face had grown a layer of flop-sweat, his jaw slack, his eyes wide.

"Chase is gone," the man with the bat said matter-of-factly. "The man he works for? He's under attack. He's under attack, so why we need to pay protection?" He squinted, leaning in a little. "That make sense to you?"

Davis nodded enthusiastically.

"Thought it might."

Davis made three quick steps backward, then turned to walk away. As soon as he did, he felt a sharp blow to the side of the head, as though his ear had exploded. He felt warmth, then hot *hot* heat, and the rushing surge of blood. He couldn't hear anything above the ringing in his head, and his neck and shoulder blared at him, locked in a new and uncomfortable state.

His knees hit the parking lot and skidded out his expensive suit. He looked up and saw that there was no blood on his hands, but couldn't shake the feeling that he was bleeding.

Jimmy Skids was laughing, his arms and legs flailing like a marionette. Every second tooth in his head was missing, and his mouth was open wide enough in laugher that Davis could see it all. He was holding the bat now.

Jimmy pulled back and swung the bat again, this time catching Davis between the eyes. This time, there was blood. Copious amounts of it. It splayed forth from the shattered remains of his nose from places it should not have, shooting out into the night air.

The man with the green bandana reached down and pushed back Davis' suit, revealing an empty gun holster. He tutted. "Should've known better," he chided. He stepped back to the step he'd started from, picked up the duffle bag of cash, and stepped back inside the barber shop.

Davis spat blood, and Jimmy raised the bat again.

CHAPTER TWENTY-TWO

"He certainly has a type, doesn't he?" Xander smirked.

Kelly turned from where she sat on the bed. She had the Robert Jordan book Tash had left open in front of her, but the same page had been open for nearly thirty minutes. Her gaze had shifted left, to the pattern of Post-Its still stuck onto the wall, and to one in the lower left in particular. "Pardon?"

"Young. Blonde. Packs a punch." He smirked.

She lowered her eyes at him. "How do you even know we're together?"

He chuckled. "I can *smell* him on you. All over you."

She shifted uncomfortably, then went back to her book.

They sat in silence for a long time, nearly another hour. She turned the pages of her novel three times, each time careful not to disrupt the feather that marked Tash's place. After a time, her head lolled back to the wall, and the big block letters stuck to it. Her hair fell back from her shoulder, exposing the large, oblong bruise on it and along the nape of her slender neck, the darkened flesh a stark contrast to her milky white complexion.

"Was that me?" he asked, his voice low.

She turned back to him, her hand going to her neck as though she'd forgotten the injury. When she touched it, she winced in pain, then nodded. "Yeah."

"I'm sorry."

She paused, flipped her thumb across the browned pages, then closed the book and sat forwards. "You really got him going."

Xander smiled humorlessly. "He thinks he wants to know where he came from. He doesn't."

Kelly puckered her lips, considered this, then nodded knowingly. "I get that." She shifted, crossing her legs, and facing him from across the room, the bed farthest from him. "He had *banks*."

Xander turned slowly and met her eyeline, sensing the shift in conversation from the tone of her voice.

"Fields, I mean," she clarified.

"I know who you meant."

"He has banks. Not a metaphorical one, not just a house with money. I've seen that, criminals with that kind of clout... back rooms with more cash than most people see in a lifetime."

Xander squinted at her, and decided she was telling the truth. There was an edge to her voice -- a hardness below the sweet that was her natural tone. The bruise on her arm was black, yet somehow she'd forgotten it was there.

"That makes sense to me. But... a *bank*," she stressed again. "A bank that anyone could walk into and think it was... a normal bank. To get a mortgage or start a kid's college fund, and turns out *he* owns it. Something so..."

"Public?"

She paused, then nodded.

He nodded empathetically. "It fucks with the head, the first time you think on it."

She turned back to the wall behind her, to the Post-It with the word BANK on it, picturing the rest of the map that had been projected there. "How far does it go?" she asked.

He watched her, her hair blonde curtains on either side of her face. Her right side came down to obscure the collar of her shirt now. Her nose stuck out from behind the curtain, curled up. "You don't want to know."

"I need to know."

He paused, licking his lips. He turned away from her for a long moment, focusing on some unseen mark on the far wall, and she thought she'd lost him. "First time I met him he killed a kid," he said finally, his voice harsh and haggard.

She tilted her head, her interest piqued.

"I went so hard on him after that. I've gone hard before but... nothing like this. I went after people he hated. I went after people who owed him money. I went *hard* after him, like, in a way you wouldn't understand."

"I understand," she said, definitively.

He turned back to her, squinted, then continued without pressing the matter. "I went too far. Lost track of what I was doing and got pinched. So, I'm sitting there in the interrogation room with this good cop, trying to make it clear that I didn't do what he thinks I did... and finally, I get sick of it. I finally give up and I say: I was after Stephen

Fields. Or something like that. I can't remember what it was exactly." He shifted, then made eye contact with her again.

Kelly was staring back at him, her complete attention on him.

"It shut down the whole interrogation. He goes upstairs and talks to his boss and makes this big fuss and everyone's shocked that I said that name. That I was going after this guy and going after him as hard as I was. And at first, I'm tickled, because I think I'm getting somewhere... and then it hits me."

"They all knew who he was," Kelly finished, nodding.

"Exactly," he spat, pointing at her. "Every single one of them got up every morning and put on the Blue and stepped out in the streets telling themselves they were protecting it, and every last one of them knew that this shit was happening right under their noses." He paused, maneuvering his mouth as though it had a foul taste in it. "I wondered how many of them knew about that kid."

She pursed her lips, stood, then walked to the other side of the room. She looked into the mirror with both her hands pressed against the small of her back, took several deep breaths, then walked back. She did not sit. She paced, anxiously.

He chuckled. "I have seen him infest public schools."

She turned on a dime and glared at him, as if wanting him to be lying but seeing instantly that he wasn't.

He shuffled again, trying to find a comfortable spot. "I have watched girls younger than you foam at the mouth because of all the product balloons they filled her stomach with. And even with their last breath, they wouldn't say his name." He bit the air. "What do you think he'd done to them, that they were more scared of crossing him even as they died of an overdose on his drugs?"

"I don't have to imagine," she snarled. Sparks radiated between her fingers, dancing like camera flashes.

He stared at her for a long moment, considering her motions and the language of her. "You've been there, I take it?"

"Yeah," she nodded. "Not like that, but yeah."

"I'm sorry." He shifted again, throwing a glance against the wall they shared with the opposing room. "Your boyfriend doesn't seem to get it."

"He's young."

Xander laughed. "He actually looks a fair bit older than --"

She shot him a glance, and for the first time in almost as long as he could remember, Xander shut up.

"He's young. He doesn't... he doesn't get just how bad it can get. When something truly sick is happening, and the world *lets* it happen, that's a recipe for disaster. He doesn't get how infectious it is. It's like *cancer*. And once that gets in the blood..."

He nodded.

"Is it in the blood?"

He paused, then swallowed. "Yeah. Yeah, it's in the blood."

CHAPTER TWENTY-THREE

Fields threw his pepper-red phone against the wall next to Smart's head, cracking the base of the old rotary unit in half but not damaging the wall at all. It was lined and thick. Smart did not flinch when this happened, even as the beleaguered ring from it filled the air in the small, echoing room. Smart did not flinch, but two of his men unbuckled the clips of their gun holsters.

"Chase is gone! Chase!" He looked to calm down for a moment, then the blood returned to his cheeks. His fists clenched so tightly the knuckles were white and the sound of his molars grinding filled the room. "He's my right arm. While I'm in here, he needs to be running shit."

Fields released his grip, ran his fingers over his face, then clenched them again, now drenched with sweat and slippery. He pointed at Smart. "This is your fuck up. This is on you. Chase is in lockup and now I get to hearing that one of his guys got offed at a drop last night. That cannot pass. If fucking hoods are starting to lose respect, the cops could be next. And then what're we doing, huh?" He thrust his finger forward again, and Smart's men put their hands on the butts of their weapons. "This is on you."

Smart waved off his men, and they relaxed. He laced his fingers together, waited, then offered them both to Fields like a cup. "You should be thanking me."

The colour left Fields' face, and for a moment he looked as though he might laugh. "I'm... I'm sorry, what? You wanna run that by me again?"

"You should be thanking me."

Fields did laugh, but ruefully. He bit his lip, reached for his own gun, and turned it on Smart.

Two of Smart's men again began to pull their weapons, and again Smart signaled for them not to.

"I told Chase not to hire you," Fields snarled. "Fucking skinhead Lurch. Every last part of this is bullshit, and it all started with you."

"It started with *you*," Smart corrected, rising to his full height. "The first deal, the first sale, the first back alley whore. It. Started. With. You. You wanted to exist half in the shadows and half in the light, and you fought enemies in the shadows and in the light. And anyone with an ounce of sense could have told you that the second --" he stepped forward, took the gun from Fields' hand, and laid it roughly on the desk beside them. "-- the *second* someone who also came from both worlds came after you, you were fucked. And here you are: fucked. Blaming everyone else."

Fields cursed. "So I should be thanking you. You lost thirty or more good girls last night. Girls we needed, before the pimps start looking somewhere else for product."

"You should thank me for bringing you into the *light*,"

Smart stressed, stepping into the beam from a nearby fluorescent bulb. It shimmered off the chrome surface near him and bathed him in the sheen of it. "Now you can operate with impunity. The way this man does. Like a man with nothing to lose."

Fields curled his lip, looked away... then slowly smiled and turned back. He nodded.

Smart smirked his ghoulish smirk, showing far too much grey gumline. "As for the girls... we have a plan to make it up. Now that we're one hundred percent in the open."

Fields eyed him for a long moment, then listened.

CHAPTER TWENTY-FOUR

Janet peered through the meshed glass window of the interrogation room. Within the room, Chase Madison sat at the far end of a long stainless-steel table, his broad form taking up that majority of its width. His hands were chained to it by a notch in its centre, and he rocked without rhythm in his chair. One leg of the chair had been filed short, Janet knew, to prevent arrestees from getting too comfortable.

Along the right wall of the room was a long glass mirror. It looked warped, like a children's toy made of cheap tinfoil. It happened to two-way mirrors, given enough time. For her first few years as a beat cop, Janet had wondered why they even had two directional mirrors anymore, if everyone knew how they worked. Years ago, she'd learned the answer: it was the feeling of always being watched, even when you aren't. The Panopticon in full affect.

"Thought I'd find you down here," came a smarmy voice from behind her. She didn't need to turn to know who it was. Even if he had taken the time to make himself sound presentable, his accent would have betrayed him. Duncan Taggart did not sound like anyone else in Los Angeles, with that weirdly muddled drawl one got from moving around the country nomadically for all their lives.

"What do you want, Duncan?" she said, neutrally.

He extended a coffee cup into her line of sight from behind her, unable to come around into her field of view in the narrow hallway.

She nodded, took it, then took a sip.

"You weren't at your desk. And when I checked the feed, you weren't in with Chase yet. So, I figured this would be where you'd be." He stood on his toes to see over Janet's shoulder and into the room. Chase sat with his shirt rolled up past his elbows, leaning forward on the cushion created by his shirt's bunching. He was moving his mouth from side to side as though his jaw were not set right. Duncan cocked his head. "What's he been doing?"

"Absolutely fucking nothing," Janet breathed, taking another long mouthful of her drink. "He hasn't asked for a lawyer even though he can definitely afford one. He hasn't asked for a drink or to take a piss, for food or to take a shit. He's just... sitting there. Like he's waiting to start sparring."

"Why're you here and not behind the glass? Or watching from the feed?"

Janet worked her jaw, in a fashion similar to Chase. "I want him to see me. I want him to know that when this happens, it's going to happen on my call. More than anything, I want something to make him unsteady."

"Well, wishes just happen to be horses today," he

smirked, sliding a sheet of paper into her field of vision the same way he had the coffee cup.

She turned back to face him for the first time, squinted, then snatched the file out of the air. She read it twice, turned it over to make sure there wasn't more, then turned back to him. "This was tonight?"

"Just came in over the wire, yeah." He frowned, staring past her at Chase, now unobstructed. "Vice should be dealing with him."

Janet glared at him. "He's mine."

"I could have the full force of the Feds down on him in minutes. *Seconds*. I'm sure there's at least a dozen federal inquiries into Fields."

"He's. Mine." Janet stressed each word, annunciating them to their fullest.

Duncan stopped himself short of prompting her again, then nodded.

She shook the paper. "Thanks for this."

"I'll be here if you need me."

She turned without acknowledging his statement and opened the door to the interrogation room, stepping inside.

"I was wondering when you'd join me," Chase smiled. He was tapping his fingers against the table in front of him. They made plump, meaty sounds with every strike, like sausages.

"Chase Madison," Janet started, her voice firm and authoritative, like an announcer. "You have been arrested for kidnapping, unlawful confinement, endangerment of a minor, conspiracy to solicit for prostitution and... just... a lot of stuff. Resisting arrest is in there somewhere, too.

Arresting officers had a clear line of sight on you from the moment you left the pier until point of apprehension."

"No, they didn't."

"Well, they say they did," Janet snapped, looking up at him from above the sheet she held. She turned it face down onto her end of the table. She shrugged at him. "Suffice to say this does not look great for you. Against my better judgment I must ask you again: are you choosing to waive your right to an attorney?"

"At this time." He turned and looked toward the mirror that ran nearly the full length of the wall to his left. He smirked. "Nobody back there this time."

She turned to the mirror, as if to check for herself.

He smirked. "Sorry. You do this enough, you learn to see the silhouettes through the sheen. There's not one of them that's perfect."

"On that note, there's no existing criminal record for Chase Madison," Janet continued. She pulled out her chair with a squeal of metal on metal, sat down on it, and produced her notebook from her back pocket. "So, I'm running on the assumption that you have felonies under other names."

"Make all the assumptions you want," Chase smiled. It was a forced smile, she knew. A politeness similar to the ones she produced when she was called into Sergeant Lake's office.

She smiled, wanly. "Things have been bad for your organization these past few... months."

He chuckled and licked his lips. He tried to wave his hands, but they were shackled. "What organization?"

"Let's start again. Over the last few months, multiple

buildings that you've been inside of multiple times for to-tally legitimate reasons have ceased to be buildings and have been converted to piles of ash." She stressed the words *totally legitimate* to make her sarcasm known to him, though she was still phrasing the statement in a way that would allow him to save face.

He ran his tongue along his teeth, then nodded.

"Glad we reached a point of understanding there," she grumbled under her breath. She clapped her hands together, bringing her voice back to full volume: "We both agree that that cannot continue... yes?"

Chase squinted until his eyes were a thin line on either side of his face, then nodded.

"We'd like to bring your employer in, to Protective Custody. For his safety."

Chase laughed at that, a full, hearty, surprised laugh that shook the table. His plump fingers laid down on it flat, then he raised one as much as possible and shook it at her. "That's a good one, that. That's... cute. I gotta say, that is the best laugh I've had all week. Thank you."

Janet smirked. "He's in danger. And until he's out of danger, everyone within a five-block radius of him is in danger." She threw up her hands. "This is a win-win. He gets protection from whoever the fuck has been hitting him hard, and we stop the violence on the streets."

In the window behind her, Duncan watched intently. He took a sip of his coffee, then fished out his cell phone.

"Except that the second I admit I have an employer and who that employer is, you'll arrest him on that long list of same things you just read out to me."

"Not the resisting arrest part," she said snidely, instantly regretting it.

He pressed his lips together and waggled his finger at her again. "Nice try."

She sighed, turned back towards the window and Duncan, and watched him for a moment. He wasn't watching her; he was on his phone. She turned back to Chase. "Let's stop pretending we're not talking about Stephen Fields a moment, okay?"

Chase stiffened.

"And while we're at it, let's not pretend that just the fact that you're here and I'm saying that name with the tape running isn't a big sign of just how far your boss' star has fallen. So maybe don't sit there and act like you still command the kind of fear you did before your buildings started burning themselves to the ground.".

He turned away from her, eyeing the nothingness behind the mirror.

She picked up the piece of paper next to her and batted it between her fingers for a moment, before sliding it face first towards him. "And while we're at it, let's also think about this."

Chase looked down. It was a police report of a murder at the Chesterton strip mall, of a man whom the Vice squad had identified as Kelland Davis. There was a photo with the report, an overhead shot of Davis, his head bashed in and its contents leaking out onto the pavement.

Chase picked up the page gingerly, reading every word of it once and then again, just as Janet had.

"See, now you've got three problems," Janet said, not waiting for Chase's gaze to return to her. "You got this fuck, whoever he is, that's fucking with you. And you've got us." She gestured towards herself with both thumbs as though she were a meme of Fonzie. "And now you've got this. Your organization taking itself apart from within."

Chase sighed. He laid down the sheet, fondled it, then gently pushed it back away from his position until it hovered on the table between them. He ran his tongue along his lips but somehow did not moisten them. When he finally spoke, he did so in a low, sullen voice: "It's going to get worse."

Janet sat straight. "Pardon?"

"The problem's not from within the organization, and it is going to get worse before it gets better. *If* it gets better."

Janet stared at him for a long moment, snapped out of it, then withdrew her notepad and began to scribble in it.

"You think this city runs easy? City this size, you think things run smooth all the time. It don't. Four million people and I'm telling you, half of them -- *half* -- fucking think they're Jesse James and shit. You think dealing with you cops and this freak is bad? Try being stuck between the cartel and some idiot pricks who think they can sell meth on a street corner and not get pinned. S'bullshit." He paused, licking his lips. "That fear you talked about, the stuff I don't command anymore? That's gonna cause you some trouble."

She stopped writing, then pushed her hair back behind her ear. "You're talking about a vacuum."

Chase ran his tongue along the inside of his top row of teeth, then clucked it and nodded. He sighed long and loud when he did. "Yeah. That's what this guy's been doing: taking out distribution networks, burning down brothels --"

Janet let a laugh escape her involuntarily, then raised up a hand by way of apology. "I'm sorry. '*Brothels*.' That got me."

He shot her an unamused glare. "He's chipping away until there's a vacuum, until there's a space that needs to be filled. And if you think for one second it'll stay vacant, you're kidding yourself." He nodded towards the folder. "S'already happening. Matter of days, and it's already happening." He paused. When he spoke again, his voice was somber. "It's pushed him to do things he wouldn't. And that was before this." He motioned around him to the interrogation room. "So, what do you think he's gonna do now?"

Janet turned back to Duncan again, who was watching the scene unfold with a set jaw and narrowed, pin-needled eyes. He nodded.

She got up from her chair and moved to the far corner of the room, to where the camera sat watching their every move. Without comment, she reached up and tugged on the cord that came out of it, the red light in its middle fading into a dull gray. She turned back to Chase: "Let's talk."

In the sweltering heat of the Homicide 12 office, one man stood in front of the feed from the interrogation room as Janet walked over to the camera and pulled its plug.

Detective Bill Hazer stood with his arms crossed, his wide frame blocking the screen from the swarms of officers that passed by. He let out a deep, beleaguered sigh, then cursed.

CHAPTER TWENTY-FIVE

Nick, Kelly, and Tash stood at the far end of the hotel room, with Nick's back to the open washroom door. They were huddled, each of them facing the interior of their malformed circle, yet clearly able to view Xander from above each other's shoulders.

Xander was chained to the radiator on the far side of the room, never out of their sight for a duration longer than an eyeblink.

"Victor's still in transit," Tash tisked, squeezing her phone to turn the screen on and check her messages, then pocketing it again. She cursed under her breath. "We have to keep him here."

"Bullshit," Xander cursed, slamming the chain of his cuffs against the rod of the radiator to punctuate his point.

She ignored him. "Once he gets here, we'll figure out how to transport him. Our contact's in touch with some people that owe us at a freight company -- it won't be pretty, but it'll get him to Payson."

"What're we going to do with him in Payson?" Kelly

asked, scrunching her nose.

Tash opened her mouth, stopped, then raised her hands. "I don't know. I can run more tests there, figure out where he came from... but we're playing this by ear, you're right."

"Whatever," Nick breathed. "Let's just get out of this town."

Kelly's head snapped up. "Wait, what?" She looked quickly from Nick to Tash and then back again. "You're kidding, right? We're not... seriously leaving without dealing with this Fields guy... right?"

Tash and Nick remained quiet.

"Right?"

"The police have his lieutenant in custody," Tash stressed, trying to sound empathetic. "It'll be dealt with. As much as these things can be." She reached out to put a hand on Kelly's shoulder, but Kelly pulled away.

"You've got to be kidding me. The man had a boat full of *children*. Younger than I was when --" she stopped. "The man has a *bank*. He owns a bank. He owns a bank and he thinks he can buy and sell kids and you're just gonna... what? Let that lie?"

"We have a little bit of our own crazy to deal with here," Nick said through gritted teeth, motioning back to Xander.

Tash's phone chimed.

"Do you think this guy's going to stop because the LAPD spanked him?" Kelly yelled, gesturing with her whole arm back to the Post-It notes on the wall, as though the map of Fields' activity contained the man himself. "Do you have any idea how many times Georgia State PD came knocking on Gavin's door before you came around? Just while I was there? He didn't blink. Even if they took kids out of there and brought them back to their parents, he didn't blink. Men like that -- they'll just keep going until you deal with them. Not the followers, *them*."

"The girl's smart," Xander chuckled from his side of the room, adjusting himself as his leg fell asleep. "You two could learn a thing or two from her."

Tash turned slowly, her lip curling as she faced Xander. Her side faced him, making her form as slender a target as possible. He wasn't sure if she'd tried it or if it were instinct to strike a battle pose. "Don't try and manipulate her."

"Into what? Stopping a mob boss trafficking children? Yeah, what an ass I'd be, huh?" He laughed without humor, leaning his head back against the pipe he was chained to. "Because this is going to get worse, you know."

Tash's phone chimed.

"Shut him up," Nick said under his breath to Tash. He couldn't even turn in Xander's direction. "I don't care what he's doing here. He killed -- he killed a lot of people. You can't just change like that."

Kelly raised her eyebrows and shot him a look.

"That's different. That's not what I meant."

Xander snickered and cocked his head at Kelly. "You'd think with those fancy eyes of his he'd be able to see more shades of grey, huh?"

"Shut up!" Nick bellowed, spinning to face him with such force that saliva few from his lips.

"Come on!" Xander screamed in return, slamming his chains against the pipe harder than he had yet, making both shake.

In an instant, Tash's gun was in her hand, leveled at the space between Xander's eyes. "Stay where you are," she said, her voice low but audible and authoritative. She was striving to lower the voices in the room to match hers.

Xander's tensed muscles slackened, save for his upper lip, which curled at her. "I've been shot before."

"In the head? Between the orbits?" she replied, pulling back the hammer on the gun.

He paused, stiffening.

"I'm an excellent shot."

"This isn't helping anything," Kelly hissed, grabbing Tash's gun arm and lowering it. Sparks flew between them as she did, and Kelly snapped her grasp back but did not apologize. "He's just gonna bring in more kids."

"Sadly, I've got to disagree with you there, hun," Xander drawled.

Tash's phone chimed. She cursed, holstered her weapon, then dug it out and squeezed the screen to life again.

"LAPD12'll be watching the coast now, and he knows it. Feds too, I'm guessing. Things are going to start to fall apart around him with Chase in custody. I've been taking apart his network, he won't be able to assign a new lieutenant. Instead he'll have opponents."

"That should make you happy," Nick snarled.

"Taking out Chase should have been the last step in this," Xander stressed, biting every word. "Fields has no idea how much of his day to day is handled by that man. That's how I could attack him for months and he not even... not even *notice*." He breathed. "There's going to be escalation now, he's going to have to make a big move—"

"Shut up," Tash breathed, her cheeks having lost some of their colour.

Kelly and Nick turned back to her, surprised by her sudden shift to a hushed tone.

She held up her screen to them. Her messenger app was opened, and the last three texts were forwarded articles from the LA Times website: 'One Dead in Gangland Shooting'; 'Two shootings reported in Gangland homicides'; 'Multiple dead in botched money drop, says Chief'.

Xander pulled on his restraints again.

CHAPTER TWENTY-SIX

Despite appearing rather large on the outside, the interior of PS 864 was intolerably cramped and confined. The walls were painted two colours: the top teal and the bottom burgundy, meeting in a jagged line. There were notches and scrapes chipped in the paint, even though the sheen on it made it appear reasonably fresh. The other side of the hall was lined with lockers, so many that they seemed like they had been created with one of those mirror effects used in the movies. Even with the sheer number of lockers, there were still coats and book bags thrown down onto the floor every few feet. The pattern of lockers was interrupted every twenty feet by a large brown door with wire mesh windows, then continued.

Smart's lanky frame leaned back against the glass doors that led out into the bright theme park of Los Angeles behind him. His arms were crossed at his chest and his legs at their ankles, and he watched as stray dust found its way from one side of the hallway to the other, the way tumbleweeds found their way across the street of a Wild West town.

The door next to him opened and his man with the swastika tattoo leaned in, a hat covering his inked head. Smart nodded at him, and he back, before the door closed again and the man disappeared.

The school bell rang, and within seconds a flood of children erupted from each of the large brown doors and made their way to lockers. The locker doors flew open at obtuse, asymmetrical angles, destroying the pattern that until then had stretched from one side of the hall to the other in the snap of a finger. Some children were already rushing past Smart, ignoring him the way children ignored adults, despite the fact that he was leaned against one of their exits. They crowded the door next to him instead, as though it were the one they always went through. As though it were unconscious.

More and more children flowed through the door, until they were bottle-necked and their progress had stagnated. Smart grinned his wide, ghoulish grin and turned back to look out the plate glass of his door.

His man stood by the furthest yellow bus away from them, the first in line. Next to him was a driver, his uniform informing his profession, standing with slumped shoulder and a hollowed face. Smart waved. His man waved back, then elbowed the driver. The driver waved back. Smart's man nodded to a group of children and the driver blocked their path, leaned down to talk to them, and then they turned and went to another bus line.

Smart smirked.

Smart pushed past the row of children still waiting to

get onto their busses, hearing the confusion and backlogging starting to happen from drivers protesting that some children were not supposed to be on their vehicles. He said nothing, but stepped forward to his man, who was sweating beneath his hat in the Los Angeles heat.

"Is it full?" he asked, without clarifying what he'd meant.

His man nodded, scanning the crowd from side to side and not making eye contact with Smart.

Smart nodded and headed up the steps of the bus and was followed a moment later by his man. The driver stared at them as they came up, his face drenched with nervous sweat as Smart ascended the stairs and looked out across the amassed children. They talked among themselves, few even noting what was happening at the front of the bus. They were safe here, their situation awareness at its lowest.

"There are boys," Smart said, counting over the group.

"About fifteen percent," his man agreed. "We couldn't get it lower without arousing suspicion, I reckon." He paused. "We can always cull --"

"Some have taste for that," Smart interrupted, cutting his man off with a wave of his hand.

"I didn't sign up for this," the driver said, his voice shaking.

Smart turned his head slowly, as if he'd been ignoring the driver as much as the children had been them. "You weren't complaining when you were helping run cocaine through young girls' intestinal tracts."

"This isn't that, this isn't --"

"It's not my fault that you couldn't think your situation through to its end. It is sad though." He paused, turning back to his man. "Can you drive one of these?"

The driver perked up, as though he were going to rise from his seat.

"I got my Class B."

Smart nodded.

His man shot the driver three times in the chest, and finally the children took notice, screaming so loud they could be heard at the back of the bus line. Smart pulled the driver out of his chair and hurled him to the narrow hall on the bus, blood seeping through the trails of the corrugated metal floor.

The bus lurched to life as his man pulled onto the main drag and gunned the engine, leaving a line of confused children in its wake.

CHAPTER TWENTY-SEVEN

"This isn't something we can ignore," Tash said, scrolling through her messages, eyes growing wider with each page she passed through. "This is... how much of this city was built on this one man's structure?"

"All of it," Xander and Kelly said in unison. She turned to him, pressed her lip, then spun back.

Nick looked between the two. "What's happening here? How are we even considering this? We came here to get the guy. *This* guy." He thrust a finger towards Xander. "That's why we're here. So, let's wait for Victor and get the fuck out of dodge. Or better yet, just get the fuck out of dodge."

"We can't leave without Victor," Tash said, shaking her head. "I'm not even totally comfortable taking one man shifts with him anymore."

Nick paused, turned back to Tash. She'd brought her phone back down to her side and was standing straight across from Xander now, her tall frame towering over his crouched physique. Despite this, he glared up at her with eyes rimmed with black shadow and hair that hid his brows and made his expression less readable. He was lowering, coiling himself as though he were ready to pounce despite his chained tether, Nick noticed, his hind legs taut like a cat's. "I don't get it."

"Look at him," Tash said, cocking her head. Her fingers moved to rest on the butt of her gun. "Look at the chaos in those news reports. The city's getting a taste of just how wide Fields' reach is... but he's known for months. He's been running against it for months, just him." Suddenly she took out her gun again and aimed it at him, so directly that it obscured her view of his face.

"Hey," Kelly started.

"Look at him. Is he even breathing heavy?"

Nick turned and looked at him, squinting his eyes until they were just thin white slits in his face. "...No."

"No. I didn't think so." She paused, then holstered her weapon again. "He's more than he's letting on he is... I'm not sure those chains could hold him, if he were determined to leave."

Slowly, Xander smirked.

"Are you saying I can't take him?" Nick scoffed.

"I am."

"I'm the best fighter you have."

"I *know*."

Nick straightened.

"We can settle this real easy if you want," Xander smirked, leaning his head back into the light again. "Let me out and we can settle this the way they used to behind The Factory out home." He cocked his head toward Nick. "You remember, don't you?"

Tash's phone chimed. She reached for it and produced

it from her pocket again.

"We've got to deal with this," Kelly said, her hand strumming against her top lip. "This isn't something we can ignore."

"No, it isn't," Tash said finally. They both turned to her. "There's been a kidnapping. Multiple kidnappings, actually. Sixty-three students from PS 864, an entire bus-load."

Kelly's hands went to her mouth.

Tash turned back to Xander, who had tensed against his restraints again. Her phone chimed again.

Fields cracked his knuckles, and the children cried. He felt the calcium deposits in each finger snap and the release that came with it, as though he hadn't done so in days. He hadn't, he realized. Not since the night of the fire.

He recalled once that one of his girls -- he didn't recall her name -- had told him that he only cracked his knuckles when he was itching for a fight. She'd run from him three times that week when he'd come home, and when he'd finally cornered her that last time he'd asked her why she ran some days and not others, and she'd told him: "You crack your knuckles. On days when it's going to go bad, on days you're itching for a fight... you crack your knuckles."

She'd regretted saying that.

He had, after all, been itching for a fight.

He'd been on the defensive since the fire, he realized. He hadn't been himself. But now, standing here a little straighter than he had... he felt like him again.

He snapped the pinky with great effort, causing the mewling child nearest him to jump at the sound of it popping. It was a young boy, one of a very small minority in the pallid, grey room. Fields turned to look at him, his lips curling despite his intent to keep his face straight. "Keep it together, Runt."

The child backed away.

The room had two doors, one of them wide open. The second was made of bars, and it was closed and locked so that Fields, Smart, and Smart's Man could peer in through them. The walls of the door were concrete and cold, each lined with numbered metal boxes that did nothing to obscure the sounds inside. The soft whines and cries echoed off them and bounced around the room, becoming a white noise of pain where no one cry could be distinguished from the chorus of them.

Fields leaned back from the bars and spoke but did not take his gaze away from the room and the sixty-three children within it. His eyes flitted from one face to the next, never staying on one for too long, and always finding a new one to rest on.

"They're all scared," he said finally and flatly, his hands resting in each of his pockets.

"They are. Extremely so," Smart agreed.

"You know how much we have to work the kids we get from across the border to act scared? Most of them, time they get here, they're already all kinds of fucked up. They're so fucked up you can't get them scared. We have to show them how to be scared, you believe that?" He smiled, leaning in. "These ones come scared. Jesus wept."

"You see it then? How working in the open can help you?"

Fields' smile faded at its edges but did not vanish entirely. "It's a lot of heat."

"You had heat before this. Now you have heat *and* this." He paused. "But I have a team taking care of the heat."

Fields nodded, scanning over the crowd of youth again. Most of them girls, and most of those white. He looked at them each as though they were items on a shelf and he were taking inventory, each face and feature a checkmark on a long list of remunerable benefits. Young. Blonde. Blue-eyed. *Scared.* "We can get a lot for this group," he said finally. He said it as agreement to Smart, without having to bruise his ego with an actual agreement. "One or two we can sell outright. I have buyers that would jump at that one in the back, with the bow. Might even start a bidding war."

"You see then. How being out in the open has its benefits?"

Fields' lip curled again, and he removed his knuckles and started to crack them again. It was harder now, their ability expired, but with work he snapped one. He nodded to Smart's Man, who closed the second door, blocking the children from them.

As the door shut, their cries grew louder, more distinct. There was no light on inside.

"On the drug trafficking side, there is a new product on the market," Smart said, slithering an arm around Fields. "The street name is Eden, but it's a clever compound of --"

"Later," Fields nodded, brushing Smart's hand away. "Get one of my girls to meet me upstairs. *Mine*, not any from this bunch." He gestured back to the locked room with the children in it, scoffing.

"There's a bit much heat on for bringing in someone you're associated with," Smart's Man warned, speaking matter-of-factly.

Fields turned back to him, smiled, and spread his arms wide. "We're in the open, now."

He snapped his knuckles, hopped up the stairs two at a time, and waited.

CHAPTER TWENTY-EIGHT

The elevator doors to Homicide 12 opened, and immediately Tash stepped back to make room for a man that scuttered in. He was holding a manila file folder in front of himself and jostling through the pages while he talked on a cell phone that he'd pinned to his shoulder with his cheek. He joined three others like him that were in the elevator behind her, and she turned to watch them for a second until the doors threatened to close on her. She stepped through, and immediately the entire room was different.

Homicide 12 was hotter than it had been earlier, despite it being later in the day. It was hot with bodies, people travelling from desk to desk, grabbing papers and people and bringing both back to where they were useful. The walls seemed to move with the heat of it, like lungs filled with hot air, expanding and contracting with every labored breath it took. The office at the back of the department was open now, and people travelled in and out with regularity. A desk had been dragged into the centre of the room with two coffee pots on it, displayed on completed cardboard boxes so that their warmth wouldn't buckle the wood.

Tash stepped into the room proper even as Officer Fredericks brushed past her. He sped down the hall, spilling coffee all the way but ignoring the pain as steam sloshed his knuckles.

"Fucking fuck!" came an aggravated voice to her right. She turned. Duncan Taggart was slamming his office phone down on its cradle three times, feeling the satisfaction of it less and less each and every time. He got up, not noticing Tash, and turned toward the forensics lab at the back of the room. Their door was open. "I need those fingerprints from the murder on Pacific, and I need them now. Not tomorrow, not when you're done your coffee, *now*."

A gangly man in a stained lab-coat appeared in the door and thrust his arms to either side, miming in equal parts 'what's up with you' and 'come make me.'

Duncan turned back to his desk and grabbed the steaming cup off it. He downed the drink, gagged twice from the scald of the heat on his tongue, then continued. His computer chimed and he turned to it, wiping dark liquid from his lips with the back of an already stained sleeve. He groaned and began to type.

Next to him, Detective Hazer sat with his head in his hands, a thick layer of sweat caked onto his pasty flesh.

A large Haitian woman with haggard breath pushed past Tash, so briskly that she almost said something, but the woman was gone before she'd have had a chance to, disappearing into the office on the far side of the room.

Tash turned to her left, where Janet stood behind her

desk. She released two Hemovel pills from their bottle into her palm in full view of the officer she was berating, then dry-swallowed them both. "Get back out there. Tell any parent who doesn't want their kid to give a statement we'll come back with a warrant to search their home." She gagged, then swallowed again. "Actually do it if you need to, but call me first. One of those kids on the other busses saw *something*, and I'll be fucked if some nervous 'rent is gonna keep us from it."

The officer nodded, turned on her heels, and made her way back towards the elevator with speed in her step.

Tash stepped forward. "Detective Nesbit."

Janet looked up for less than a second even as she was opening her desk drawer, then turned away again and continued her search. "I don't have time for any of your bullshit right now, actually," she said dryly.

"I have information you might find --"

"And I have sixty-three missing kids. Sixty. Three. Along with a spike in gang violence I haven't seen since..." she paused, thinking for a moment. "A spike I haven't seen. So, I personally could not give a fuck what Arthur Shane is up to at this exact moment, you'll be amazed to know I'm sure." She turned and yelled over Tash's shoulder: "I need Holloway and his team downtown, now!"

Tash turned to follow the direction of the voice, and watched as four men jumped to action, stepping away from a pegboard filled with photos and running to the exit in tight formation. She'd never seen men run so fast in so straight a line before, not even when she'd been overseas. Hazer got up from his desk with his phone pressed to his ear and marched out of the room as quickly as he

could, following the path of Holloway's men without realizing it.

She turned back to Janet with urgency, placing both
knuckles on her desk. "The man from Fields' network you
have in your custody."

Janet stopped, laid down the phone receiver she'd just
picked up, and straightened her back. "Pardon me?"

"There were more men there that night. More people
that escaped across the beachhead. They were not all
Fields' men."

"You're very close to an arrest right now, you understand that, yes?"

"One of those men is in *my* custody," Tash clarified,
spreading her fingers out across the desk as though she
were building evidence. "I think... I think we can use him
to stop some of this madness."

Janet squinted. Behind Tash's head, Taggart raised
from his desk, finally noticing the activity. Without thinking of it, he reached for the butt of his gun.

Without warning, the fire alarm blared to life, drown-
ing out the constant sounds of people going back and
forth. Several people stopped and pressed their hand to
their ears, and the large Haitian woman emerged from
her office. "What the hell is this?!"

"Fire alarm!" Taggart responded, yelling to be heard
above the blare. He made his way over to Tash and Janet.
"Must be a glitch in the system or else --"

As if on cue, fire erupted outside the bay window of
Homicide 12 and the sprinkler system came on, soaking
everyone with frigid streams.

"Fuck!" he yelled, grabbing Janet by the hand, and

leading her out of the office.

Tash stepped forward to the window and peered out, pressing both hands flat against it. Below were three men -- she recognized one of them from the pier -- each of them with guns strapped to their arms. There was a large fire between them and they were kicking over barrels, each one spilling its contents into the flame and making it erupt again, sending shoots of flames up and out until the entire eastern edge of the building was walled in fire, caught by the dried brush of Los Angeles. She watched in horror as the first officers, Holloway's men, stepped out the front door and were immediately gunned down by the arsonists.

"Wait!" she screamed, turning quickly to Duncan and Janet. Duncan stopped, pressing his hand forward and halting the elevator doors.

"Is it a false alarm?" Officer Fredericks yelled out down the hall, holding his gun aimed down toward the ground with both hands. He was moving from foot to foot, the anxiety of the alarm bells reaching him.

"No," Detective Hazer said, stepping down the hall with his key ring already displayed. "We're under attack. Fields has men outside."

Fredericks' eyes bulged and he raised his weapon a little, out of impulse. "Pardon?"

"Fucked up times, kid." Hazer growled. "We've got to move him, either way. We need to get him to a safe location."

Fredericks nodded, stepping out of the way of the interrogation room as Hazer approached it with his key. He fumbled with it, then finally snapped it to one side and the door opened.

Chase Madison sat with his shoulders hunched, try-ing to protect his bald head from the sprinkler system that rained down on him despite the fact that his arms were chained to the table. "Yo, what the fuck, man?" he screamed as soon as they came in, without even taking note of who he was talking to.

Hazer went to his side with the keys and tried the first one in Chase's handcuffs.

"The Department is under siege," Fredericks said. He was holding the door open with his body and turned from Chase to the hallway Hazer had come down every other second. "We need to get you out of here."

Hazer put the key ring down.

"Wait, what?" Chase barked, looking from Fredericks to Hazer. "No man, you can't let him do this! You've got to --"

Fredericks turned just in time to see Hazer raise his gun to the side of Chase's scalp and say, "Fields sends his regards."

Fredericks raised his gun, but it was just in time for blood and brain matter to spray along the white wall of the interrogation room. It was there for barely an instant before the stream from the sprinklers sent it streaming down towards the floor. "No!" he screamed.

Hazer dropped his gun and laced his fingers together along the back of his head.

CHAPTER TWENTY-NINE

Xander glared at Nick and Kelly from across the room, his hands in such a strained position that they buckled back against the constraint of his restraints. The two of them stood all the way across the room from him, Nick on the chair with his legs splayed wide to either side of it and Kelly standing between him and Tash's bed, the map of Fields' activity always in the corner of her eye. Tash's gun lay at the edge of the table nearest Nick, ready to be picked up at a moment's notice.

"He hasn't had to use the bathroom," Kelly said, looking at Xander as though he were a photograph of himself as opposed to an actual person who was in the room with him. She turned to Nick quizzically, not asking him a question so much as waiting to be refuted.

"No, he hasn't," Nick agreed, never once taking his eyes from Xander, who met his stare as much as he was able.

She paused, looked at the map, and then looked back at Xander. "What *is* he?"

"I'm in the room, you know," Xander interjected,

his tone of voice somewhere between menacing and annoyed.

"He's an asshole," Nick drawled. "He's always been an asshole. That's why we should get clear of him as soon as possible."

Kelly balked, spinning on him. "What has gotten into you? This is a problem. You're... This isn't who you are." She paused, wavering from foot to foot as she chose her words. "You are the most sure-sighted man I've ever known. You don't see problems, you see *solutions*, and you *act* on them. That's what... that's the man that sees me, that saw Gavin. I can never be like that. This isn't... you."

"Maybe I see the solution, and this *is* it," he responded without malice, not turning away from Xander to regard her.

"She's seen the world for what it is," Xander said, cocking his head towards the map wall.

"Shut up," Nick retorted.

"She's seen the forces at play underneath the street, where there's nothing but *rats* and filth and everything else you don't like to think about when you go to bed at night on your down sheets. She sees now that the dark doesn't exist just in the corners of life, but right out in the open. That your school bus driver can be on the take from the mob, and that that mob can own the bank where your parents saved for your student loans."

"I said shut up," Nick returned.

"He has a point," Kelly said, bringing her arms up to hold herself as she did.

Nick squinted.

"Maybe he sees something you don't. I mean look at this," she gestured back to the map. "This is a fucked-up world. Maybe he looked at it and he saw just how fucked up it is, and it fucked him up a little, but that *doesn't* mean he's wrong --"

"He's a killer, Kelly."

She winced.

Xander tilted his head toward her.

"So, he's an asshole." Kelly huffed. "I've dated tons of assholes. You're an asshole." Nick turned to her, putting Xander in his peripheral vision for the first time in well over an hour. She tapped the wall with the map of Fields' activities on it. "Maybe it takes an asshole to deal with this, you ever think of that?"

Xander laughed, then hummed. "Man, you sure can pick them, can't you?" He grinned. "No more than me, I suppose. But it's nice to see. Makes me think that maybe she'd have been my biggest advocate too, if she were alive."

Nick spun on his heels, jolting a finger through the air at Xander. "Shut up, do you hear me? Shut. Up."

Xander's eyes flitted towards the gun on the table, very briefly, while Nick was in mid-spin. He did not catch it.

"Nick," Kelly chided, putting her hand on his chest and pulling him back. It took very little effort; he was used to moving with the motions of where her hands led him.

"You don't see it, do you?" Xander said, narrowing his eyes at Nick. "You don't see how much that killer comment hurt her?"

Nick stopped, turned, and looked at Kelly. She refused to meet his eye. "Why would that?"

She met his eye, and his words caught in his throat.

"You might have the sight, Nicky, but I'd learn you some body language. Your girl here was very *very* on the same page that something drastic needed to be done about Fields. She might not have even realized she was there... but she was. And the way she carries herself, hugs her arms like that... she's standing up but not far beneath the surface is a much younger girl who doesn't like this. She's someone who has been here before... and here you are, just ignoring it."

Nick's nostrils flared.

Xander winked. "I wonder what else she's let slide that's escaped your sight, huh? I'd say quite a bit, seeing as I can *smell* the two of you all over each other."

"Fuck you," Nick cursed, reaching for Tash's gun and bringing it up in line with Xander's face.

"Nick, no!" Kelly screamed.

"It won't kill him," Nick snarled. "It won't. But I'll --" He stepped forward against Kelly's tug, now a scant few feet away from Xander.

Xander tugged hard on his handcuffs, feeling the bone of his thumb squeeze in at an unnatural angle.

The door to the hotel room opened and Tash stepped in, barely acknowledging the scene that met her. She was soaked still, her hair matted and wet. Kelly and Nick turned back from Xander, stepping outside of his striking range, and his muscles relaxed.

"What happened?" Kelly asked, even as Tash sat in her chair.

"Fields attacked LAPD12," she said, her voice exhausted.

Xander looked up.

"There are a few dead... Fields' lieutenant is one of them."

"Fuck," Xander cursed. "He must have been flipping."

Tash glared at him, sighed, then pushed herself to her feet again. She stepped over to him until she was even closer than the striking range that Nick had found himself in, moments before. She leaned to one side, saw the ragged red mark along his right thumb, nodded, then turned to see Nick over her shoulder. "The next time I tell you to be careful with a prisoner, that's me trusting you enough that I don't have to say not to engage with the prisoner... Understood?"

Nick nodded.

She turned back to Xander, locking eyes with him. She reached into her pocket, produced her cell phone, then put it away again. "Still no word from Victor." Her mouth warbled. "There are sixty-three children missing," she said firmly, annunciating every word.

Xander nodded.

"What is going to happen to them?"

"They'll be sold. The lucky ones -- the real lucky ones -- will be sold at auction. That's maybe five percent. Those we can save, even if we let this go too long... we wait for a big money buyer or two to come into town, we figure out where they're meeting, we make our sting."

"We?" Nick balked.

"Quiet," Tash snapped. She turned back to Xander. "And the rest?"

"We've got days. Hours maybe for some of them. I've

been releasing Fields' prostitutes for months, chipping away at his stock."

"Killing them," Nick snarled.

"Getting them back to their *parents*," Xander stressed, turning to glare at Nick over Tash's shoulder. "He's more desperate for girls than anything else. It's... it's a problem of my own making, but he'll want these girls out and on the street fast, making money, making clients happy."

She gestured back towards the map on the wall. "You know his network."

He straightened. "Better than anyone. Better than he does."

Tash nodded. She reached back into her pocket, but this time instead of producing her cell phone... she produced a key. "I need help to make this right."

Xander's eyes widened slightly, then he nodded.

Smart put down his phone with a gentleness that belied his nature, his thin, bony hands finding their place on the table and perching it there. He turned to Fields, who was sitting on the edge of his bed across the room, his shirt off and a cigarette in his hand. "Chase has been taken care of," he said without emotion.

Fields nodded, taking another puff. There was a woman on the bed behind him that was clothed only in shadow, but Fields acted as though he was alone. His eyes were rimmed with red flesh, his cheek tugging down on them and giving him the look of someone perpetually tired. His skin was loose, especially the pink distortions around his scars. The room was hot and humid, but despite all this...

he felt right for the first time since this ordeal had begun. He was himself again.

"What do we do now?" Smart asked, standing so straight that his tall frame almost reached the ceiling.

Fields took another long drag from his smoke. "Get rid of the kids," he breathed, exhaling grey clouds into the atmosphere. "We need them in the system by end of day."

CHAPTER THIRTY

Nick and Kelly pushed the bed back out of their way and then moved the writing desk away from the wall until it was in the centre of the room.

"I actually don't think you're supposed to move these," Nick said, under his breath.

Kelly shot him a look. "There's a lot of things you aren't supposed to do in hotel rooms." She paused. "Stop complaining and you'll get to do some of them, later."

He grinned.

In the corner of the room next to the radiator, Xander smirked as Tash crouched down next to him. "You know they really do make a cute couple."

"They do," Tash agreed. She turned back to Nick. "You have the gun?"

He raised it.

She turned back to Xander and raised the key. "Any funny business, and there will be hell to pay... We understand each other?"

"I understand but... That's a weak threat. The gun won't hurt me."

"The metal in your body will focus a blast from Kelly," Tash said with finality, raising the key again. Behind her, Kelly's fingers crackled with electric blue energy.

Xander stiffened. "Got it."

She selected the key and carefully placed it into the lock of his left hand and turned it. The latch snapped free and the cuff came loose.

"Finally," he breathed, sliding his left arm forward and dragging the chain through the radiator grate until the chain had worked itself all the way through and out the other side. He gripped his newly freed wrist and rubbed it. It wasn't as raw as Tash would have expected it to have been, but it was still quite tender and red. He stood for the first time in over a day. "You cannot imagine how good that feels."

Nick raised his gun to point it at him.

Xander paused, his step stuttering. "You've got to be kidding me."

"Not even a little," Tash smiled, bringing the loose cuff up and snapping it around one of the loops of the table leg, fastening Xander to it. She reached into her pocket, produced her phone, and tossed it to Kelly.

Kelly caught it and brought it to the bed, where she opened it and scrolled past several pictures until she arrived at the map of Los Angeles. She made it full size, then slid the entire phone into a small cardboard cube with a lens attached, projecting a jittering, blurry mess along the salmon pink wall. She maneuvered the placement of the box until it lined up properly with the Post-Its that had been on the wall, then stood straight quickly. She bounced with the motion and clapped her hands together.

"These are the Fields locations we know about -- are there more?"

"I'm bored of this already," Xander grumbled, tugging on the chain connected to the thick table and pulling it tight.

Kelly sighed, stepped around the bed, then leaned over the opposite side of the table toward him. "I know you're a good man."

Xander and Nick stood straighter, in unison. "I'm sorry?"

"I echo that," Nick agreed.

Kelly frowned. "No matter what he says," she motioned toward Nick. "He wouldn't have known you if you weren't a good man. He wouldn't have held onto you all these years if you weren't a good man. Because *he's* a good man." She paused, holding Xander's eye and forcing him not to turn away. When he met her gaze fully, she continued, "Something happened to you. I'm not going to lie: I don't care what. We're not going to have a moment. But for one second, remember when you were the type of man who would stop this from happening to others, instead of the type of man who punished men who did this."

Xander stared at her a long moment, swallowed, then nodded sheepishly.

"Now that that's out of the way," Tash said, stepping past Nick and plucking her gun out of his hands as she did. She gestured with its butt toward the map projected on the wall.

Xander huffed, a sound that made his throat sound sore. He stared at the floor for a moment, the discoloured carpet from where the bed had been moved, then looked up at the map. "If we're talking places big enough to hold children, then we're talking about his whorehouses. No two ways about it." He pointed to the map, indicating cross streets, and Kelly started to apply Post-Its. "He had at least ten when I started."

Kelly paused at the number, looked over her shoulder at him, then continued.

"I scuttled three to the wind. Security has gotten tighter around the rest since then... I didn't want to risk the girls, so that hit that backburner until I could figure out a safe way to annex them. Sadly." He paused.

"Something wrong?" Tash asked.

He shook his head. "Just remembering. Central City East had two... no, Kelly, down from there. Watts has one. There are two more on Skid Row... The rest are in Hyde Park." He paused again, biting his lip. "The ones in Hyde Park are the worst. There's one run by this asshole -- Clayfield -- I took a chunk out of him months ago trying to get a bead on Fields' drug trade. He's been hiding ever since, and I've been hoping he'd pop up again."

Kelly plucked her sharpie off the bedside table and flicked it between her thumb and forefinger. She stepped back and looked at the map, the curve of her hip blocking the beam of light and making a projection of their form. Her eye lingered on the word BANK in bold letters as it did every time, and she shivered. "That's where they end up," she said finally, sticking the edge of the market in her mouth.

Nick turned to her. "What do you mean?"

Xander raised an eyebrow at Tash, who motioned for him to pay attention.

"The whorehouses. That's where the kids end up, right? That's where the supply chain ends."

Xander squinted, then nodded.

"So there's no way he's keeping them there, is there?"

"I don't follow," Nick frowned.

"Sure you do, think about it. Stop thinking of them as kids for a moment and think of it the way they do, as gross as that sounds. It's fresh product. And if there's one thing I know about the men who run whorehouses --"

"They like fresh product," Xander finished. He cursed under his breath. "You're right. Wherever he put them, he'd be in danger of losing them there before they could be sent out to the other houses in the system." He paused. "It'd be bad anyway, now that I think on it. If there are rival gangs trying for his territory, they've got to be poking away at the brothels, too. They're vulnerable, if anything."

Kelly pulled down the Post-Its she'd applied.

"Wait," Nick said, raising his hand to stop her. "This is... this is it, isn't it?" He turned to each of them, but neither of them had the glimmer of recognition in their eyes, even Kelly. He frowned, then stepped over to the map. There was excitement in his tone for the first time in days. "We don't know where they are now, but we know where the supply chain ends... Right? So why not just save them there? Stake out the brothels, wait for the delivery, then BAM!" He slapped his right fist into his left palm. "We've got them."

Xander worked his jaw, turned to Tash, and sighed.

"What?" Nick said, his smile fading. "What's the problem?"

"He is," Tash said, narrowing her eyes at Xander. "He said it himself. He took down three of them and they upped the security."

Xander curled his lip, sniffed hard, then nodded. "Vice started to be able to build too many cases from testimonies, once the girls got home and got clean. Fields couldn't have that shit. Last few times I tried to scuttle a house the pimps almost killed the girls." He paused. "All the girls. They start seeing signs of stress, that's what they'll do now."

Nick's face fell. "We hit them at once then. We --"

"We don't have the numbers," Tash interjected. "And even if we did, one bad move at one and they'd send the word out to the others. Either way: dead children."

"That's not even considering the choice ones, the ones he won't let into the open market," Xander said.

"Or what might be done to them before they reach the end of the supply chain," Kelly added.

"Alright, I get it. I suck." Nick frowned, stepped aside, then lit up again. "What were they going to do with those kids from the boat?" He turned to Xander.

Xander squinted. "Deliver them, probably. In a big truck. Maybe in a shipping container, but there's risks in that. Probably just... a big truck."

"Is it possible they're just... in a big truck. Driving around, waiting for orders?"

Xander turned to Tash, and the both of them seemed to have a nonverbal conversation, separate from the others. Eyebrows moved and nods were given, until finally Xander wavered, stared at the map for a long moment, then turned back. "I'm gonna say no, but you're on the right track. It'd draw too much attention, and if there's a break in the communication anywhere -- *anywhere* -- the rivals could take it over, easily. Another time, you'd be right. But not now."

The four of them stared at the map for a long moment.

"They're in Safehouse Red," Xander said finally, rapping the knuckle of his free hand against the table so hard it made a dent. "I'm such an idiot."

"Care to share?" Tash said, standing.

"Before I started really making a play for him, I wanted to make sure there was nowhere Fields could go to be underground. I'd learned my lesson with Clayfield; the last thing I wanted was for him to scurry under the fridge and me have to wait until he felt safe again to come back into the open. So I found out where his safehouses were... There were a lot of them. He colour-coded them for how much danger he was in. Blue, Green, Burgundy... whatever. I burned the lot of them to the ground, but I never managed to find Safehouse Red." He sucked in air through his teeth, angrily. "That's where he's been, that's where they are."

He pulled against the chain, not out of an attempt to escape but out of anger, kicking the chair. "Stupid."

Kelly turned back to the map, her hands open. "Just hold on. It's gotta be big, right? Really big. Big enough to hold sixty plus kids."

"Yeah," Xander growled, still angry at himself. "Not as big as you'd think it'd have to be... not big enough to be humane, but yeah. Pretty big."

She nodded. "Big. Right. And he has to have had it for a while, right? Safehouse Red, that's his main one. His most secure one. The most secret, probably the oldest."

Xander squinted. He turned to Tash, who returned his look, before they both turned back to Kelly and her map.

"Go on," Tash said with encouragement.

"So it's big and it's been there a while. And it has to appear normal, otherwise it'd attract the rivals, like you said. It can't be a brothel or a condemned building or anything like that. That says keep away to normies but to squatters and criminals, that's a welcome sign." She paused and smirked at Nick. "Believe me, I know."

He smiled at her. "And it has to be secure."

She wagged her finger at him. "Yes! Yes. Big, old, doesn't attract attention, and secure. Probably bigger than we're thinking, if it *really* doesn't want to attract attention. Like if there's a public face to it, and the badness all goes on in the back, it'd have to be twice as big."

Xander's eyes widened slightly. "You've got it."

She turned sharply, her hair spinning. "I'm sorry?"

"You've got it. You've figured it out." He spoke with disbelief at first, but it quickly faded into admiration. He smirked and laughed, with the barest hint of humor to it. "I could kiss you, if I didn't think you'd shock me into next year for it."

"I don't... I don't have the answer."

"Yeah you do. You have from the second you looked at it." He gestured towards the map. "Look again."

She turned back toward the map and stepped back from it, obscuring it with her hip again until she was behind the projector and could take in the fullness of its view.

Big. Old. Normal. Secure.

The Post-It note in the lower left-hand corner of the map read BANK in big, bold letters.

CHAPTER THIRTY-ONE

Smart opened the doors to the bank's vault and turned on the lights, revealing the caged second door and the horde of scared children inside. Milagros and Hector stepped forward to stare in, and as one, smiles spread across their lips. Hector stepped forward until his head touched the bars, running his fingers over the sparse hair of his mustache as his gaze travelled from child to child.

"It's a good bunch," he said, smiling from ear to ear.

"It's Los Angeles," Smart scowled. "You get all the pretty people from the rest of the country and you put them in one place and fuck, and you're shocked their school system produces good looking kids."

Hector laughed, standing and clapping Smart on the back. "You are a smart man. I can see where you get your namesake."

Smart opened his mouth as if to correct Hector, then stopped himself. He grinned his ghoulish grin from ear to ear, showing too many teeth, the space between them unnatural.

"This... this will be good," Milagros agreed, waggling

his finger at the vault of children. "This will make us money. And Fields, you say he himself again?"

"He just needed a win," Smart said. "And to be reminded that the shadows were no place for him."

"The streets are wash with blood," Hector laughed, clapping Smart on the back again. Smart looked at the hand disdainfully but said nothing. "The Czechs and the Russians are stumbling over themselves to take the territory they think Fields has lost, killing one another. When the dust settles from this, we'll have the whole city." He grinned and gestured back to the vault. Several of the children jumped from his sudden movement. "And still, you give us this. Chaos reigns where you go, Mr. Smart. And from that chaos, we can make profit."

He clapped Smart again.

Smart smiled, then turned off the lights in the vault.

CHAPTER THIRTY-TWO

Xander pushed the thin paper wide, spreading it until it covered the surface of the table he was chained to. It was mostly phonebook pages, that thin sort of newsprint that made even those thousand-page relics at least partially reasonable to carry. He had a hard time spreading them with one hand, and when one found its desired space, he pinned it in place with a thumb tack, driving it down into the sandalwood.

Nick took a large chunk of the tacks and started at the other side, beyond Xander's reach, until the entire table was covered. Xander displayed his hand and Kelly put the black marker in it, and he immediately drew a large rectangle, then leaned forward and drew a second, then to the edges of his reach and drew a third.

"There's three floors to the bank, and only the first floor is accessible to the public. The rest is just offices. Storage. Servers. At least that's what it says on the maps." He added four lines to the lower righthand corner of the rectangle closest to him, the first floor, then four more at the opposite end. "There's one main entrance, it takes up the whole southwest side. It's big, it's glass: you can't miss it."

"You also can't sneak up on it," Tash frowned.

"We're not sneaking," Xander corrected, pointing the marker at her. He drew a long L-shape that divided most of the ground floor, and in the null space to the northeast corner made three divides in it. He tapped the centre of the L. "The main area has the outfacing stuff. Bank tellers, customers, chairs. The type of thing you expect when you walk into any bank in America." He tapped the divided area beyond the null space. "Back here there's two offices, stairs, and the vault."

"That's where we'll find the kids?" Kelly ventured.

He shook his head. "I don't think so, no." He leaned forward and drew a rectangle on the second floor, roughly above where the vault was on the first, then patterned the rest of it with haphazard lines. "There's a second vault on the second floor that feeds down into the first through an elevator."

Tash rumpled her brow. "That's smart. Keep a majority of the cash out of sight, so if anyone knocks the place over, they think they got it all."

He nodded. "And I'm sure that's the reason it said on the design permit, but in reality that's where the lock boxes are kept, and all the things they don't want to cops to see if they come knocking. Dirty money. Drugs. Hot guns."

"Kids," Kelly breathed.

"Kids." He took a deep sigh, tossing the marker to Nick. "The top floor is like the second, save for the vault. All office spaces."

Nick took the hint and started to fill in the offices on the third floor. His strokes were more careful than Xander's, each one shaking with hesitation.

"Basement?" Tash asked.

"You don't get basements in LA, usually," Xander drawled. "The environment doesn't cooperate well with them. There's a roof access though, in the northeast corner of level three."

Nick nodded and added it, then slid the marker back against the table.

"If I had to guess, I'd say Safehouse Red is right on that top floor," Xander said, nodding his head toward it. "Probably the offices closest to the roof access. That's where the most security will be."

"Not with the kids?"

"No... he values himself too much. That also happens to be where the central security is." He leaned over at put a large X on the office at the southeast corner of the third floor, as far from Safehouse Red as it could be while still on the same floor. "Twelve or thirteen servers worth of some of the highest redundancy-proofing you've ever seen. Backups upon backups that control the heat, the AC, the security systems... and the bank vault locks." He ran his tongue around his mouth. "If one system goes down, they flood the whole security apparatus to a third-party location. If that goes down, it cycles back. But of course, we don't know where the second server is, so all that's a bit moot. If one goes down, we're toast; it calls out and backup comes in. It might be cops, but more than likely private security. Either way, it is at that point that the whole thing is officially FUBAR."

"Will it hurt the kids?" Kelly asked, strumming her lower lip.

Xander stared at the mark he'd made, picturing it. "I don't think so. But I can't rule it out." He frowned. "I hesitate to call any security system perfect, but this one comes close."

"But you did it," Tash said, lowering her eyes. "You did this, once."

"I got into the lower vault, sure. I paid attention to drop times, knew when it would be open. Also, I did it the old-fashioned way: with a gun. I'm not suggesting you leave yours home or anything, but I think if we go in here expecting that to work, we'll find ourselves outgunned fairly quickly."

She nodded.

"I broke into this place when it was just a bank. A mob bank, sure, but still just a bank. Now it's a fortress; it just *looks* like a bank."

Tash stepped closer to the table and leaned over it. "Three floors means three teams. Means they'll have to be spread thin."

Xander nodded.

She clucked her tongue. "If we can get me up to the top floor, I think I can take care of the security servers. I think."

Nick shot his head up. "Since when can you --?"

"I can do it," she said curtly, and he took the hint. She looked back to Xander. "You join me to give me enough time to deal with it, Nick and Kelly stick to the stairwell between the first and second floor. Between the two of them they can control the crowd."

Xander nodded. "It's a good plan."

She nodded.

"It will fail."

She raised her head to glare at him.

"The stairwell thing is a neat trick. Very strategic. You learn that overseas?"

She narrowed her eyes at him. "I knew that long before I went overseas."

"Strategically it's sound. Tactically it fails. There's one stair system. They *will* get flooded with men. You were right from the start: it needs to be three teams."

"Three teams means either you alone or someone alone with you," she glared. "Neither of which I'm comfortable with."

He frowned, ignoring her. "We put two in the middle, right outside the upper vault so we're ready when it opens. We put them there and we make a big fuss: so big they can't ignore it. Those two draw in the fire from the other floors. Keep one on the ground floor to work the crowd and stop anything new from getting up, all the while the person on the top floor works the security system."

"No," Tash shook her head. "No way. That's putting me on the top floor and either you on the ground alone or you with one of my kids. That's not happening."

"You're not going to be on the top floor," Xander said matter-of-factly, then turned and pointed to Kelly: "She is."

Kelly stiffened. "Pardon?"

"That shock you gave me to the chest, what kind of control do you have over that?"

"I --" she stammered, unsure of what to say.

"It's good enough to start a heart without flash frying the human attached to it... right?"

She nodded.

"Twelve servers, and they all need to be fried at once. You connect in and you control the charge, no more than an amp. Two at most. You get that charge to run all the way through the system, then you turn them all up at once, before either one has a chance to remote-access out... Can you do that?"

Kelly winced, thought for a moment, then nodded.

"Kelly," Tash hissed. "You've never --"

"I can do that," she insisted. "If it's like he says, I can do that."

"There's no way they've changed out the system," Xander assured her. "I went in with a gun. There was no hole in the system as far as they're concerned. No reason to change it." He turned back to Tash. "If you go in, there's a fight right away. We're battling and trying to watch your back so you can open the vaults, and while you do... nobody's watching the kids. It goes south, fast." He pointed to Kelly. "She has what's needed to get onto the top floor without causing a stir."

Tash straightened her back. "She's sixteen."

"What am I missing?" Nick asked.

Xander shot him a look.

"Oh... oh fuck no. That is not happening."

"It's okay," Kelly nodded.

"She is sixteen years old," Tash snapped, slapping her palm down on the table. "She has been through enough in her life without --"

"That's why she'll get in. Fields will see that history on

her as much as I did," Xander said, burying his knuckle into the desk. He turned to Kelly. "Sorry."

"It's okay."

He turned back to Tash. "Do you think he cares? Hm? Do you think the owner of the largest prostitution ring in Los Angeles will care that she's sixteen? Do you think he'll card her?" He paused, letting the questions sink in. "She's *exactly* his type. Young. Blonde. Cautious. The type of cautious that only comes when you've been hurt before." He turned back to Kelly again. "Again, sorry."

"I can do this," Kelly breathed, placing a hand on Tash's bicep. "It'll be okay."

Tash cupped her hand with her own.

"It will, actually, because before anything can happen Dickhead and I are going to make an awful mess on the second floor," Xander continued, nodding to Nick.

"We are?" Nick said, raising an eyebrow.

"We are. We're gonna make a play so big that it draws all the guns for hire down from the top and up from the bottom. Kelly's going to have her peace to deal with the security system, and there'll be few enough on the bottom floor that Tash can take them down so we don't get overwhelmed." He paused. "And she can be there if we get bottle-necked and need to come down through the second vault into the first."

Nick leaned forward, eyeing the map and the places Xander had indicated. "It's a solid plan, Tash."

Tash looked at the map for a long moment, pressing the knuckles of her right hand into her lip. She nodded. "It is."

"Only problem with it is it doesn't need you," Nick

sniped, turning to Xander.

Xander lowered his eyes but did not respond. He turned to Tash. "The *real* problem with it is the problem that no plan can account for: the security. We don't know what we're dealing with. Fields' guys I could have contended with, but enough of them are out of the picture that the ones he's got on staff I haven't dealt with, and the new guys he's hired..."

"The guy with the tats," Nick said.

Xander nodded. "Mercenaries, more than likely. Although I don't know from where. They're the wild cards. I don't know how many or what to expect from them."

"I do," Tash said in a low voice. She stepped back to the bed, retrieved her tablet from her bag, and brought it back to lay it on the table. "And it's not good. The men are all ex-military, white supremacists from what I can gather. I'm not sure where they're linked to, but I'm willing to bet they were trained before the military found out just how fucked-up they were. I'd like to think it was before they got deployed... but that's probably how they got tied up with this man."

She loaded a picture onto her screen. It was two images, divided down the middle. One was a blurry nighttime photo of a man that looked like a ghoul, with sunken eyes and a pronounced forehead. Next to it was an official headshot of the man, the type you'd see on a mug shot or military badge.

"That's Smart," Xander said, his voice filled with venom. "Where'd you get this?"

"I filmed us picking you up the other night. I've had one of my contacts scrubbing the footage, IDing everyone on the file since."

Xander straightened, faced forward, then turned slowly to make eye contact with her. "I'm sorry, you did what?"

"I filmed you. When we caught you."

He scrunched his face together, fought the urge to say something, then turned back to the tablet. "What do you have on him?"

"Well first of all, his name's not Smart. It's Smrt. Actually, it's Alessandro Bianchi, but he's gone by Smrt for the last decade or so."

"Sounds stupid."

"It's Bosnian for Death."

Xander paused, turned to her, then looked back at the screen.

"He's Italian. Italian mob maybe, I'm not sure. I do know that he crossed over into Bosnia no less than three hundred times towards the tail end of that conflict. We couldn't find good records, but there's a lot of talk on cleansings. He had a list of towns, and the towns on those lists don't exist anymore. Rapid expansion. Some say he smuggled the kids out; some say he killed them all. Hard to say for sure, but whatever he did over there, it earned him his name."

"Smrt," Xander said under his breath.

She nodded. "Smrt. The last time he came back, he had a bunch of his skinheads in tow and came across the border with them to the west."

"Lucky us."

"He's been for hire since. It's a high price tag." She paused. "Fields must have been desperate."

Xander narrowed his eyes, then turned to the clock on the bedside table. "It'd be better to make the hit at the end of the day. He'll be trying to move out the kids a little after then... but before then it'll be too suspicious bringing Kelly in." He nodded to the tablet. "Can I read up on this?"

Tash nodded.

He picked up the tablet, scrolled past the picture, and started to page through the file Tash had been sent on Smrt.

"You pushed him too far," Tash said, after stepping closer to Kelly and Nick. She didn't turn to him when she said it, and her voice was thick with contempt. "They're monsters, but... there were other ways."

Xander did not respond. He started to scan down through a lengthy document that was marked as classified.

CHAPTER THIRTY-THREE

Duncan pressed Janet's shoulder in, popping it properly back into place. She winced, cursed, then started to rub the sore area as he took his hands off her.

"Thanks," she said, her voice low. "I can't stand that EMT."

Duncan looked past where she sat on the edge of the picnic table to the EMT truck that waited on the edge of the parking lot and the burnt grass. The one in front tended to Sergeant Lake, helping her breathe with a respirator and pantomiming deep breaths. His hairline receded unevenly, and he had acne so bad on his cheeks that Duncan could see individual marks even from across the property. He had a smile that oozed grossness. "Yeah, I can see that."

He sighed and turned back to the bordered off LAPD12. He could see fire crews moving around inside through the bay windows of Homicide 12.

"Where'd you learn to do that?" Janet asked, testing her shoulder's range of motion, and finding it as free as it had been when she'd woken up that morning.

"Before I came to LA, I pulled mostly remote assignments. Places where EMT means Electronic Money Transfer and nothing else. Except not really, they don't have that either. Places where if you got hurt, you had to know how to deal with it yourself or it might not get dealt with."

She nodded and followed his line of sight into the building. "You worried files got lost?"

His mouth warbled. "I've been backing up the Shane files... but yes. Yes, I'm worried we've lost things. Fucking bullshit is what this is. If I never have to deal with the fucking bastard for the rest of my life, it'll still be too soon." He turned back to her. "Are you okay? You need anything?"

Janet paused, smiled, then shook her head.

Kelly sat on the edge of her bed in her and Nick's room, wrapping the crook of her arm with cotton cloth as he paced back and forth. Her expression was calm and methodical, the expression of someone going through motions they'd gone through many times before, though she hadn't. It was an expression she'd mastered long ago: the ability to go somewhere else, for her mind to shut down while her body kept working, without comment or emotional connection to the acts.

When she wrapped two layers, she dipped her fingers into a canister of aloe vera at her side, applied it liberally to the surface of the cloth, then started wrapping again. She tested the motion of her arm to make sure she wasn't constricting it, found she wasn't, and continued.

"I don't know how you can be so calm," Nick said, so

quick she didn't so much hear him as she knew what he'd said.

"I'm not," she said, continuing to stare into a blank spot on the wall. Tash had postulated for months that moisture or aloe would help with conduction control, and now she was putting the theory to the test, wrapping her elbow and wrists with infused bandages. She did so with a static stoicism that seemed to make Nick more and more tense with each pass of his pacing.

"You seem calm," he said, gesturing at her with his whole hand and then running it through his hair. "You seem... you seem like you're not questioning this at all."

"I'm not."

He spun on his heels and turned back to the door that joined his and Tash's rooms. It was closed, but he gnashed his teeth at it as though he could see through it. "I should go right in there and fuck him up. He can... Fuck, I hate this plan. I don't trust him, and I don't trust this goddamn plan."

"You sure it's not me you don't trust?"

He turned back to her suddenly, his hands on his hips. "What?"

She sighed, tied off her bandage, then rested her hands in her lap. "What did it feel like, back when you met me?"

He smirked.

"No... sorry. Not meeting me. The other part... rushing in head on. Going into a dangerous situation. Heading into that house even though you could see it for what it was, because it's you. Of course you saw it."

He winced. "Scary," he said, finally. "But... right.

There were these butterflies. Anxiety. But it didn't press me down, it kept me going. It felt... it felt right."

She raised an eyebrow at him.

He lowered his shoulders. "I get it. I'm sorry." He looked back at the door, and as it sat there, his snarl started to return. "He's the *devil*, Kelly. The devil himself. He was an asshole back when I was a kid in high school and --" he paused, then stopped.

"And it got someone you loved killed."

He turned back to her, relaxed again, then nodded.

"That's not me," she said, standing and stepping over next to him. She took his face in her hands and led him back to his bed, the lowered him until he was sitting on it. It brought him down to her height, and she leaned in and kissed him.

He expected the kiss to stop and tried to start to apologize, but she kissed him harder and leaned him back. He put his arms back to brace himself against her decent. She pulled back slightly, enough that he could see her whole face. "Hey, we don't have time."

"We have time."

He winced. "It *is* him I don't trust. Not you. Never you. We don't have to --"

She pressed her lips to his again, brought her hand to his collar and led him down to the swell of the bed. "I'm leaving to do something extremely dangerous in forty-five minutes," she said, her tone factual and to-the-point. "We're gonna fuck before then."

He laughed, and she leaned in and kissed him again, bringing her hands to his chest.

Xander leaned awkwardly out the window in Tash's room, his left hand cuffed to the thick metal frame of it. He puffed on a cigarette that he intermittently let dangle lazily from his lips as he looked over the city below, blowing swaths of gray smoke into the atmosphere.

"They're good kids," he said absently.

On the other side of the room, Tash looked up from checking her ammunition but did not stop loading mags into their carrier. "They are," she said, without needing clarity about who or what Xander was talking about. She loaded another mag, picked up two more, then paused, weighting them. She turned to him. "Do you have anyone?"

He smirked, turned back to her and shot her a wry look, then took another drag of his cigarette.

"It can help with this part of it. The dread."

"I'm about to fuck up a big plan of Stephen Fields. Despite what your eyes and ears might be telling you, I'm happy as shit."

She frowned. "I'm serious. You get to a point where all you can see is the mission. It helps to have someone to..." she rotated the mags, as though turning them around to find the words "... orient yourself, I guess. Force you to have a work-life balance."

"You have someone like that?" he drawled.

"I do. And I like to think I'm the same for them."

Xander turned back, smoke cascading up into his eyes and travelling out into the Los Angeles air like horns from either side of his head. "And how's that mission doing? All accomplished, I guess?"

She paused, freezing.

"Thought as much." He turned back towards the window.

She laughed angrily, binging both mags into their holsters. "It's a good plan, you know. Yours. Solid."

"I know."

"We could do it without you, though."

He turned back, narrowing his eyes at her.

"Could be me and Nick causing the fuss on the first floor, enough to drive everyone down away from Kelly, long enough for her to do her thing."

"Leaves the kids vulnerable."

"We'd be quick."

"I also think you're underestimating my ability to piss Fields right the hell off."

"Oh no, I don't think I am." She stepped toward him, reached into her pocket, and withdrew his pack of cigarettes. She patted out another and handed it to him... then took her keyring off her belt and brought it forward, unlocking his final restraint. She nodded at him slowly, holding his eye.

He squinted.

"It's a better plan with you," she said finally. "I'm trusting you with this. With them."

Xander worked his jaw as he rubbed his newly freed hand, then turned back to the window ledge with greater freedom and lit his second smoke.

High above the Cedarwood Plaza Bank, Stephen Fields sat in his cramped and crowded room, watching on the television as cleanup crews struggled to get the last of the water out of LAPD12. The scroll across the bottom of the screen informed of escalating gang violence, while talking head pundits argued over the situation.

"The truck will be here at eight to take the first of them," Smart said, stepping into the room without knocking or announcing himself. "I think you should be on that route. You've been in one place for too long."

"Yeah," Fields nodded, nonchalantly. He gestured towards the screen with his remote. "They're arguing over why this happened. Talking heads, arguing the sociology of it." He chuckled softly to himself. "One'll come on and say that this is why we need sterner laws, then another'll pop on and say it's class warfare. That people are oppressed to the point they lash out at the cops." He laughed again.

"It's chaos," Mr. Smart nodded, stepping in through the narrow hall to see the television.

There was a woman on Fields' bed that came into view when he stepped around. She looked at him.

He looked past her, as though she were not even there. "Chaos bleeds as soon as you cut through the skin of the world, I have found."

Fields smirked, running his hand over a chin peppered with several days of stubble. The smirk spread into a wide, toothy smile. "I can work with this." He stood up and lit a cigarette. "Let chaos reign."

CHAPTER THIRTY-FOUR

Kelly Saunders stepped into the main foyer of the Cedarwood Plaza Bank to the steady clack of heels she had never worn before. They rubbed at the edges of her feet uncomfortably, pushing her joint up at an awkward angle that splayed her bare legs to their fullest extension with each step. Her legs extended to the ends of a short red dress that was loose enough to shift and move with any breeze that Los Angeles deemed fit to provide, and her movement. It was rhythmic: the motions and the fabric and her step in concert with one another, her straight curtains of blonde adding their own bounce and volume while they framed her plunging neckline.

Sleeves covered her arms and she held a small black bag clutched to her side.

The bank was emptying of patrons, but several still lingered at tellers. Some waited in a seating area that was distinguished from the main hall by nothing but the feng shui. There were few enough people that she could move freely from one place to another, but still more than she would have liked, and she felt that same bubbling of anxiety in her middle as she had before, about to boil over. She touched that spot on her chest reflexively and was surprised to be reminded that there was nothing covering that segment of her flesh. It did not help her anxiety.

There were still too many people there, but there were less than there had been twenty minutes before, she knew. And they were sparse enough that she could see the people who would not be conducting their business and leaving: the men who stood behind along the wall behind the tellers with large bulges under their jackets and shaved heads covered by caps. The men in the security guard uniforms that looked too lanky to have held that position for any length of time. The men who flanked either side of the vault, embedded into the wall twenty feet behind the closest cashier, locked shut.

Their gazes followed her as she stepped by, each and every one of them. Their gazes were like laser sights on the guns they concealed, and she could feel the tiny red dots of their attention at different places all over her body. She swallowed and stepped past, doing her best to keep her eyes forward on her destination.

She stepped up to the lone free teller, a woman in her late twenties with brown hair and large hooped earrings that came down to her shoulders. The woman smiled broadly at Kelly and chewed gum as she talked. "What can I do for you?"

Kelly smiled wanly, a thin thing on lips that were painted the same shade of red as her skirt. "I'm here to see the man upstairs."

The teller winced for a moment but didn't let the facade of her smile fade. She turned to her computer and clacked the keys, the screen's reflection in her glasses showing one window closing and another popping to life. "If you're here to see a banker, we don't usually schedule appointments this late in the day. Was there a delay, because I can see who is in, but it may not be the one you--"

"I'm not here to see a banker," Kelly said flatly. "I'm here to see the man upstairs. I have something for him."

The teller paused, the hairs on her arm slowly rising to stand on edge. Behind her, the broad man with the handlebar mustache that she'd seen at the pier stepped forward. He was wearing a flak jacket that made him seem even wider than he had that night, with the word SECURITY pressed across the bust line in cheap vinyl.

"What's the problem?" Dale said with authority.

Kelly turned her attention to him without missing a beat, barely blinking. "I'm here to see the man upstairs. I have something for him." She paused, making sure she remembered the name just the way Xander had said it. "It's from Mr. Burov."

Dale's bushy red eyebrows raised, just slightly, and he motioned with his head for Kelly to step around to the saloon door the tellers used to get back behind their desks.

The teller shuddered, moving back to her computer and waiting for what she hoped would be no further customers until the end of the day.

Kelly came around to Dale's full view and his gait stammered, briefly, upon the full sight of her. He smirked despite himself and pushed open the saloon door, letting her in past him and taking the opportunity to get the full view of her he hadn't been able to from the front. The dress was backless and plunged as much as the neckline had, its fabric loose.

He motioned for her to step towards the vault and she did. Her hackles raised, she wished she could back away from him, but wasn't sure she could in those heels. She stepped toward the vault until she could touch it, then turned back around to face him, producing a scant smile.

"You say you're here from Burov," Dale said, his voice gravelly.

She had dealt with enough men like him to know that that affect was false, though. She could hear it in his tone, in the way the O-sound dropped when it should have raised. They were both pretending, she realized: she pretending to be charmed, and he pretending not to be. "I have something from Mr. Burov." She was careful to use his title, and never just his name. "He heard your boss had some interesting trade come in. He wants to make peace."

Dale squinted, sighed, then raised a finger and spun it in the air. "Turn around. Hands on the wall."

She swallowed. She'd been prepared for this. She turned and placed her palms out, laying them flat against the vault. She sparked on contact with the metal, and she fought the urge to look back and see if Dale noticed.

Without warning, she felt his hands on her hips, rough and calloused. His thumbs pressed into the exposed small of her back and his fingers splayed out to surround her meager frame, then both travelled up, dislodging and raising the loose cotton of her skirt as he did.

She swallowed again, closed her eyes, and tried desperately not to react. She thought for a moment that she could *hear* his smile and tried to ignore it.

He raised his hands until the fingers were just under the swell of her breasts, then pushed them in to feel beneath. He let her go, then ran his hands down both her arms, upping her bicep fully in his wide grip. He lingered at her bandaged elbows and her breath caught in her throat, but he persisted.

He stepped back. Her skirt had been raised by his action and he could see even more of her leg than he'd been able to before, and even the swell of her lower back. He examined it, raised a hand to strum his mustache, then squat forward and took her by both ankles, moving them apart.

She winced.

He wrapped his hand around the inner track of both her legs and slid his way up, tracing the structure of legs that seemed all the more smooth and milky white when contrasted against the roughness and burned redness of his own. He moved past each knee, cupped the back of them, then moved up to embrace the meat of her inner thigh.

"You can *see* there's nothing there," she snapped, finally unable to hold it back.

He stopped, grinned, and released his grip. "They pay me to be sure."

"I'm sure they do." She turned back around, despite him not having given the order to.

He reached for her purse and slid it off her shoulder, taking the strap of her dress with it and exposing the pale flesh of her upper arm. "Sorry," he smiled.

She tugged the garment back into place.

He opened her purse. Inside was a handgun laid perfectly on its side, a tube of lipstick in the same shade she was wearing, and nothing else. He tisked. "Really?"

"Just for protection."

"Yeah, you're real protected." He snorted. "There's nothing else on you. If Burov didn't send you in with this, what's this gift you have to deliver for him?"

Kelly met his eye. When she spoke, it was plain and factual, as though it had been obvious the entire time. "*Me*."

Dale swallowed, turned and looked over his shoulder to make sure no one was watching, then closed the purse with the gun and lipstick inside it. He took Kelly by the crook of her arm and led her past the vault to the first flight of stairs.

CHAPTER THIRTY-FIVE

"She's in," Nick said, staring forward at the windowed walls of the bank from his perch half a block down the street. The three of them -- Nick, Tash, and Xander -- sat in an open-air coffee shop that was situated just outside of the bound of the Cedarwood Plaza: the type of business that took advantage of a popular locale, but refused to pay popular locale pricing. He stared forward until the last wisps of her hair disappeared into the mouth of the stairwell.

Xander nodded, taking a sip of his espresso. He did not meet either Nick or Tash's gaze, instead looking around at the graffiti that served as the cafe's decor whether it desired it or not, gazing from a large blue dragon to a man with flames for eyes. "Good," he said without addressing them.

They paused a long moment. Tash had a full cup of coffee in front of her but had not touched it, and the steam from it was not subsiding. A server had come over three times to refill it, found that it was still unconsumed, and had walked away with a miffed expression on his face.

"What's the teller look like?" Xander asked, while looking back at the rack of teacups displayed along the back wall.

Nick furrowed his brow, then turned back to the bank. "Youngish. Brown hair. Glasses."

He nodded but said nothing.

Nick turned back to him. His hands shook and he tried to steady them. He reached up and took out his contacts, revealing the pure white of his eyes, and didn't even bother putting them away. They fell to the ground, immediately invisible amid the uneven concrete. "We should go in," he said, so quickly his voice tripped over each word.

"She needs to be up the stairs," Xander said. He checked his phone, closed it, and slid it into his pants pocket.

Tash turned to him, then looked around at the street, then back again. She kept one hand against the side of her head, and the other on the bend of her elbow.

"There's no point in this if we don't give her the time to get in a position to take advantage of."

"That's what I'm worried about, in so many words," Nick huffed, leaning back on his chair and rattling his fingers against the glass table. He turned back to Xander, who was looking at a young woman at a table near theirs and smiling flirtatiously. Nick scowled. "Could you keep your head in the game and pay attention, please?"

"We're being watched," Tash said without looking at either of them, finally taking a sip of her coffee and using it to obscure the movement of her mouth.

Nick stiffened, then turned his gaze out onto the crowd on the street.

There was a man on the far corner wearing all black. His shirt bulged his frame more than the rest of his form would have implied were possible, his bulletproof vest adding to his girth. Several meters away were two black vans, each parked and running, though there was yet no driver in them. One had a man leaning against it who was smoking a cigarette and holding it with three fingers in a way he'd never seen before. He was staring across the street towards the cafe, but not at them, and was ignoring the fact that the tips of his toes were obscuring traffic.

There was a man dressed all in black at the cafe bar, ordering a large tray of coffees and talking to the woman behind the counter in a way that made her visibly uncomfortable.

Nick's mouth went dry and he took a drink from his cola. "I fucking hate this plan."

Kelly stepped into the narrow room at the top floor of the Cedarwood Plaza Bank. The second floor, from what she'd seen of it, had looked professional: like every office building she'd ever been in. Clean tile, doors equal distance apart. The third floor was rougher, less finished. A large section was carpeted in the way banks had been in the eighties, and the fibers were worn and scuffed in multiple places. Dale had opened the door just to the left of the stairwell, just where Xander had guessed it would be. She'd stiffened when he'd tried the knob: it looked like the entrance to a broom closet and she thought, for the briefest of moments, that she'd been made after all.

But it had opened to the narrow hall she was now

stepping through, with boxes stacked along one side and making it even narrower. The room was pale orange with bad lighting and bad paint. Stephen Fields sat on the edge of his bed, a small television resting on a box a few feet in front of him. When he turned and saw her, he turned it off and stood.

"What is this?" Mr. Smart said, appearing from behind the corner. "A princess."

The word made her spine twitch. He said it with two elongated S-sounds that made her skin crawl. He laced his boney fingers together, making a triangle.

"Burov sent her over," Dale said, staying outside the room. "Sounds like he wants in on the buying round."

Fields smirked, buttoning his blazer in front of him. He nodded to Dale, who took one last look at Kelly from the backside, licked his lips, and closed the door behind him.

"If Mr. Burov is willing to bargain, your problems are becoming fewer," Smart said, his voice as thick as cold butter.

"I'm not here to negotiate for him," Kelly said plainly. "I'm here with a peace offering. He wants in on the deal with the kids."

Fields smiled. "And what's on offer? The territory he claims is already mine."

She let her head loll to one side, spilling her golden hair down over one shoulder like a brook catching the burning light of an autumn sunset. It exposed the opposite shoulder, pale and white and small. She met his eyes with her own, big and blue atop freckled cheeks, and did not answer, verbally.

"You can go," he said to Smart.

Smart's jaw clenched. "We have to prepare for the movement."

"I'll be there," he assured, not breaking his gaze on Kelly and waving Smart away.

Smart sighed, then turned and left the room.

Fields continued to stare at her. He stood at least a foot taller than her, and in the cramped, tight room it was impossible for him to be anywhere but directly in front of her. He stared at her and she stared back, looking up at him with those cobalt blue lenses that had transfixed many before him. They were singular, a current of electric blue running through them at all times. He smiled thinly, reaching up and cupping her shoulder gently, and finally her spine faltered, and her gaze fluttered. He moved around her, and she turned her head to keep him in her peripheral vision as much as she could.

"How long you been working for Burov?" he said, making his way to the other side of the bed. He withdrew a bottle of white spiced rum from it and unspun the top with one smooth motion, letting it fall to the floor. There were two glasses on his bedside table, both dirty with lipstick, and he filled them both halfway.

"Two years," she said, watching his hands and making sure the only thing that went into the glasses was alcohol. Despite herself her tongue was dry in her mouth, making her voice catch.

He bobbed his head. "That's a long time to be doing your work and me have not noticed you."

"I don't work," she said, letting a trace of defiance slip into her voice. She pivoted her hips as she spoke so that she could face him without turning fully around. "I was his."

He paused, examined her from toe to head for the first time since she'd entered the room, then nodded. "Was?"

She met his eye but didn't answer.

He smiled, then stepped back over to her, holding both glasses by their lip with one hand, pinching them together. With his free hand, he took her by the bare flesh of her shoulder and turned her until she faced the boxes that lined the wall. He applied firm pressure to her collar, lowering her until she sat at the edge of the bed below him. He held out one of the glasses until it touched her bottom lip. It stank of another woman's perfume, putrid and chemical.

"I'd rather n--"

"There are a few things you're going to put in your mouth you'd rather not," he said, his voice losing any attempt to soothe and becoming low, authoritative, and frightening. "You're gonna convince me you like them all."

She paused, then nodded. She took the glass from him and took a sip, the liquid hot and burning her tongue and filling her nostrils with the spice. She tried to lower it, but he brought his hand up and tilted the bottom of the glass, and brought his free hand up to her neck, tilting her head back. She choked, liquid trailing to either side of her mouth, then swallowed as much of it as she could. He let the taut flesh between his thumb and forefinger ride the soft cleft under her chin, releasing it in patterns to let the liquid travel down her throat. When it was gone, he released her, and she lunged forward in a coughing fit despite herself.

He picked up the other glass, took a sip for himself...
then lowered it to her level.

She held her chest, struggling to get her breath back
from the burning sensation in it, then looked up at the
glass and finally, to Fields.

"Take it," he said. It was not a request.

She took the glass.

"Drink."

She brought it to her lips again and took a sip through
pursed lips, ready for him to do the same thing again and
force her to have it all. He did not. She shuddered.

He smiled, reached into his pocket, and produced a
cigarette. They were so close in the cramped space that his
knee touched hers, and he was still as far away from the
bed as he could have been. He lit it with a match, exhaled
smoke at her, then smiled his best Sinatra smile. "Next
time I do something you don't like, you're to act like you
do. You understand me?"

Her hand went to the spot on her neck where his had
been without her realizing it, but she nodded.

Fields smirked. "You know I was just talking about
those kids downstairs; there's a lot we're going to have to
teach them. You get them in too young, you gotta teach
them everything." He raised one leg and placed it on the
bed beside her, then leaned forward onto it. "I should put
you through your paces, if you're gonna work for me."

"I'm not for sale."

"You will be." He took off his belt but did not dis-
card it. It remained coiled in his hand, like a cobra. "How
about sultry, you know how to act sultry?" She nodded.

"Sexy? I think you know how to act sexy." She nodded. He brought the arm holding the belt and leaned it over his knee, so that the cold of the buckle just barely touched the top of her chest. "What about scared? I was saying that's the one thing we're not gonna have to teach those kids. What about you... you know how to act scared?"

He grinned.

Despite her attempts to maintain his gaze, her eyeline fluttered to the pattern on the belt. It was segmented and well worn, frayed along its edge from violent misuse. She forced herself to turn back to him.

"Can you act scared?"

"I don't need to," she said finally, voice quavering.

He removed the belt, letting it touch her cheek as he did, then took her drink glass from her and raised it back to her bottom lip. "That's a good girl."

She leaned her head back.

CHAPTER THIRTY-SIX

"How are we going to do this?" Nick asked, as he and Xander both touched their boots to the pristine clean of the bank's foyer floor.

Xander turned to scan the row of red chairs surrounding the marble table to one side of the room, then brought his attention to the tellers. His gaze landed on the third desk in, where a young African woman was counting bills. Her nametag identified her as Cindi, with an 'i' instead of a 'y'. "It's gonna happen on its own," he replied under his breath, even as the lanky security guard made his way over to him.

"Sir, we're closing."

"I'm just here to make a withdrawal."

Cindi looked up. Suddenly her eyes were dinner plates, with quivering black pupils in their centre. She spun, palm up, and pushed it down towards a large red button on the side of her desk.

"Xander," Nick hissed, seeing the scene play out in slow motion.

"You're going to have to go, sir," the guard said, placing firm pressure on his forearm.

Xander turned and his jacket erupted, a hole pushing out from the pocket his hand was in. At the same instant the guard's knee spurted blood, first in a V-shape out the back side and spraying onto the floor behind him, and then from everywhere. Xander removed the jacket and withdrew his weapon in one smooth motion, turned, and took aim at a second approaching guard.

The alarm blared, and suddenly the tellers were out of sight. More men appeared from behind the stairwell's mouth and stepped forward, hoisting rifles that they quickly brought to bear. Xander turned the gun on the closest of them, fired, and watched the bullet puff off his vest.

"Fucker!" Nick yelled, turning and bringing his hand down with all his speed on the last guard's collarbone, sending him to the floor. The guards were gone now and all that were left were skinheads.

"Get to the stairs," Xander snapped, firing his gun again.

The alarm blared and Mr. Smart burst through the door of Fields' room. Kelly jumped to her feet and wiped alcohol from her lips into the sleeve of her dress.

"What the fuck?" Fields glowered, even as Smart crossed the room in two great strides and took him by the arm. "When I'm here, you don't --"

"We are under attack," Smart hissed, tugging at his arm.

Kelly leaned and rolled off the side of the bed, shoved her fingers down her throat, and sicked up a large mouthful of burning clear liquid.

"You little slut," Fields snapped through gnashed teeth. "Is this Burov's idea of a --"

"It's time to leave!" Smart yelled, pulling him with great force.

Fields tugged forward, composed himself, then followed Smart from the room.

Kelly shoved her fingers down her throat again, heaving up alcohol twice more before steadying herself and raising to her feet, wiping her lips into her sleeve again and smearing her lipstick into a joker's smile. "Motherfucker," she growled, then started to make her way out the hall after him.

She reached the washroom and slipped, falling to the side despite the fact that she'd abandoned her heels and was in her bare feet. She caught herself on one of the boxes, tried to right herself, then finally pushed herself to her feet. The pattern on the worn carpet spun beneath her.

"Mother. Fucker."

Nick pushed a large man with cauliflowery ears back down the stairs towards the first floor. In the single frame where his feet were unsteady, Nick dropped and kicked at his knee and sent him veering back down the staircase back first, knocking several others who were oncoming back as well. One found his way past them and Nick reached into his peripheral vision without having to turn into it, pried a fire extinguisher from the wall, and collided it with the man's cheek, sending him back down with the others.

Xander fired the last shot from his gun into the chest

of a man with a large 88 tattooed over his head, sending him to the ground and screaming in pain. Behind him was the Upper Vault, the one break in the pattern of offices and brown doors that segmented the hall for as far as the eye could see.

As Nick watched, almost all those doors opened, and men with guns began to emerge. "Xander!"

Dale came down the stairs from the top floor hurling obscenities. He withdrew his gun just as Nick caught him in the jaw, slamming him against the wall once, and then again. He wasn't proud of it, but in that exact moment, for Nick: it felt right.

Xander was grabbed by the shoulder and spun around. A large man with sagging jowls and a sparse beard of long hair grabbed him by the throat, put the barrel of his gun flush with Xander's shoulder, and fired four times, rending the bone beneath to shreds.

Xander brought his opposite elbow up, connecting it to the man's jaw, dislocating it. His face hung freely from itself as Xander clutched his shoulder, cursed long and loud, then withdrew the hand to reveal the inky black blood that was flowing from him. He grinned, cursed again, then withdrew his claws and raked them against the face of the man who was stepping up behind him. "Black Womb lives, motherfuckers."

Tash stood in the lobby of the Cedarwood Plaza Bank alone, her feet planted to either side of her and her form turned so that she presented the smallest target to the doorway. At once, the two black vans that had been parked down the street were blocking the rest of the street from view, and men started to pour out.

The first opened the door and she raised her gun, firing twice. Explosions of blood erupted from both the man's kneecaps. He screamed and fell to the floor. The second man in line stopped, backed up, then the lot of them opened fire on the door.

The door shattered and spider-webbed, but no bullets made it through.

She smiled, raised her weapon, and waited.

Kelly pushed open the last door on the right of the long hallway, and immediately the heat of a baker's dozen servers all running hit her. Her face went flush, and her hands gripped her sides, her face losing its colour in the extreme heat. She turned and vomited again, this time not of her own free will.

She cursed the one word that would have made her father slap her back in the day, then stepped fully into the room and shut the door behind her.

The servers were tall, the sort that stood above normal height and threatened to push the ceiling. They were black, like marble monoliths that stood, diving the room into sections it was impossible to see around, filling it with shadows and crevices to hide in. Each one had blinking red, yellow, and green lights.

She stepped to the one nearest to her and rolled up her sleeves. They fell back down. "Fuck," she cursed, then ripped them free at the shoulders, revealing the tightly wrapped bandages at her elbows and wrists. She sat next to the server, squeezed two triggers on either side of it, and opened its access panel to the world.

The world spun around her and she stopped, steadying herself. She bit her lip hard to try and focus herself, reached out, and found a bundle of wires thick enough to hold a charge.

She closed her eyes, took a deep breath, and tried to concentrate despite the fact that the world was a tilt-a-whirl around her.

CHAPTER THIRTY-SEVEN

Three men shoved Xander back against the stairwell. He grabbed at the largest's face with his clawed hands, rending the flesh beneath it, even as another pulled a long buoy knife and plunged it through Xander's bicep, embedding it into the wall behind him and stapling it there.

He felt the true Womb beat against its cage in his right side, pumping steadily for release, as he watched Nick take down a man across the room by forcing him into the Upper Vault head first.

The knife twisted, and Dale rose to his feet, a bloody smear obscuring one side of his face. He screamed, then brought his fist down against Xander's cheek: once, twice, three times.

The Womb surged in his gut... and Xander felt his vision close in with blackness until he couldn't see anything aside from the blares of light that came with each strike.

Tash fired again, catching a man's hand just as he attempted to enter the foyer. He screamed, turned back, and three of them moved to the side of the door.

She shifted positions now, to watch the back hall for people coming from there as well.

At the mouth of the foyer, the man she'd kneecapped still screamed.

"Sorry again," she said through clenched teeth. "I don't usually use guns."

Sweat found its way down Kelly's chin, dribbling off of it in big, statically charged droplets that hit the carpet and expelled their charges like electric shocks. She kept her eyes closed: each time she'd opened them before, the feeling that the room was spinning around her had threatened to break her concentration.

She could feel the charge like she never had before, each particle of it forming a map of electric blue lines in her mind's eye. She wasn't fueling the charge, not yet, but was a part of the circuit: the power went in her right arm and flowed through her, regulated by her, and when it came out her left, she was a part of it. It wound its way through wires and connections, through circuit boards and breaker chips, forming a mental map of cobalt energy amidst the blackness of her eyelids.

She felt the line resist and pushed a little of herself -- just a little -- into the system.

The line made the leap, and suddenly the second server came into view.

"Nick!" Xander bellowed, as loud as he could to be heard above the blaring alarms.

Nick spun on his heels quickly, watching as Xander pulled his arm free of the wall in a torrent of wrenched flesh. He tried to stand, but was struck by a blow from Dale, who was standing directly in front of him. Despite that, no block had been attempted.

Xander raised his head and swollen eyes, and suddenly, Nick knew. He turned and elbowed a man coming after him, grabbed him and forced him to the floor, even as Dale leaned back for another blow.

"Your nine o'clock!" Nick screamed.

Xander brought up his claws and connected them to Dale's neck, and suddenly the redneck's arms fell, no longer raised and powerful. Xander shoved him back with gritted teeth and smiled, applying pressure even though he could not see the result.

"Six!"

Xander spun, striking out with a clenched fist and connecting with an oncoming assailant.

"Twelve! Gun!"

Xander turned and leapt, even as rifle fire protruded the air. He plied the gun from the man's hands, pulled it back, and sank the butt of it deep into the man's temple. He turned toward Nick for instruction. When none came, he took several slow, deep breaths. Tinges of light began to appear at the edges of his vision.

"Thanks," he said, his voice ragged. "Good eyes."

Nick nodded, his fists up and ready for more men.

Kelly winced. Her nose was bleeding, adding copper to the salt taste that her sweat and tears were dribbling into her mouth. Twelve servers shone in her mind's eye now, and the strain to keep the charge going at a steady gate made her ears ring. She could hear nothing and see nothing, and all she could feel was the heat of the wire she clasped and the weight of the world changing its centre of gravity on a whim. She gasped, breath coming in giant gulps every few moments as she tried -- desperately -- to concentrate.

Beneath her fingers she could feel the consistency of the wires changing, and her nostrils caught the stench of burning plastic.

She winced and opened her eyes. They shone an electric blue.

Tash fired another shot even though there was no one at the front door, then turned and clipped a man who had come in through the back in the shoulder. She straightened her arm and glared at her watch. "Come on, Kelly."

On the third floor Kelly strained. The last server refused to come into view. She opened her mouth and blood and spit flowed from it and she screamed. She screamed out all the pain and rage of the last three years of her life and felt it surge through her fingertips like fire, first burning them and then numbing them as it left her and shattered its way through the system, each circuit bringing itself to its fullest load at once and surpassing it.

Nick stared down the hall toward the offices, waiting

for more men to come as Xander struck another in the neck and watched him tumble down the stairs towards Tash's position.

Next to him, the door to the Upper Vault unhinged itself and swung open.

Nick's eyes lit up and he unclenched his hands immediately. "The kids!" he yelled, turning on a dime and stepping through the door into the vault proper.

It was empty, save for three large bricks of cocaine and a safety deposit box large enough that it looked as though it could have held a rifle.

Cold sweat started on Nick's forehead. He turned to step back through the door just as Xander shut the iron bar interior of the vault behind him and its lock snapped shut.

Xander smiled at him. "Bet you didn't see that one coming."

CHAPTER THIRTY-EIGHT

Tash let off a warning shot that was close enough to keep a large man with an automatic rifle from entering the foyer, then pushed out her mag and slapped another into place in one clean, smooth motion. She looked at her watch again and cursed. "Come on, Kelly. Come on."

At once the alarms stopped and she heard the faint clink to her left of the Lower Vault door becoming unlocked, gravity taking hold and swinging it open. Elated, she smiled broadly from ear to ear... until she heard the soft, escalating sounds of children, first whining and then all but screaming.

Face white, she kept her eye and gun trained on the door but sidestepped until she was in view of the open frame.

Inside were the children for PS 864, all sixty-three of them. "That motherfucker," she whispered, hitting her leg in frustration even as she fired another warning shot at the door.

From somewhere above, she heard the low rumble of a powerful engine, and the steady frum frum frum she recognized as turbines. As she watched, the men who she'd held at bay outside began to scatter, and the first of the two vans roared to life.

"Mother. Fucker."

Nick slammed against the bars of the vault, tried the lock, then slammed his foot against them three more times in rapid succession.

Xander watched from just out of arm's reach with a quiet, cold demeanor.

"Stop this!" Nick yelled, spitting. "This wasn't a part of the plan!"

"No, this was absolutely part of the plan... just not yours." He stretched his weary muscles and withdrew his cell phone from his pants pocket. He turned it on, checked it, and then tossed it through the bars to Nick. "There's enough charge on there for one call. Call Tash, tell her where you are."

"It doesn't have to be like this. We can get Kelly and get the kids and get out and... and that can be the end of it."

Xander almost laughed at that. "You say that, but... really there's only one way it ends. On a long enough time-line, every experiment ends in death, Nicky. You can learn that now, if you like, and save yourself a lot of pain down the road."

"I knew it. I knew it from the second I saw it was you... I knew you were a piece of shit."

Xander paused, stared at him for a long moment... then nodded. "Yeah."

He slammed the outer door of the vault shut, sealing off Nick's repudiations, then turned and made his way quickly to the stairwell to the upstairs. He stopped along the way and squatted down next to an unconscious white supremacist, rolled him over, and picked up his handgun. He checked the mag, shoved it into his pants, and moved forward.

On the stairs, he picked up the fire extinguisher Nick had dislodged, then ascended.

"It's okay," Tash said, scrambling with the lock she was holding in her hands and trying to soothe the youths inside the vault at the same time. She turned over her shoulder every few seconds, but it had been minutes since there had been sight or shadow of the men outside.

In the distance, she could hear sirens.

Xander stepped onto the third floor and found it calm. It was a cluttered, dystopian version of the second floor: but calm and still all the same. Without the blare of the alarms, one could have been forgiven for calling it peaceful.

He leaned into the narrow hall of Safehouse Red, his gun raised and ready.

"He's not in there," came Kelly's voice from down the hall. He turned suddenly and found that she'd opened the door and was stumbling out, holding her head. "He bolted when the alarms started. That Smart guy grabbed him."

Xander nodded, turning his attention back up the

stairs. "He didn't go down. We would have seen him."

"Did it... did it work?" she asked. She was stretching her fingers, the skin between them dry with flakes of melted plastic caked to them. "I mean, are the kids..."

"The kids are safe," he stated, holstering his gun, and raising the extinguisher. "Tasha has them."

She furrowed her brow. "Wait, what? That wasn't the--" she stopped, her lagging, alcohol-soaked brain catching up to the situation finally. "Wait, where's Nick?"

"I'm proud of you," he said, finally turning back to her. "That was a hard thing I got you to do. The electricity and... the other thing. You're the strongest of them, I want you to remember that."

Sparks began to shoot through her fingertips, and she stepped closer to her. "What did you do to--"

He turned the extinguisher hose on her and expelled the plumes of white retardant, pushing her back with the force and dissipating the charge she was building into the atmosphere. She coughed, still unsteady on her feet, and fell to the ground.

He dropped the fire extinguisher, took out his gun, and headed up the stairs to the roof without another word.

The wind from the helicopter blades blew everything back and forth in swirling tornadoes of Los Angeles heat as Xander stepped onto the roof, his heart excited and beating harder in his chest than it had in months. Across the expanse of the roof, two men stood near the chopper, ready to embark. One was tanned with black hair and a blazer; the other gaunt, his stark white hair billowing in the contradictory drafts of the helicopter blades.

Xander smiled, his heart racing, his vision ebbing at its corners. He fought it back. "Stephen Fields!" he yelled, loud enough to be heard above the roar of the engines.

Both men turned as one.

Fields stared at him across the empty expanse of the rooftop, his jacket flapping in the night air. He squinted, staring back at Xander, the both of them locked in place for a long moment and them both understanding: this was the end of their long game.

Xander raised his gun and fired, clipping Fields in the chest and sending him back towards the side of the copter. His vision delved in, narrowing to needlepoints, as Mr. Smart moved to the side and drew his own weapon from beneath his coat, turned it, and fired. The shot struck Xander in the cheek and shattered it, screaming in pain and once again sending his heart rate soaring, reducing his visibility from little to nothing. In his gut, the true Womb sputtered, exhausted as it sent its black blood to heal the gaping wound in his cheek.

The world around him was a black as pitch, not a single ebb of light coming through. The throb of the copter blades drowned out any sound that he could use to orient himself, filling his head with noise. He'd turned when the shot hit him, and was now unsure which way was north, but the wind belted at him.

He arose to his feet, turned slowly, and raised his weapon to firing height.

"Alessandro!" he yelled, again at the top of his lungs.

Far to his right he heard the gravel shift and a low, guttural sound. He turned and fired at its source.

The bullet pierced Smart's throat in its centre, sending blood and matter back onto the window of the helicopter. He raised his hand to his throat and they were instantly covered in blood, their deep red a stark contrast to the chalky white of his flesh. He fell to his knees, hair billowing and getting caught in the sticky heat that flowed from him, as the copter took off behind him.

Xander pressed forward, hearing Smart struggle to speak last words and stay upright. He heard him try to grip his gun but keep slipping, his hands slick with blood, until eventually he fell to the side and let out one final, horrible gaggle of air.

He stepped to the right of where Smart lay dead, to where Fields had been left, and found the rest of the roof to be empty. He cursed loudly, raised his gun to point in the direction of the whirling blades, and opened fire until his mag was spent.

Kelly coughed, shaking retardant off of her arms as she stumbled down the bank's narrow hallway to its first floor. There was a sea of children there, lined up row by row in the bank's main room as Tash attempted to calm them. She had a phone to her ear, and her tone said that she was talking to the police.

"That's right, all of them. They're all here. Please, send medical. A few of them look like they're in bad need of nutrition and I don't --" she turned, seeing Kelly stumble into frame, and clapped her phone shut. "Are you okay?!"

"I'm drunk," she coughed, warbling on her feet, and bracing herself against the wall.

"Pardon?"

"Where's Nick? He must be --" She stopped, seeing the colour drain from Tash's face, then turned and ran back up the stairs, suddenly finding sure footing.

"Wait!" Tash screamed after her, taking a step but stopped when she heard the children behind her. She cursed.

Kelly bounded back up to the second floor and spun around, her matted hair whipping from side to side. "Nick?" she yelled, turning to look at the face of every unconscious male she passed, regardless of body type. Sweat was making trails down the cake of white fire suppressant that coated her, making her a lined geisha, her lips still the bright red of her dress.

She turned to leave again, growing more and more frantic, then stopped and turned back. The second-floor vault was closed. "Fuck" she hissed, ran up to it, grabbed it by the handle and pulled.

Nick stretched his arms out from between the bars of the vault and she clasped them. She hugged him into the iron of the cage, and she pressed the white chemical of the extinguisher into his eyes, and neither cared. They pulled apart long enough to press their lips to each other, she grabbing his face in both her hands and holding it tighter than she'd ever held anything she could remember, then hugging into him again.

"Why do you taste like rum?" he asked, laughing.

"It's a story," she snorted, leaning back and kissing him on the forehead. He took note of the bruise on her neck and raised a hand to it, but she intercepted and kissed his fingers. She turned the hand around and found the burner cell still palmed within it. "Why didn't you call?"

Nick grinned wryly.

Fields' helicopter landed at Terminal Free airfield on the outskirts of the Hollywood Burbank Airport. The air whipped around him as he eased his way out, holding his right hand to the bloodstained pectoral muscle of his left.

There was a car waiting for him on the lot, and he hobbled towards it. "That car had better have opioids and a medical technician, I shit you not, or I am going to lose my goddamned mind."

"Lose it then," Duncan Taggart said, stepping out of the driver's seat and swinging his gun around to be level with Fields.

Fields stopped in his tracks, his face suddenly sallow and dull. His cheeks hung as his mouth went slack, and at once he fell to his knees.

Janet Nesbit got out of the passenger-side door and stepped around, her weapon drawn and ready. There were sirens in the distance.

"Stephen Fields," Duncan said, his voice great and magnanimous, "You are being taken into federal custody for kidnapping, attempted murder, and solicitation of a minor... and many other things that I'm sure we'll figure out. You have the right, to remain, silent." He inched his head forward. "But I wouldn't."

Janet smiled.

Fields let his arms fall to his side, the weight of everything finally crashing down upon him, and fell to the ground with salt tears on his cheeks.

CHAPTER THIRTY-NINE

Nick stretched his arm until the joint popped. It was still sore from one of the blows he'd taken -- he wasn't even sure which one. They'd all started to blur together. He sat on the edge of his hotel bed, his shirt off, rotating the arm back and forth until it felt as though it were in position.

Kelly popped three painkillers that Tash had given her. She wasn't sure what they were, only that they weren't over-the-counter. "I don't think I'll ever have rum again," she drawled, still tasting it on her tongue.

"You'd had it before?"

She turned and looked at him over her shoulder, her gaze incredulous.

He shrugged, accepting.

She smirked. Her top was off as well, laid over the desk in front of her as she examined the extent of the bruise Fields had left on her neck. It had darkened and was now a perfect imprint of his thumb along the bridge of her chin. "Why'd you call the cops?" she asked, not turning to face him or even addressing him in the mirror.

He paused, then smirked. "I could see it. Just... the ten steps aheadness of it. I could see that it wasn't going to go his way, no matter how well he'd *thought* he had it planned. In that moment it was just... obvious. The way out of this loop, the thing he wouldn't do."

"He'd gone to the cops before."

"Early on. Not since he'd started this mess. Not since he'd pushed Fields into slipping. But by that point, he was too far gone. He'd committed to a path and just... had to see it through to its end. He had blinders on, but I just... saw through it."

She smiled at him, then nodded.

"I told you about him. That he couldn't be trusted."

"You did."

"Why didn't you believe me?"

"Well, you were wrong."

Nick stiffened. "What?"

"You were wrong. You found out that the perfect little hometown you remembered wasn't so perfect after all... and it made you angry. It messed you up. It happens, to all of us. It happened to me before I even left home, for Christ's sake." She turned to him, smiling. "It made it so you couldn't see."

"The man locked me in a bank vault."

She smirked. "You got out."

"I cannot believe you're defending --"

"I would have done the same thing," she said, cutting him off without being impolite. "That's what I learned through this. I started off not wanting to get involved... but then it pulled me in. The weight of it. And yeah, I may not be able to see all the avenues you can. Maybe if I could, I'd make different choices... but I can't. So, I'm saying, I would have done the exact same thing."

"You would have locked me in a vault."

She paused, swallowed with great pain and difficulty, then turned back to her mirror. She made eye contact with him through his reflection. "I would have killed that fucker," she said, stretching her neck back and tracing the line of her bruise again. "And you would have tried to stop me. You would've told me Tash and Victor won't have me if I'm a killer, or you would have brought up being worried about some other shit... so yeah, I'd have done the same thing."

He stared at her.

"You wanted me to take action, that's the action." She turned back around to him. "Do you hate me?"

He stiffened, turned, narrowed his eyes, then returned her gaze. "Never."

"Then you can't hate him. Because there's a big part of me, I'd say probably filled up to fucking here," she gestured up to the height of her bruised neck, "that thinks Fields got off *way* too easy."

Nick paused, then nodded.

She stared at him for a long moment, bathed in the Los Angeles sun streaming in from the window. "If it ever got that bad... if we met someone who *really* deserved it, and I did something about it... what would you do if I left the team?"

"Start a new team," he said, without hesitation.

She brought herself forward and kissed him. He wrapped his arms around her and held her as tightly -- and as gently -- as he could.

Tash sat on the balcony of her hotel room, watching as the sun set over the Los Angeles skyline. There were purples and reds and deep, deep blues in concentric rings around the last ebb of the sun, each one winking out in turn as the world turned it further and further from view.

Despite the night, the air was hot, so hot that she couldn't get comfortable. It made her grateful for the tickets on her nightstand, and the fact that soon she would be back in Atlanta.

She shifted her shoulder uncomfortably, clicked her tongue against the side of her mouth, then reached into her breast pocket and withdrew a battered package of cigarettes. She laid them on the glass table in front of her, stepped back a pace, then turned back toward the sunset to watch the last sliver of it vanish.

"I was surprised when you took down Smart," she said, crossing her arms. "I was expecting you to kill Fields."

Xander stepped out from behind her, walked over to the cigarette pouch, and scooped it up. He opened it, lit one, then slid it back into his pocket where it belonged before stepping to the other side of the balcony. "I didn't have a clear shot."

"Another time you would have found one, I think. Or am I reading you wrong?"

He took a puff from his cigarette, leaned over the rail, and let the smoke trail out of his open mouth without forcing it.

"I thought not."

They both stood like that, both facing west, for a long moment, flashes of sunlight leaving them.

"Do I have to worry about you anymore?" he asked,

without turning around.

She moved to her edge of the rail and leaned back against it, placing both sore palms against the cool of the metal. "You've never had to worry about me."

"I mean --"

"We're leaving tomorrow. Tickets bought. I think we'll catch a show before we go, but... yeah. We're gone."

He nodded.

She licked her lips. "The trick of the war is knowing how to leave it."

Xander turned until she was in his peripheral vision.

"They train you for months how to be there. How to act, how to fight, how to kill. But when you come back, man, they just dump you back in with society. They don't retrain you. You don't know how to shop. How to laugh. How to eat in a crowded restaurant."

"I ain't been to war, and whatever this is, I didn't train for it."

"No?" she asked, raising an eyebrow. "That file I pulled from Coral Beach says otherwise."

He turned away again.

"You said you weren't built to last this long... what did you mean? Was that just a turn of phrase... or did you actually mean you were *built*?"

He didn't answer or turn around.

"You were, weren't you? That's what was happening in Coral Beach... The big thing I got called out for and missed. That's why you have multiple powers... they frankensteined you together. That's what you are... isn't it?"

"I'm me," he said gruffly, turning slightly to see her out of the corner of his eye. He finished his cigarette and threw the burning ember down towards the street below.

"I've never been anything else."

She frowned, her eyebrows curling up in pity. "I'm sorry I couldn't have helped you."

"You got the kid out of it," he said, stepping up and over the rail, dangling off and preparing to drop the half story to the floor below. "That's worth it. You got him out of there before that place could get to him. Before it could --" He paused, his lips curling. "Before it *trained* him."

Tash nodded.

"They are good kids. They hate me, for good reason... but they're good. They'll make a difference. People that good, even just living good lives... they make a difference."

She stepped forward, extending a small slip of paper towards him. It was a business card. "They'd learn to like you."

He turned his head fully around, eyebrow raised.

"I don't just let people on my crew go. No matter how far gone they might seem... I get them back. Every time." She held out the card, his hand unwavering.

He reached out and took it, looked at it, and pushed it into his front pocket. "I'm not in your unit."

"As far as I'm concerned, you are." She swallowed. "You call that any time you decide you're ready to try things a better way."

He clenched his jaw, turned, and prepped himself to fall.

"Wait," she said.

He paused.

"I don't know how your chemistry works, but I have a pretty good idea. That black blood... that has to come from somewhere."

He turned to her, squinting.

"It doesn't have its own circulatory system, from what I could tell. It goes through your veins, the same as your blood." She waited for him to respond. "You have two hearts competing for control of the same territory. It plays havoc with your blood pressure."

He twitched in her direction.

"I think you're right. I think whoever made you, they didn't intend for you to last this long. The system --the balance your body operates at -- it was never meant to be this strained for this long. I think if you don't find a way to stop the transformations... I think you'll just stay blind. Or stroke out. Either way, it won't end well."

He nodded, slowly. "Engen," he said finally.

She stiffened. "What?"

"Engen made me this way."

He dropped from the balcony to the next floor down. When she reached the edge and leaned over where he'd stood, he was already gone. She huffed, looked at the darkened sky, then turned back and went inside her hotel room.

She packed away the remainder of her clothes and turned the television on, not choosing any channel. She just wanted the noise. She set her alarm, retrieved her gun from its holster, then removed its mag and emptied the chamber, storing it carefully.

She paused.

Sticking out of the back joint of the gun was a glob of red flesh, pinned between the frame and the hammer. She squinted, looked back to the balcony, then stepped back into the bathroom.

She returned with a swab and a collection kit.

EPILOGUE

Stephen Fields sat in his holding cell. He was alone. There were no other detainees on his block, only empty beds in empty cells. It was deafeningly quiet, although the concrete walls made it so that every sound, were there any, could be heard from all the way across that level. He sat in his orange jumpsuit, palms pressed firmly against the hard mattress, staring blankly at the chipped floor where the bars of his cell met it.

From down the hall, he heard the security door un-latch. He did not look up. Someone walked with a steady gait up the hall, the solid click clack, click clack of their heels patterned and familiar immediately. It was the walk of a serviceman, the walk of a man trained in the art of walking.

Fields kept staring at the spot on the floor, and when the clacking heels stopped, a metal tray of food was slid into his line of sight.

It was a fine cut of lamb, seared to perfection and still billowing steam. There were stalks of asparagus arranged neatly on the plate, mashed potatoes in garlic sauce, and little baby carrots. There was an unlabeled drink carton on the tray, with a plastic white glass overturned next to it.

Fields looked up.

The guard smiled down at him with a mouth that was unshaven and one blackened tooth. "The latest shipment came in, sir. Things are being distributed now."

Fields smiled, picked up his tray, and touched his fork to his lamb.

It melted like butter.

Jimmy Skids sat on the steps of the Chesterton strip mall, his hands strumming against his knee. He watched as a man approached tentatively, looking from side to side every few squares of concrete, even though the parking lot was empty. When he got close enough, the man nodding at Jimmy.

Jimmy nodded back. "Good homes, Louis."

"Fire blanks," Louis smirked, repeating the code from memory. "You carrying?"

"The usual. And we got this new stuff too, just came in. S'called Eden, and man... it is something." He chuckled to himself. "Earns the name, I'll tell you that."

Louis nodded, reached for his wallet, and started counting out bills.

The glass door to the barbershop behind Jimmy opened.

Louis looked up, and his smile faded, his eyes growing wide. He turned to run, dropping his wallet as he went.

Jimmy shifted to turn around and was on his feet before he knew what was happening, pinned tightly against the window of the barbershop and cracking it.

Xander leaned in, eyes thick and black, and smiled. His pulse quickened, and he did little to fight it. "We're gonna have a talk... about where you get your product."

AFTERWORD

This book was just plain a blast to write. It took me a few times to get started (I actually made it over 30,000 words into a draft that was completely scrapped. That doesn't happen with me once I have something plotted) but once I figured out the core of it, it flowed.

Kelly Saunders is amoung one of my favourite characters, and the idea of getting her into a room with Xander Drew was immediately appealing. All of these characters pair off of each other very well, and I think they'll have to meet again sometime in the future.

This was a really fun book to write, and I hope it was also a fun book to read.

I'd like to thank my editor Erin Vance for all her help on this text; her input to the Engen Universe has been invaluable.

This book is dedicated to my partner, Ellen Curtis, who makes me a better writer. Every day.

Matthew LeDrew
November 27, 2020

ENGEN TIMELINE

With over twenty novels spread over three different series by many different authors, the Engen Universe of titles is growing every day and into genres we couldn't have imagined! From the original ten book *Black Womb* thriller series, its crime novel sequel series *Xander Drew*, our flagship adventure title *Infinity*, or single-novels like *Jacobi Street* or *light | dark*, there's something in the Engen Universe for everyone with more books by more authors on the way soon!

...But how do the events relate to one another, chronologically? While some astute readers have guessed at the potential timeline (some accurately, some not), we're going to finally set the question of the Engen Timeline to rest.

Turn the page for an up-to-date guide of the ever-widening world of Engen, featuring the works of Ali House, Ellen Curtis, Erin Vance, Matthew Daniels, Andrea Hackett, Sarah Thompson, Jay Paulin, and Matthew LeDrew!

In the 10 Years Prior Black September

"Reptilia" by Matthew LeDrew
published in *light | dark*.
Danger descends on a small secluded town in the form of a deadly virus with fantastic and terrible side-effects. Can a small group of doctors escape alive?

Compendium by Ellen Curtis
Three short stories forming the basis for the Engen Universe's ties to suspense, genetic engeneering, and the supernatural. Features the stories "The Tourniquet Revival," "Falling into Fire" and "At Midnight, the Dawn."

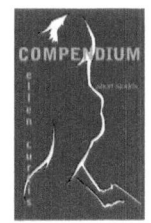

"The Theogony" by Matthew LeDrew
published in *light | dark*.
A tale of young Theo Flaherty of the *Infinity* series and his time admitted against his will to the Black Springs hospital, where he learns to paint, and seeks out his father.

Black September

"Revving Engen" by Matthew LeDrew
published in *light | dark*.
A direct lead-in to both *Infinity* and *Black Womb*, Tasha travels to Coral Beach, Maine on a hot tip about a recently discovered young man with incredible abilities.

Infinity by Ellen Curtis & Matthew LeDrew
Faced with a destiny he's uncertain of, the enigmatic Victor must bring together four unique people with very special abilities… or face the tasks ahead alone. Guaranteed to excite!

Black Womb by Matthew LeDrew
Fifteen years ago, something happened in Coral
Beach, Maine that resulted in the present death of
a seventeen-year-old boy. Now four high-school
students must try to solve the mystery... before
the killer picks them off.

Jacobi Street by Matthew LeDrew
When a mysterious painting shows up at an art
gallery he works at, Bob must work with Eddie
and Sloan to track down its sinister origins and
convince the people living on Jacobi Street of
them, before its too late!

Transformations in Pain by Matthew LeDrew
When two girls are assaulted and one is
hospitalized, the residents of Coral Beach must
put their shared tragedies behind them and stop
the man responsible, as well as unlock the secrets
behind the true nature of the Womb...

Year One: October

Smoke and Mirrors by Matthew LeDrew
The approaching trial of Genblade brings closure
to the people of Coral Beach, until people start
showing up dead in the same manner they did
when he was at large.

"Scarlett" by Andrea Hackett
published in *light | dark*.
Introducing Scarlett, the slightly damaged hunter
on a mission to save others from the monsters
from her past.

"The Inevitable" by Ali House
published in *The Lightbulb Forest*
A young woman must contend with the
emergence of a frightening new power alongside
the emotional high of a first date.

The Tourniquet Reprisal by Curtis & LeDrew
A man lives in Atlanta, Georgia that people
don't talk about, but everyone knows he's there.
He arrived a year ago and turned a gaggle
of uneducated youth into something new,
something to fear.

Roulette by Matthew LeDrew
As the teen suicide rate in Coral Beach starts to
climb astronomically fast, Xander travels to Los
Angeles to fight his most terrifying adversary
yet… and learns that the only thing worse than
looking for release… is finding it.

Year One: November

Exodus of Angels by Curtis & LeDrew
Victor's enigmatic past is illuminated when
Jaycee accompanies him to visit a new friend
in the paliative care ward of the Black Springs
hospital, where Theo also happens to be
searching for a cure for Leigh.

Ghosts of the Past by Matthew LeDrew
Coral Beach faces its most awesome threat when
one of Engen's past mistakes is unleashed upon
the unsuspecting populous. Friends and enemies
unite to fight a common enemy… but will even
that be enough?

Touch Your Nose by Matthew LeDrew
Simon Monk must infiltrate the San Fransico
branch of Shane Industries, a massive company
with deep ties to the Engen Universe. Where do
his true loyalties lie? And can he get out without
causing harm?

Ignorance is Bliss by Matthew LeDrew
After being set through the ringer one too many
times, Xander decides that his life with Julie
needs a little more attention... which is bad news
because a new villain has come to town with his
sights set on Adam Genblade.

"Gristle While You Work" by Jay Paulin
published in *light | dark*.
A short story centering around the rise of a new,
and possibly cannibalistic, serial killer in the
Engen Universe.

Becoming by Matthew LeDrew
For months Xander Drew has been doing his
level best to keep the streets of Coral Beach clean,
which means it's time for the forces of darkness to
strike back... all at once.

Inner Child by Matthew LeDrew
Julie is hospitalized with life-threatening wounds
to both body and soul. But the real threat comes
from the hospital walls themselves, as a demonic
presence makes itself known to Xander and his
friends.

End of Year One

Gang War by Matthew LeDrew
The Tees, a homicidal gang of evil men, has finally been taken down by Xander Drew. But his victory is short lived, as retired Tees are mysteriously killed. With a town of suspects, anyone can be the culprit… including one of their own.

Chains by Matthew LeDrew
Sociopath Derek Smith has been freed from prison and is praying on the weak; and none are weaker than August Styles: a pregnant girl with Down Syndrome who has run away from home.

"Omega" by Ellen Curtis
published in *light | dark*.
A sinister division of Engen begins a series of experiments on pregnant women in a fashion eerily similar to those that created the original Black Womb project.

The Long Road by Matthew LeDrew
Xander meets the American people — and realizes that the world is harsh and wicked, but can also be soft and gentle, even loving. Xander Drew comes of age on the road, and sets his new direction.

Year Two

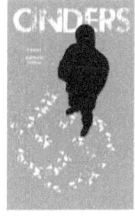

Cinders by Matthew LeDrew
Detective Horton enters a violent and dangerous world he didn't know existed beneath the veneer of order and structure that he has based his entire deductive method around.

Sinister Intent by Matthew LeDrew
One of the killers Detective Horton could not
catch has resurfaced: a serial killer who flaunts his
sinister intent in front of the Los Angeles Police
Department, making it so that no one is safe.

Faith by Matthew LeDrew
Xander's mysterious and troublesome past returns
to haunt him on the streets of Los Angeles; a place
where even more people can get caught in the
crossfire of the games of death and deceit that
makes up his life.

Flickers in the Night by Matthew LeDrew
Lisa Rowdan is hunted by her haunting -- and
powerful -- ex-boyfriend Ryan through a lonely
city street. Can she escape him?
One of over twenty great sprine-tingling short
stories!

Garden of the 8th Circle by Curtis & LeDrew
Victor brings Chad, Abby, and Alice into a
dangerous conflict a decade in the making,
fighting an out of control cult for the fate of a
young soul. Meanwhile, Theo investigates a
mysterious event in Los Angeles.

Family Values by Matthew LeDrew
Xander and his new friends Crowley, Lisa, and
Tim investigate a series of kidnappings and
murders that stretch back decades, all of which
have the same similar twist: victims being found
after years of being missing.

Fate's Shadow by Matthew LeDrew
When one of Xander's old cases comes up for trial, Megan Greene returns with it. The former friends are led into conflict regarding her client's innocence. However, they put their difference aside when they both become targets of the vigilante known as Shiro Gilbert.

First Aid by Matthew LeDrew
Xander takes his feud with mob boss Stephen Fields to the streets, and his attracts the attention of the *Infinity* team. Before the arrive, he'll have pushed the mob boss into an all out gang war, the likes of which the city will never recover from.

Exposure by Erin Vance
Joshua Deering just wanted was to pass his final photography project. But that's not what happened. But hindsight is 20/20, and now creepy cemetery guy Adrian, Josh, and Josh's two friends are being stalked by nameless, violent strangers.

The Future

"Remers" by Sarah Thompson
published in *light | dark.*
In the not-too-distant future of the Engen Universe, young athletes are the targets of a scouting program to create the next stage of super soldier with cybernetic enhancements.

DARK STORIES FROM ENGEN BOOKS

THE HOWL BECONS

Growing up without his father, Tyler had no way of knowing the horrible secret that has plagued his family for generations. To free himself and find the cure, he will have to look beyond himself and into his dark history.

"A very ambitious novel… the horrors of everyday life can be worse than anything in fiction. The idea of using werewolves as a metaphor – to me this pushes the book a bit above much of what is out there… Brad [Dunne] is a very good writer and obviously has a deep background."
— Andrew Peacock

WESTON'S WAR

Something evil grows in the heart of Colorado. Bill Weston was a man of the West. He knew it – its land, its people, its stories. It was where he plied his trade, hunting men for money. His life wasn't easy, but it was predictable. That all changed when he captured Faraway Sue and he was led on a trip through the Colorado forests

"Take a little Zane Grey. Add a little Penny Dreadful. Read with Sam Elliot's voice. Discover Jon Dobbin's masterful The Starving."
— Darrell Power,
Great Big Sea

The early years of **Xander Drew** as he struggles with the evils of his small rural hometown of Coral Beach, Maine. Cursed with the heart of the Womb and the gift of seeing the world around him for what it really is, Xander must learn the hard lessons about the nature of humanity to traverse the minefield of criminals, gangs, and abusers that stand between him and ultimate happiness -- but most of all that **sometimes it takes a monster, to catch a monster.**

"THE WRITING OF ITS GENERATION- - VISUAL, TO-THE-POINT AND IN-THE-MOMENT."
- *The Northeast Avalon Times*

The Coral Beach Casefiles series by Matthew LeDrew:

For more information, please visit

www.engenbooks.com

infinity

The world is changing, and we have to change with it. That was the one thing that Victor was really sure of when he started looking for special people: people who could change the possibilities of the future from something certainly grim... to something *infinitely* positive.

Now four unsuspecting people from different backgrounds and walks of life have been thrown into the mix together, and nothing will ever be the same. But there's a difference between hoping for a better world and actually having one, and there will always be resistance to change.

Book One:	Infinity (October 2010)
Book Two:	The Tourniquet Reprisal (October 2012)
Book Three:	Exodus of Angels (April 2016)
Book Four:	Garden of the 8th Circle (August 2020)

Related Books:

Compendium (October 2009)
light|dark (April 2012)
Roulette (October 2009)
The Long Road (May 2014)
Touch Your Nose (May 2018)

Written by the superstar author team of Ellen Curtis (*Compendium*) and Matthew LeDrew (the *Xander Drew* series).

Destiny doesn't wait for anyone.

THE XANDER DREW SERIES

Prologue: The Long Road (May 2014)

COMING SOON FROM ENGEN BOOKS:

MOMENTS

The Shane Killer has returned to finish the job he started in *Family Values*, decimating the ranks of one of the largest companies on the planet. Last time Xander was distracted, but this time his full force will go towards solving this mystery. Can he and Duncan put their differences aside to stop a killer?

ABOUT THE AUTHOR

Matthew LeDrew holds an Honours Degree in English from the Memorial University of Newfoundland with a minor in Anthropology, and studied Journalism at College of the North Atlantic in Stephenville, Newfoundland. He was honoured to be a jury member of both the 2018 NLBA awards and the 2020 Arts and Letters Awards.

He has written twenty-two other novels for Engen Books: the ten book Coral Beach Casefiles series, *The Long Road, Cinders, Sinister Intent, Faith, Family Values, Fate's Shadow, Jacobi Street, Touch Your Nose, Infinity, The Tourniquet Reprisal, Exodus of Angels, Garden of the Eigth Circle* the latter three of which with co-author Ellen Curtis.

He lives in St. John's, Newfoundland.